ACTIVITIES OF
DAILY LIVING

ACTIVITIES OF DAILY LIVING

A NOVEL

LISA HSIAO CHEN

FIC
Chen, L

W. W. NORTON & COMPANY
Independent Publishers Since 1923

Copyright © 2022 by Lisa Hsiao Chen

All rights reserved
Printed in the United States of America
First Edition

Excerpt from *The Fatalist* by Lyn Hejinian. Copyright © 2003 by Lyn Hejinian. Used by permission of the author and Omnidawn Publishing. Excerpts from *Out of Now: The Lifeworks of Tehching Hsieh* by Adrian Heathfield and Tehching Hsieh. Copyright © 2009 by Adrian Heathfield and Tehching Hsieh. Used by permission of the authors and The MIT Press.

For information about permission to reproduce selections from this book, write to Permissions, W. W. Norton & Company, Inc., 500 Fifth Avenue, New York, NY 10110

For information about special discounts for bulk purchases, please contact W. W. Norton Special Sales at specialsales@wwnorton.com or 800-233-4830

Manufacturing by Lakeside Book Company
Book design by Beth Steidle
Production manager: Beth Steidle

Library of Congress Cataloging-in-Publication Data

Names: Chen, Lisa, author.
Title: Activities of daily living : a novel / Lisa Hsiao Chen.
Description: First edition. | New York, NY : W. W. Norton & Company, Inc., [2022]
Identifiers: LCCN 2021052467 | ISBN 9780393881127 (hardcover) |
ISBN 9780393881134 (epub)
Subjects: LCGFT: Novels.
Classification: LCC PS3603.H45 A64 2022 | DDC 813/.6—dc23/eng/20211028
LC record available at https://lccn.loc.gov/2021052467

W. W. Norton & Company, Inc., 500 Fifth Avenue, New York, N.Y. 10110
www.wwnorton.com

W. W. Norton & Company Ltd., 15 Carlisle Street, London W1D 3BS

1 2 3 4 5 6 7 8 9 0

FOR EKH

Why do people want to do a project at all, instead of just living on into the future unfettered by projects? The following answer can be given to this question: above all else, each project strives to acquire a socially sanctioned loneliness.

—BORIS GROYS

Real duration is that duration which gnaws on things, and leaves on them the mark of its tooth.

—HENRI BERGSON

ACTIVITIES OF
DAILY LIVING

A dock outside Philadelphia on a still night. A slight figure slips off an oil tanker, quiet as a thief. He walks fast, head down, until he reaches a street with traffic lights and hails a taxi.

Where to?

New York City.

He pays the driver fifty dollars in cash.

The young artist has come all the way from Taiwan. He's not yet twenty-five and already he's renounced painting. He knows Paris is no longer the center of the art world, New York City is, and he knows hardly anything about New York City except that it's where he needs to be.

Yet once he arrives in the city, he doesn't make art. It's all he can do to keep himself alive. For the next four years, he washes dishes, cleans restaurants for $1.75 an hour, the going wage for someone without papers. When he isn't working twelve-hour shifts, he paces the floor of his rental loft on Hudson Street in an industrial, guttering part of Lower Manhattan. To be an artist, you have to make art. But where to start?

One night after the restaurant closes, he sets up a 16mm camera and films himself performing his nightly routine: wipe the tables, stack the chairs, wax the floors. The film, forty minutes long, is the same forty minutes he spends on the clock. But alchemized. He sets the film aside.

Then one day while pacing his loft, it hits him. He doesn't need to go searching for a project. He's already inside one.

He builds himself a cage.

2016

Time is filled with beginners. You are right. Now
each of them is working on something
and it matters. The large increments of life must
    not go by
unrecognized.

—LYN HEJINIAN

THE BEGINNING OF THE PROJECT

What are you up to these days? a friend might ask.

I'm working on a project, Alice would say.

The real answer is the project doesn't exist. But calling it a project makes it a thing.

What's the project about?

The project is about an artist, says Alice. The Artist.

The first time she encountered the Artist she was a girl and he was in the pages of a magazine. In the photograph that accompanied the short article, he was tied at the waist with rope to another artist—a woman, taller, older, white. They stood apart to show the distance—eight feet—the rope afforded them for the year they'd be bound together.

Alice remembers studying the Artist's slim frame; his long hair, which shagged past his shoulders; the double pocket shirt he wore stuffed in his jeans. She felt kinship with his Asian face. Even now she can recall how he stared back at the camera with the look of a man uncomfortable with being seen yet who needed an audience. The work perplexed her. Somewhere in that perplexity must be the art.

Most people Alice talks to about her project do not recognize the Artist's name. She might, if the conversation persists, try describing a few of his performance works:

He's the artist who locked himself in a cage for a year—

Who punched a clock, on the hour, every hour, for a year—

Who lived outside in the streets of New York City for a year without going into any buildings—

Sometimes in response there might be a nod of recognition; more often than not, their faces are blank as hard-boiled eggs.

You could say the Artist's performance works, his extreme acts of physical and mental endurance, are the heavyweights of projects, the kaiju of projects. A lazy twitch from the tail of one of his projects could level a metropolis of lesser projects. Yet for most of his career, he remained an underground figure, for all the usual reasons. He didn't become famous the way other artists synonymous with the downtown art scene of the 1980s became famous—Basquiat, Haring, Sherman, Schnabel. He didn't share a booth with Warhol at Max's Kansas City. He didn't do lines in the unisex restroom at the Mudd Club. He was in and of the margins, one of a loose community of artists who made up an alternative to the alternative art scene. Very few people had actually witnessed any of his performances, but the truth was, you didn't need to. You could be standing on a tenement rooftop at a party listening to a stranger describe, in an incredulous, conspiratorial tone, what the Artist had done and forget about him for years, only to have a casual mention uncover the memory like the sound of a mountain.

The artist Tim Etchells has described his first encounter with the Artist's work. This was at a cinema in Sheffield in 2001. By then the Artist had driven himself further underground with a series of hermetic, bewildering performance pieces that resulted in his disappearance from the art world altogether. A year before the talk he gave in Sheffield, the Artist had emerged briefly, after more than a decade of silence, to announce that he wouldn't be making art anymore to a public that had largely forgotten him. That was more than sixteen years ago.

The talk that Etchells saw was about the Artist's body of work—six performances pieces in all—before his self-imposed exile. The Artist explained that after spending a year confined in a cage that he'd built in his downtown loft, he embarked on his next project in April 1980: Every hour on the hour for an entire year, he punched a time clock. He clicked through a slideshow—snapshots of himself as a much younger man standing in the same spot with the same slightly doleful yet resolute look on his face.

This is day 53. This is day 54. This is from day 55. In the dim illumination of the theater the Artist stood very straight. His tone was impassive. He offered no interpretation, no betrayal of feeling. From his seat in the audience, Etchells felt sunk. He felt as though a hole had opened up beneath him. The hole unnerved him because it also felt familiar; it was not a new hole but one, he realized, that had been there all along. The Artist's work had made it visible.

"I was silenced by what I saw," Etchells wrote. "I think I was frightened."

Was what he was seeing art—or pathology? Etchells wasn't

sure. The Artist's performance pieces were ephemeral, vanished acts. Yet they were freighted too with the labor of their making, the days advancing drop after drop, one barely distinguishable from the last, into the black well of the hole.

This is a project about looking down into that hole.

ONE YEAR PERFORMANCE 1978-1979

September 30, 1978

<u>STATEMENT</u>

I, **SAM HSIEH**, plan to do a one year performance
piece, to begin on September 30, 1978.

I shall seal myself in my studio, in solitary
confinement inside a cell-room measuring
11'6" X 9' X 8'.

I shall NOT converse, read, write, listen to the
radio or watch television, until I unseal myself on
September 29, 1979.

I shall have food every day.

My friend, Cheng Wei Kuong, will facilitate this
piece by taking charge of my food, clothing and
refuse.

Sam Hsieh

THE NEW YORK ART WORLD

When the Artist first arrived in New York City, he avoided the subway and went by another name—Sam—for the same reason: to evade the police.

His first apartment was near 180th Street at the very top of the island of Manhattan, an overcrowded share with other Chinese migrants. Eventually he made his way down to Greenwich Village. Passing through the marble arch in Washington Square, he encountered people with easels painting portraits and buildings. *Here is the New York art scene*, he thought.

SoHo he stumbled onto by accident. The neighborhood—a postindustrial Wild West of cast-iron warehouses and former industrial factories—electrified him. By then, a handful of bars, galleries, and cafés had opened, you could still be out in the middle of the day and see no one except for a few people slipping in and out of what looked like derelict buildings. The Artist knew he had to make his way back there one day. He made a mental note of the address of a building: that would be his bread-crumb trail. Then he forgot the number. It would be another two years before he'd find his way to SoHo again.

By 1978, the year of his first performance piece in his adopted city, the Artist had made few, if any, inroads in the art world. But he'd been doing his homework, steadily compiling a list of artists, writers, critics, and gallery owners in town. He bought a typewriter, a roll of stamps, and a box of envelopes and mailed each person on his list a copy of a one-page artist statement that began, *I, Sam Hsieh, plan to do a one year performance piece to begin on September 30, 1978 . . .*

One recipient, the poet Jackson Mac Low, wrote back:

"May I ask you a completely serious (not meant negatively) question: why do you do such performances? They do not seem self-fulfilling or such as to give much pleasure or insight to audiences, but there must be more to them than is apparent. Please try to let me know."

DISRUPTIONS IN CONTINUITY

The word *project* comes from the Latin *projicere*, as in *pro*—forward—and *jecere*—to throw.

Alice had done this, looked up the definition of *project* while procrastinating on her own project. She'd also done this: read blogs by project managers who put it this way:

A project has four phases: initiate, plan, execute, and conclude.

A project must have a beginning and it must have an end.

Curiously, embedded in the layered definitions of *project* is its own undoing: the *project* is "an idle scheme; an impracticable design; as in, 'a man given to *projects*'" (Webster-dictionary.org).

Alice was one who had been given to projects. Experimental film shorts; an apocryphal ghost tour of Manhattan Chinatown; a Gothic space opera; wayward "hypertexts." More than a few projects, yes, of impractical design. These projects lay forsaken, beached on their sides like large kitchen appliances after a tornado; some swam amphibiously in scum water in perpetual pre-project formation; others, more developed yet stalled, were walled up in folders on her laptop.

And yet a new project was stirring, showing signs of life, her project about the Artist. She didn't yet know what form it would take, only that she would work with the same raw material that he had: time.

But right now, at this minute, she absolved herself from thinking or doing anything about the Project. She was on a red-eye from New York to California to visit her father, and, for Alice, in-flight time was time already accounted for based on the foggy theory that the transport of her body at high speed through space and time should release her brain from undertaking any great exertion. She felt released and relieved to be off the clock from her freelance work, and from having to keep a meticulous record of the hours and minutes she spent on each assignment for invoicing at the end of the month.

Most of the video editing jobs she took on lasted no more than a month. The TV shows she worked on sometimes ran together in her head, but they seemed mostly to fall in two categories: aspirational makeover, or fractious family-owned businesses in the American South. She'd come to think of her role in these assignments as Caspering, after the friendly cartoon ghost. She was the person they hired to fill in for someone on leave or who was recently let go. It was her job to make their absences appear seamless—stitching in the music, editing the dialogue, color-correcting and grading, time-syncing between one scene and another. It was work, she supposed, that was invisible to begin with, but it paid all the bills and was, with the exception of a few harrowing weeks every year, steady.

Last week she'd wrapped up a gig editing promos for a meal delivery start-up that specialized in vegetable-forward global cuisine. Just as she'd started to worry about ginning up the next job, a former classmate got in touch. They'd studied classics together in college. Would Alice be interested in doing contract work for the new digital-only vertical he was managing? The staffer who'd been working on the account was scheduled to be out on maternity leave. The show, her former classmate said, was called *Bring On the Feels*. He paused, as if to let the drama of the name sink in—or to make sure Alice registered that he was appropriately detached, in a droll, ironic way, from the mainstream inanity of the entire enterprise. It was hard to know which, and this too she remembered about him, his straddling of two points of view, which made him seem smarter than most people, and without passion. The assignment would be helping to package together short viral news stories of the uplifting variety—a cancer survivor owner of a rescue dog with a cleft palate parachuting together out of an airplane—that kind of thing.

Yes, she was interested. When Caspering, it helped to have a story driving things along, even if the story was as hyper-calibrated as a designer drug. Otherwise, the job felt too much like selling toothpaste. She'd done that too—sell toothpaste, polishing promos for a fluoride-free, paraben-free, and cruelty-free brand that cost more than fifteen dollars a tube and came in flavors like English Cucumber and Peppermint Stick.

The pilot announced something about headwind and a delayed arrival time in that cowboy drawl all pilots seem to affect to settle people's nerves. As the plane leveled to cruising altitude, Alice read a magazine profile of a British actor who'd starred in a reboot of an apocalyptic road movie franchise. She tore out recipes for complicated salads she'd never make. When she was done with that, she watched *Westworld* on the little screen in front of her—the movie from the 1970s, not the TV reboot—and fell asleep to the soothing rhythms of a long-running sex crime procedural.

It was the end of January. This was the first of three, possibly four trips Alice planned to make that year to see the Father. Since his retirement from the carpentry shop where he'd worked nearly his entire adult life, the Father had been slowing down. Days might go by when he didn't leave his house, where he lived alone. He'd moved several times since he and Alice's mother divorced, always in Berkeley, their first city after arriving from Taiwan. Alice's older sister Amy lived an hour's drive away and checked in on the Father regularly, but she was a single mom of a nine-year-old working full-time at an optometrist's office. The sisters triaged. Since last year, Alice had been visiting more frequently for longer stretches. She took the Father to medical appointments and to get his hair cut. She tried to troubleshoot things around the house.

On her last visit, she'd found the Father parked, as he often was, in front of the television. She could tell from the snarling and gunfire that he was watching the zombie show.

The Father leaned forward in his chair, pointing the remote at the TV to turn it off. As he shuffled slowly to the dining room to talk and smoke, he told her that he'd watched the same episodes of the zombie show so many times that he'd begun catching what he called "mistakes." In one scene he'd watch a zombie get his head cleaved by an ax, only to spot the same walker a few scenes later as one in a horde of zombies trying to mow down a fence.

"How many times do you think you've watched the same episode?" Alice asked.

He shrugged. "I've lost count. It doesn't matter. I can't remember what happens in them anyway."

Alice shrugged too. The Father's memory was not what it used to be; this particular lapse struck her as among the least worrisome.

More worrisome was this: problems with his hands—gripping things, balancing things. Problems, definitely, with his brain. He got frustrated easily and was quicker to lose his temper. Why had he recently stopped reading his paperback thrillers, Connelly, Koontz, Clancy? Because he falls asleep when he reads in bed, he explained, and the books fall on his head and startle him awake. It took a minute for Alice to realize this was a white lie. He stopped reading because he was forgetting words, forgetting plots.

The morning she arrived in the Bay Area, she called the Father before making her way over to his house and asked, as she always did, "Do you want anything from the outside world?"

Yes, he said. A nine-volt battery and antihistamines from CVS. A package of baloney from Safeway. "See you soon, baby doll."

The first order of business was to take the Father to see his doctor, who had recently relocated to a sleek office park in Emeryville. The gently landscaped walkways and newly planted trees and bushes made Alice feel like she was walking inside an architectural model. The waiting area, painted a light aquarium-blue, had been newly appointed with matching green and blue furniture. But the women at the front desk were the same and greeted the Father with warm smiles. Still bleary-eyed from her flight, Alice went to the restroom to splash water on her face and came back to find the Father tapping his cane lightly on the carpet and looking out the window at nothing.

When the doctor entered the exam room, the Father cracked, "Nice haircut. You look just like Yul Brynner."

The doctor chuckled, touching his dome lightly. "That's fine with me. I like Yul Brynner. Especially in *The King and I* and *Westworld*."

Westworld! Alice's brain flickered. Hadn't she just—well, yes, she had, and here it was again. This was an instance of frequency illusion, a.k.a. the Baader-Meinhof effect, a whiplash trick of the mind and distant cousin of déjà vu. Your brain, swimming through oceans of data, catches on to something newly learned or conspicuously arcane; a sequencing or synchronicity takes hold, and you're left feeling the uncanniness of its reoccurrence.

On the plane, she'd lacked the patience to watch the film— she'd seen it at least a few times on TV as a child—from beginning to end. Instead, she'd fast-forwarded to the good part, when the robots at the robot theme park start going berserk. The first sign that all is not well in *Westworld* is an animatronic rattlesnake that fangs a guest, breaking skin. Then a medieval knight-bot gores a paying customer in a sword fight. Things can be said to be truly going ape-shit when Robo-Yul, a diamond-eyed gunslinger programmed to take a bullet, refuses to die.

Is Yul Brynner still alive? the Father and doctor mused.

"He most certainly is not," Alice said loudly.

As a child, she'd seen Yul Brynner's public service announcement on TV against smoking. The actor, a five-pack-a-day smoker, stares straight into the camera—his skin gray, yet his voice as

Yul as ever—and warns, "Don't smoke, whatever you do. Just. Don't. Smoke." By the time the PSA aired, he was already dead from lung cancer. The Father was up to two packs a day.

In *Westworld*, Robo-Yul is the Terminator before there was a Terminator. He marches, his back straight as a plank, his boot spurs jingling the terrifying jingle of death. He marches right out of the Old West corral into the mead hall of Medieval World, cuts past the marble fountains and pleasure gardens of Roman World. The anachronism of his cowboy hat is queasy-making. Disneyland, to avoid such incidents of de-synchronicity in its amusement parks, built a vast network of underground tunnels to shield visitors from the sight of a pirate texting in Bear Country. But Robo-Yul could give a fuck.

Alice made sure the doctor performed a prostate exam. She also persuaded him to write the Father a prescription for an anti-depressant, which didn't take much persuasion at all, actually. This made her suspicious of the doctor even though it was her idea.

Just as it seemed the appointment was drawing to a close, the doctor said to the Father: "I want you to do something for me."

"Uh-oh," the Father said.

"I want you to draw me a clock."

"With the hands and numbers?"

"Yes, with the hands and numbers."

The Father asked no more questions and set upon the task. This ready compliance to authority—except when it involved something he didn't want to do—had always troubled Alice about him. She made a mental note to research safeguards against phone scams that target the elderly. The Father gripped his pen and pressed down on the paper with great seriousness, the same look he got on his face when he signed checks.

Across the room, she froze in her chair. She knew all about this clock-drawing test. She'd learned about it a few months ago from a TV show about early Hannibal Lecter. All season long Hannibal has been cannily gaslighting a colleague, a high-strung criminal profiler who has been skirting dangerously close to the cannibal's secret. Hannibal manages to convince this colleague into thinking that he himself might be the dangerous psychotic he's been trailing. The profiler, aghast at his own deranged impulses, subjects himself to the clock-drawing test. The drawing he makes—a flabby Dalí clock-face with all the numbers skittering into a heap—seals his fate. Hannibal's nemesis is locked up in a psych ward. Hannibal is triumphant. To celebrate, he executes a buoyant meat mold set in aspic.

Her throat tight, Alice resisted the urge to peer over the Father's shoulder. But, surprise! His drawing of the clock was perfectly normal, the numbers in order, hands tucked neatly inside the face. The Father was not criminally insane, nor did he appear to have Alzheimer's, his greatest fear. The only peculiar thing was that his clock was about the size of a quarter.

RAVENS

Alice and James were trading stories on the phone about the brains of their fathers. Hardly anyone they knew seemed to talk much on the phone anymore. But what started out as an accident—a butt dial that turned into a dumb joke about a talking butt that then evolved into an actual phone conversation—became routine in their friendship.

James's father was in his eighties and had recently suffered a stroke. Not a catastrophic one but serious enough to lay him out. James said it hurt to see him spent down like a week-old helium balloon after a party. His father had been a looker in his day, tall, broad-shouldered, with hooded eyes that made him look a little dreamy. When she was alive, James's mother used to joke that she had to beat other women off with a baseball bat. James had his father's eyes, although their effect was muted behind his horn-rimmed glasses.

Early on after the stroke, James's father wasn't talking, so it was hard to tell how much his mental faculties had been affected. And yet when the old man encountered something or someone not to his liking, he amazed everyone with the fierceness of his kicks, his skinny leg slicing through the air like a sword.

Alice shared her stories too of taking her father on a disastrous trip to Target where he became enraged by the inexact sizing of men's underwear, a fury that he then unleashed like buckshot at his fellow shoppers as he propelled himself out of the store. The same thing had happened a few months ago at Costco.

"Well, at least they still got fight in them," James said. "It might be terrible to behold but I'm going to claim it as a victory."

"Where are you?" Alice could hear the beeping sound of a truck backing up and cars whooshing by.

"I'm standing on a corner in Williamsburg waiting for veal."

"You're what?"

James explained that he'd been chatting with a guy in his pay-what-you-will meditation class. The guy was the only other Black man in the room, an electrician in his sixties who had converted to Buddhism many years ago and no longer ate meat. The electrician made an exception, however, if the animal died in a humane way, which, of course, was a rare event.

"Medium rare?"

"You're stupid. It turns out this guy has some kind of arrangement with a meat farm upstate, grass-fed artisanal-type shit. He gets a heads-up whenever there's a cow or pig on the farm that's died of natural causes. And he's not the only one. There's like two other people here on the corner with me. They're jonesing. I'm just here for the scene."

Alice laughed. She loved this about James, his willingness to follow the floating byways of life. "What else is going on?"

"Mythology."

A few weeks ago, James had come across a beat-up copy of Edith Hamilton's *Mythology* on a stoop in Crown Heights. It was the same mass-market edition he'd read as a boy, with the cover image of Medusa's decapitated head writhing with snakes. Alice nodded. As a girl, she'd received the same edition from the Father, a find from one of his flea market expeditions. She couldn't get enough of those crazed, shape-shifting tales. Curious, James had flipped to the section about Odin, the Norse god, to refresh his memory of the immortal chieftain hailed by white supremacists. His rereading had failed to deliver much insight, but it had revived his knowledge of Odin's two pet ravens. One bird was named Munin, or Memory, and the other, Hugin, or Thought. Every morning Odin released his birds and every night they flew back, alighting on Odin's shoulders to whisper to him all they had seen of the world. James was haunted by the image of his father as a hoary old Nordic god waiting for his birds, the stand-in for his brain, to return every day.

"Or maybe we're the ravens," Alice said. "We're the ones bringing the news from the outside world, reminding them of who they are."

"In that case, we're going to need a whole mess of ravens. Or is that what you'd call a murder? Hold up, I think the veal guy is here."

More and more Alice found herself thinking on the machinery of the brain and its sprongy parts, which led to gloomy thoughts about her own inexorable decrepitude. She was thirty-nine, with a cat but no partner, no children, although, to be truthful, children had never been more than an abstraction, nothing she'd ever thought to work at to make happen. Who would perform daughterly duties when she became old and infirm? She'd never observe, at the granular level like a mother would, she thought, a child's developing brain. She'd not watch as they learned how things work or blurted those ingenious koans children are known for. She wouldn't observe the moment they figured out how to be devious and clever. But she *was* watching an old person's brain fall apart, little by little, and strange and awful as it sounded, it was as full of marvel in its own way.

Later that night in her apartment, Alice searched online for Odin's ravens, scrolling on her laptop as she slurped her dinner of ramen and pre-washed spinach from a bag. She shoved the cat's nose away from her bowl and his feet off the keyboard.

These ravens flapped across her screen:

—The ravens the Vikings kept in cages on their ships and which they released to the open sea to gauge the proximity of land.

—The ravens in Roman myth, once as white as swans, enlisted by the gods to inform on the deeds of man. A raven informed on a nymph lover of Apollo's for making time with a mortal. Apollo killed the nymph, and, for good measure punished the messenger by turning the raven black.

—The ravens in an Old Norse poem about Odin, which contained this central enigma:

Hugin and Munin
fly each day
over the spacious earth.
I fear for Hugin,
that he come not back,
yet more anxious am I for Munin.

Without Hugin, we'd be nincompoops. But who would we be without Munin? Without our memories we could be anyone, or no one.

The cat was crowding her laptop again, flashing his starfish asshole in her face. She typed in a new search. It isn't a murder of ravens, it's a murder of crows. A gathering of ravens, she learned, is an *unkindness*.

APHASIA

People get old and forget words. We know this. The Father and Alice would be chatting and he'd stop, struggling for the word that described, you know, the part of the leg between the knee and the foot.

"The calf?"

"Yes, yes, calf, calf!"

She liked this game, finding the right word. It made her feel useful and she was good at it.

The Father knew three languages to forget words in— English, Chinese, and Vietnamese; the last two he learned in the Army during the Vietnam War. Later, when the Father's problem with words revealed itself to be more serious than run-of-the-mill senility, they learned its name: expressive aphasia. He could understand what was being said to him and he knew what it was he wanted to say; he just couldn't get the words out.

Alice found it strange that the Father's trouble with words aggravated him so much more than the fact that he'd forget, on occasion, how to turn a shirt right-side in, or slide a belt through the belt loops of his jeans. His hands, he complained, were bad.

All last year Alice and Amy had been trying various stop-gap measures to manage the Father's decline. There was Meals on Wheels and the home health aide they arranged to drop in a few days a week. There was a volunteer-operated driving service that took him to appointments if neither of them could make it. There were the hours spent researching diabetic socks, Velcro slippers, soap holders that suction to tile not just porcelain, a chair for the bathtub, plastic food containers with easy peel-off lids.

The problem was nothing worked. Rising from the bath chair they'd gotten him, the Father hit his head on the showerhead, so the chair didn't work. The shoes pinched his toes; why wouldn't Costco carry his favorite sneakers anymore? There must be something wrong with this jacket because he couldn't figure out how to put his arms through it. Shopping their way out of his problems didn't work, either, but, like small talk, it performed the necessary function of disguising an immense melancholy.

Aphasia was a source of intense interest for the philosopher Henri Bergson. Bergson was convinced that somewhere at the heart of the aphasic person's condition lay the answer to his life's question: Where, exactly, did memory reside? In the realm of the spirit, or in the realm of matter? For five years Bergson pored over the literature—scientific studies of people possessed of normal intelligence and with perfectly intact speech organs, yet who, for reasons unknown, could no longer form language; research on individuals in full command of their wits but whose vocal cords no longer worked or whose tongues could not be made to curl or fall back. The fact that being afflicted with aphasia did not foreclose the full range of emotions, thoughts, and memories was a revelation. It meant, Bergson believed, that the brain could be separated from thought and matter from memory, and this meant that a soul could exist—persist, even—beyond the fleshly depredations of the body.

"Come on, brain!" Alice heard the Father mutter to himself from the other room as he struggled to shove his legs through his pants.

ACTIVITIES OF DAILY LIVING

Alice had been looking at photographs taken of the Artist's first performance work in New York, known informally as *Cage Piece*. For the purposes of his project, the Artist allowed himself no reading material, no television, no radio, no writing, and no speaking—nothing that would distract from the undistilled passing of time in the prison of his own making. In many of the pictures, he's staring off into space. There are pictures of him lying on his thin cot, sometimes with his legs crossed at the ankles, sometimes sprawled out, his expression alternating between a stoic mask and the sulkiness of a teenage boy. Here's one where he's taking a sponge bath; another of him etching a mark on the wall (*day 53, day 54*). He relieves himself in a slop bucket. There are only a few photographs—one with his head buried in hands—where he appears to be broken by the stillness and sameness of his days.

Despite the solitude of those images, the Artist wasn't entirely alone; someone took those photographs from the other side of the cage: Cheng Wei Kuong.

Cheng Wei Kuong was the Artist's friend from back in Taiwan. They'd gone to art school together, studied with the same painting teacher, and even roomed together for a time in New York in a loft on Hudson Street. That's where the Artist built himself a cage from pine dowels and two-by-fours. In addition to taking daily photographs, Kuong was also responsible for keeping the Artist alive by bringing him food every day and emptying his bucket of shit and piss. Alice guessed it was probably Kuong who put up posters in SoHo and the East Village announcing the four public viewings of the performance-in-progress, one for each season of the year. (Anecdote: a woman climbed the stairs up to the loft, peered around the room, and demanded, "But where's the art?")

Alice could find no online trail of Kuong, at least in the English-language press. His name appeared only as a credit for the photographic archive he'd made of the Artist's performance, and in one spare reference the Artist made in an interview. The Artist said every day his friend Kuong brought him a take-out meal of beef and broccoli over rice. Over time, the monotony of this dish became so aggravating to him that one day he threw the beef and broccoli to the floor, which he felt badly about afterward.

Did Kuong stay or return to Taiwan? Did he continue to paint or make his own art? Was he living in a brick split-level in Bensonhurst? Was that him, the liver-spotted patriarch in a Yankees baseball cap, surrounded by his large family at the dim sum parlor on Eighth Avenue last Sunday?

The Father had a beloved if not original gag. "Pull my finger," he'd insist. Doing so released a fart.

In the Father's favorite picture of himself, he's sitting on a toilet. The photo was taken soon after he left the Army in Vietnam. In the picture he's hunched over the bowl, elbows resting on thighs, his brow slightly raised. The shutter clicked so suddenly he didn't have time to register surprise. He has the look of someone whose contemplations have been interrupted, whose last thought, the kind that preoccupies a moment of privacy, lingers as a shadow.

Whenever the Father tells the story of how the picture came to be, he chuckles good-naturedly. A buddy flung open the door to the can and took a quick snap. A good joke. All his life he has not minded being the butt of a good joke. He enjoyed this one so much that he had T-shirts of the photo made to share with family and friends. The joke was the seriousness on his face.

When he wanted to describe an unconditional state of happiness, he compared it to being "like a pig in shit." He used to mortify Alice's mother when they were still married by wearing a T-shirt emblazoned with an advertisement for Ex-Lax. Shit was funny. Shit was crazy. Shit inevitably went down.

No one knew exactly when the Father fell. It had been less than a month since Alice's last visit, which had been largely uneventful. No: There was one thing. He'd looked a little wild because he'd grown a beard, a nest of wires that looked like it wanted to leap off his face. She'd never known him not to be clean-shaven. The armpits of his white T-shirt were stained, which she hadn't thought too much of at the time, figuring he had just let his dirty laundry pile up.

Amy was much better than Alice about checking in on the Father regularly by phone, but she didn't call every day and he didn't answer every call. He must have lain on the floor for at least a day and a half before his cleaning lady found him. He was dehydrated, delirious, yet nothing was broken, thank god. Amy dropped Ezra off at a neighbor's with snacks and a few of his favorite toys and drove to the hospital from San Jose. At the hospital, she found the Father roaring at the nurses and doctors. His fury would burn, then simmer to a black pitch, only to fire up again. He yelled. He threatened.

This behavior, the nurses explained to the sisters, was not unusual. There was even a name for it: sundowning. They clung to this new word, a dinghy bobbing on the sea of their know-nothingness. They learned that sundowning, triggered by the approaching lateness of the day, was prevalent among elderly patients, especially those who suffered from dementia. Once it hit them, they were like werewolves enraptured by a full moon, raging with mania. What causes sundowning is not entirely clear, but medical experts agree that the sensation of timelessness produced by prolonged stays in institutional settings—where daytime and nighttime become indistinguishable—makes it worse.

Alice wondered how the Father would draw the clock now, because, since his fall, his brain seemed, well, more out of whack. Did he have dementia? His doctor had never used that word. To Alice, dementia meant Alzheimer's, that blank fog of incomprehension and memory loss, and the Father didn't fit that profile—at least not exactly and not yet. Was his angry delirium temporary or permanent? Alice thought ruefully of his drinking. The Father drank. There had been dry periods, but mostly he drank. Surely his drinking had something to do with all this. He was a mostly private drinker, careful to hide his drinking from others. Alice never fully understood how much his drinking played in her parents' divorce; looking back, how could it not have? There were no drunken episodes, no loud fights. But to her mother, Alice thought, the Father's drinking, his dreaming—all of that must have felt like an abdication in the years when money was tight. And now this: Drinking was the pass the Father had given himself to let everything else go, including his health. It made Alice pissy. Bitter thought: Was there an onset before wet brain? Moist brain? Maybe he had that. Her moralizing was a wicked lash. But then she'd watch him sleep fitfully in his hospital bed, feel her heart twist in her chest, and set the lash aside before she'd find herself judging him all over again. Judging him instead of worrying about him was like delivering a hard slap against an itch: relief of a different feeling.

How had he fallen? Later the Father would insist he fell in the bathroom because work was being done in it. He recalled long rods crisscrossing the floor and electric lights shooting out from each end. It sounded mad, like Dan Flavin was his handyman. His hands wouldn't do what his mind wanted them to do. He cried easily.

When a new doctor or charge nurse entered the Father's hospital room, they would glance in Alice's direction and ask if she was the nurse on duty.

No, Alice would explain. I'm the daughter.

This case of mistaken identity was understandable. The Father was actually her stepfather, and he was white. He had grown up in a Pentecostal family in a former coal-mining town outside Mobile, Alabama. The Father's father drove a truck and built their home with his own hands using wood beams and other salvaged materials from houses on the other side of town that had been demolished to build the interstate. The Father's brother was a devout Tea Party member; his sister played the organ at church and taught Sunday school. The Father was the outlier, the one who left.

The other reason for the misidentification, which would be obvious to anyone who spends more than a few minutes in a hospital in California, is that the world of the sick and dying is ministered almost entirely by Black, Latinx, and Asian women. Alice blended in with the other health workers. That was okay by her. She was in awe of the nurses.

By the time she and the Father had entered each other's lives, she was already three years old. As a stepparent, he never had to wipe her ass clean of shit. As his daughter, she'd probably have the resources not to have to wipe his ass, either. At least she hoped.

It wasn't until she was college age that she saw herself and her father as others might see them, sitting across from each other in a restaurant in Oakland, Chinatown, or in a shopping plaza in El Cerrito, which they often did, bent over their menus. It was the same idly curious look she now gave to other diners who looked like them, an older white man with a much younger Asian woman.

After three weeks in the hospital, the Father was released to another institution: a skilled nursing facility, or SNF, in Oakland. A nurse had taught Alice and Amy how to pronounce it—"sniff."

The SNF was loud and dissonant and grief-struck. Every day for his physical and occupational therapy, the Father traveled a short distance by wheelchair from the main building through the parking lot and into a smaller building that housed a small gym and a facsimile kitchen where patients learned to open cabinets, work the stove, and eat with utensils.

Already he was walking slowly with the help of a walker. Good. But he had trouble with his fork and, on one occasion, threw his shoe across the room in frustration. Every week the therapists reported on the Father's progress to the insurance company. Once he *plateaus*, they explained, insurance will cut him off and he'll be sent home.

At the hospital, and later at the skilled nursing facility in Oakland, shit was referred to as "BM"—short for bowel movement.

"When was the last time you had a BM?"

"Did you have a BM today?"

One can't say *shit*—that's swearing. *Excrement* is a mouthful and even more foul. *Poop* is infantilizing; *number two,* too coy. As with so many matters that people prefer to leave unnamed yet must be said aloud, an acronym delivers the truth, slant.

As the Father recuperated at the SNF, the question of whether he would, in the future, be able to walk to the toilet, take a shit, and wipe himself clean loomed large in Alice's mind. She and Amy had talked about it in circles. His facility with performing these tasks would determine how and where he lived once he was released. The Father was heavy. Who would help him to the toilet? What would happen if he needed to go in the middle of the night?

In the lingua franca of this strange land of the sick and ailing where the Father had washed ashore, going to the bathroom was considered an activity of daily living, or ADL. In the months leading up to his fall, the Father's handle on ADLs had already been slipping. He was afraid of falling in his tub, so had stopped bathing with any regularity. He stopped shaving or wearing clothes that involved zippers and buttons; somehow he managed to keep making his daily brew of coffee, but he grumbled about how difficult it was to pour water into his coffeemaker.

Some wiseass with a mordant sense of humor came up with a mnemonic for ADLs: Dressing. Eating. Ambulating. Toileting. Hygiene.

Despite his weakened state, the Father did not lack for energy to wage a campaign, which started at the hospital and carried on at the SNF, to watch Super Bowl 50 in his own home. Whenever Alice visited him, he'd ask again and again when the Super Bowl was, convinced it was a week away even though it was a month out.

The closer the countdown to Super Bowl Sunday got, the more anxious the Father became. He wanted so badly to be in his chair at home in front of his TV with his favorite snacks, his cigarettes, and a whiskey in hand. If no one would take him, he said, baring his teeth, he would call a cab himself! He didn't care if he had to crawl or shoot people to get there!

Naturally, Alice and Amy began using the Super Bowl as a carrot. If you eat this or do that, you'll be strong enough to go home and watch the Super Bowl. But as the weeks dragged on at the SNF, it became clear to everyone, including, finally, the Father, that he wouldn't be going home anytime soon, although he never conceded this defeat aloud. Instead, he began marshaling his spirits around the only possible alternative: watching the game in the facility's larger common room where the game would be broadcast on a big-screen TV, much bigger than the one he had at home—the exact eventuality that Alice had been stealthily building up in his mind for weeks by talking up the big screen every time she wheeled him around the building.

Then came the week of the big game. As she pushed the Father in his wheelchair through the corridors, he rallied the other residents to join him on Sunday, while she stood behind him, nodding and smiling imperceptibly like a butler. By then he had come to be on friendly terms with a few other patients who were well enough, or cared enough, to hold a conversation, including a former Navy pilot who appeared to listen with attention yet never spoke, and a rather fussy, distracted woman, also in a wheelchair, who talked too much and worried with her hands.

"I'm going to be there," he said, his hand pressed over his heart, "and my daughter will be bringing snacks." His interlocutors nodded distractedly. Most of them rarely smiled.

On the morning of Super Bowl Sunday, she went to the CVS on Telegraph Avenue to load up on the Father's favorites, chili-flavored Fritos and fried pork rinds. It was a bright, cloudless day. She took the bus and got off on Piedmont near the old-fashioned ice-cream parlor where the Father used to take her and Amy for black & tan sundaes when they were young. From there it was a walk up a slight incline to the facility, a block and world away from the main commercial drag.

This was an area of Oakland known as Pill Hill, so called for the hospitals and skilled nursing facilities clustered there. Later when she read the short stories of Lucia Berlin, she realized she was riding the same bus lines that the narrator of "A Manual for Cleaning Women" took to get to her clients' homes—the 40 on Telegraph Avenue, the 43 along Shattuck. Once you cross into Oakland from Berkeley, the streets widen out and the bus stop benches start advertising local funeral homes. In Berlin's stories the bus passengers were either young and Black or old and white. This was in the early seventies. Now they were nearly all old and mostly Black.

But if she caught the 40 bus in the early afternoon, young people let out from Oakland Tech High School would come on board. They didn't smoke or play their radios as they had in Berlin's time. They bobbed their heads to music streaming through their headphones. It occurred to her that the women in Berlin's stories were the type the Father favored: blunt-talking yet feminine, crackling with jokes; women who didn't take shit from no one and who didn't take themselves too seriously, either; women who crossed their legs when they smoked. Like him, they were skilled at hiding their drinking behind their sly humor and their manners. They were private with their sadness.

When Alice arrived at the facility, she found the Father lying flat on his back in bed staring at the ceiling. The TV in his room was blaring as usual, but he paid it no mind. He told her his stomach was upset. Earlier that morning when the charge nurse made her rounds, she discovered that he hadn't had a BM for some days. The decision was made to give him a suppository. Now he felt that he might "go" at any minute. He was afraid to get in his wheelchair and join the others in the TV room. He was convinced that people would laugh at him if he shit his pants.

She wanted to tell him that if there was one place where shitting one's pants would be met with forbearance and empathy, this was it. Instead, she promised she would wheel him back the second he gave her the signal. This seemed to assure him.

By then a larger group than usual, fifteen deep, had gathered in the large common room. At this hour the room was stifling: the afternoon sun glared from the floor-to-ceiling windows and made the TV hard to see. The activities coordinator, a short blond woman in a Raiders jersey, had wheeled out two carts of party food: a few liter bottles of root beer, Coke, and orange soda, a big bowl of Doritos, and trays of vegetable sticks and ranch dip. There was even a platter of chicken wings.

At least a few other residents seemed to have family visiting too to watch the game together. But most pulled up solo. Alice noticed the pretty, older Japanese woman with long, silver hair she had spotted when she first visited the facility. The woman's seething at the nurses ("Get the fuck away from me!") was Alice's indoctrination to the mercurial moods of the residents and the bitter sorrows of living in an institution. Another time Alice saw her squatting, spider-like in her bed, peering at the contents of her diaper. Now she seemed to be in some kind of daze, her head nearly touching the tabletop.

The Father took a few desultory sips of soda from a straw but refused food. He looked weak. In the second quarter he leaned over and told her that he wanted to leave, meaning he felt like he was going to shit his pants.

Once, at a party in the Lower East Side, Alice met a man who lived for a while on a houseboat that was docked in the Gowanus Canal in Brooklyn. In the course of conversation, it was revealed that the houseboat did not have a bathroom or a shower.

So how, exactly, did he shit?

He explained that he went to a nearby gym where he was a member, and that this arrangement worked because he was fairly "regular." He mused at how odd it was that he had become accustomed to talking to strangers or near-strangers about his bowel movements; indeed, it may be one of the few things people remembered about him.

The Artist seemed to have anticipated this natural, prurient interest in his bathroom habits.

After the year he spent punching a time clock, the Artist embarked on his third major performance piece. The performance, which he began in late September 1981, involved spending an entire year outdoors in the city without shelter or cover of any kind. The Artist made copies of a map of Manhattan and for each day of the performance he marked his peregrinations— where he slept, ate, and defecated.

Absent a home, downtown Manhattan became his home, he said. Chinatown was his kitchen; the drained swimming pools and sliver-sized parks of SoHo became his bedroom. In winter, the Meatpacking District, where blood from the slaughterhouses ran in the gutters and fires blazed in open garbage cans at night, was his fireplace. His bathroom was the West Side piers, the same abandoned waterfront along the Hudson River immortalized by Peter Hujar, David Wojnarowicz, and Alvin Baltrop, where hustlers, the horny, the homeless, and the runaways gathered among the crumbling docks and warehouses for sex, sun, shelter, and relief. Alice was amused to see in the exhibition catalogue for *Outdoor Piece* a photo of the Artist, his bare backside facing to the camera, squatting at the lip of a pier, primed to take a shit.

The Artist considered all the photographic documentation of his work, along with the maps and the cage he constructed, to be nothing more than what he called *trace evidence* of the work itself. What's happened has already happened; we are left constructing meaning from the leavings.

The Father spent the rest of Super Bowl Sunday in constipated knots. Alice wheeled him back to his room as he requested. The nurses coaxed him off his chair and installed him in a bathroom. Then they rushed off to deal with a more pressing crisis, the soles of their sneakers squeaking as they rushed down the hallway with a mechanized gurney. After a few minutes, the Father began cussing for help. He was in agony sitting on the toilet. She spoke to him from the other side of the door, assuring him the nurses were on their way. For the next half hour she boomeranged between that door and the nurses' station. A few times she pretended not to be by the bathroom when she was, so she could monitor the modulation and frequency of the Father's yelling without actually having to deal with him.

Nearly an hour into this ordeal, it was determined that the Father would be better off back in his wheelchair, where he could at least be more comfortable. Meanwhile, the nurses had gathered in a huddle to discuss his case. A decision was made to consult a medical reference book.

This was worrisome. Alice, a lifelong champion of books, became their skeptic. How could a pre-digital object made from the skin of trees possibly contain the answers they needed? Were they druids? Warlocks?

In any case, the book was proving difficult to locate. The nurses vanished again. The father looked exhausted. He had withdrawn somewhere deep inside himself. More waiting.

And then, it happened: The Father shit himself. As the shit roiled out of him, he cried out in a voice she had never heard before, "Oh! Oh!"

The locus of his torment wasn't physical pain. He keened because the moment he had been dreading all day—his whole life—had broken open. Relief and shame came spilling out.

Annie Ernaux published a slim book, *A Man's Place*, about her father after he died. Her parents operated a modest grocery and café in Seine-Maritime, a provincial region in northern France where Flaubert set *Madame Bovary*. Everyone in town knew her parents and their little store, which struggled financially once the supermarkets moved in.

Over time, Ernaux wrote, her father "became what was known as a human man, a simple man or a good man."

But what did Ernaux mean, *became*? Wasn't the father the

same person he'd always been? *Became* because it was the daughter who had changed. Years of private schooling and university had elevated her to the ranks of the bourgeoisie. Ernaux's father found himself on the periphery of this metamorphosis. It annoyed him, sometimes, to see his daughter studying all day. He blamed books for her bad moods, the sullen look on her face. He was dumbfounded one day to hear her chattering away to a customer in English. "The fact that I had learnt a foreign language at school, without ever visiting the country, was beyond his comprehension." So he too had transformed, becoming to her how he had always appeared to others, someone other than a father. This is when the child stops being a child.

Once, the Father said to Alice, "You know, I'm uneducated . . ." as a preface to a point she now couldn't remember. It hadn't occurred to her that he considered himself uneducated. He enlisted in the Army soon after graduating from high school. The draft was still years away. Because he scored high on the DLAB—Defense Language Aptitude Battery, a military test that gauges your knack for picking up new languages—he was dispatched to the Army's language institute in Monterey to learn Chinese and Vietnamese. He spent the war at a base in Phu Bai eavesdropping on intercepted enemy communiqués.

Alice was the one dumbfounded by her father, a small-town boy from the South who spoke and read Chinese fluently, who had survived a brutalizing war and landed among expats in Taipei, subsisting on Sun Li instant noodles, tuna fish sandwiches, and beer. When they weren't smoking hash or playing bridge, the Father and his American friends taught conversational English to Taiwanese students, which was how he met Alice's mother.

The Father was a woodworker by trade and knew all there was to know about the different types of wood; he could tell in an instant how poorly or well-made a piece of furniture or window was by looking at the joint work and the quality of the materials. Furniture made from particleboard, like the cheap, self-assembly desk she bought from IKEA, upset him.

A college degree didn't account for much in Berkeley, the city where Alice's family settled after leaving Taiwan. Their social universe was made up of social workers, carpenters, graduate students, waitresses, acupuncturists, pottery makers, and organic farmers. There were parties in the backyard of the last house where they would live together, hand-cranked ice cream, foam coolers sloshing with ice and beer, and once, a pit dug in the ground to roast an entire pig. As the years passed, it had become harder for Alice to recall her parents physically together in one place, how they looked at each other, the rhythm of their talk. But in these backyard recollections she could feel their proximate warmth like an aura—the Father with a cigarette glued to his lower lip, testing the pink of the burgers and wise-cracking with her mother and her waitressing friends while they sunned their bare legs—there in that world they'd built which contracted now like an iris shot in a silent film, the black screen closing in on a white dot not so much forgotten as run out.

It never occurred to her that her father's lack of formal education—or her gaining of it— would change them. Even so. When she surveyed the narrow room at the skilled nursing facility in Oakland that the Father was to share with two other old men, Alice found herself hoping that, because the Father was a *simple man*, it might mean he'd adapt to these diminished surroundings more easily. If it had been her mother, Alice thought, she would have agitated for a better, more private room. Did that mean she loved her mother more? The Father did not complain, although he did confide to Alice in a quiet voice that the elderly Korean man in the bed next to him who never seemed to speak or move was a Vietnamese gangster.

Of course the Father hated it there. Anyone would. Yet part of him also seemed resigned to his fate. What choice did he have? This passive acceptance of his lot, with no possibility of an upgrade, no angling for more, no questioning of authority— all that was familiar to Alice, meaning she too tended to take shit for granted. This was the part of him—of them—that she exploited for her own peace of mind.

Now the Father sat in his shit in his wheelchair. While they waited, the shit dripped and puddled to the floor under and around the chair. Alice went to check with the nurses. They asked her to describe the consistency of the shit. Pudding. No, runnier. Like chocolate milk.

While they waited, she stuck her head in the activity room across the hall to check on the football score. On TV was some kind of tribute to halftime entertainers of years past. Whitney! Michael! The Stones, U2. There was Prince at Dolphin Stadium, his hair bound in a bandanna, insouciantly tearing into his guitar in a fierce downpour. She reported to the Father, who was fond of Peyton Manning, that the Broncos were ahead. He responded with a small smile as though receiving news from a distant planet.

The Father sat in his shit because it didn't make sense for the nurses to squander what little time they had to change him, only to have to change him again before they identified a solution. Rationally, this made sense. Irrationally, he was still sitting in shit. Alice did not want to touch shit. She wanted the shit to be someone else's job. But no one else was stepping in. Only then did she head for the bathroom down the hall, yanking long strips of toilet paper and rolling them around her fist like boxing wraps, and wipe the shit beneath her father. She breathed out of her mouth. The shit was unexpectedly slick; the toilet paper mostly swirled it around on the floor.

At last a nurse appeared with a plan of action, a tall woman in purple scrubs with straightened hair that fell in a dramatic waterfall down her back. The plan, she said, was to adminis-ter an antidiuretic to combat the side effects of the supposi-tory. Alice stepped away so the nurse could change the Father's briefs in private. The curtain hooks scraped along the rod. When she returned, the nurse emerged from the bathroom with the Father's Costco sneakers in her hands; she had washed the shit off them, even cleaned the grooves in the soles.

Alice nearly cried over this act of kindness. Later, in a note-book, she carefully wrote down all the nurses' names at the facility, starting with the pretty Armenian nurse who made her father giggle with her impression of Road Runner (*meep meep!*) when she changed his briefs. She wrote down their names so she could greet them with respect, but also, cannily, like a politi-cian's aide, to call in future favors.

Alice had never seen certified nursing assistants or CNAs up close in action. This made her curious about what it took to become one. She found an essay online written anonymously by a former

CNA. The CNA wrote about the sadness of her patients. She wrote about the bright, false cheer of relatives who drop in for the holidays, the inadequate consolations of bingo and checkers; the transition from underwear to pull-ups to adult diapers. She wrote about the rigors of keeping track of each resident's dietary needs, transfer requirements, shower schedule, the level of oxygen in their tanks, when they needed their blue boots and hand splints changed.

Mostly the CNA wrote about time. Ten minutes is what it takes to thoroughly and gently clean a resident who has soiled her briefs. But when management announces cuts to the number of CNAs on the floor from four to three, ten minutes is too long. The decision to take the time or not take the time is like slow-drip moral suicide. Cut your own break short to do it right, or rush through the task like a machine. Caring, she wrote, should not feel like stealing time.

Alice was in awe of the nurses and nursing assistants, how they maintained an even tone; the broad range of improvisation they deployed—playful, firm, warm, cajoling, scolding— to get their patients to do what needed to be done as they deliver us our loved ones, smelling faintly of soap, properly medicated, nails clipped, buttoned, zippered, groomed. She bowed down to the nurses whenever she could no longer take the Father's sundowning. She bowed down when she stepped through the automatic doors of the hospital, of the rehab center, when she peeled off her visitor sticker and breathed in the early evening air, that intoxicating atmosphere—she could practically taste it—the taste of her freedom, her life splitting from his life, gratitude at having left that whole shit show behind.

THE LIST

At the Father's request, Alice brought a small spiral-bound notebook to him at the rehab facility. She attached a pen to the notebook with a string and kept the notebook in the drawer by his bed.

The idea was that she would record the words he'd been forgetting so he could have them readily at hand. What would these words be? She was genuinely curious.

Constipation
Walker
Wheelchair
Bowel movement
Void
Bladder
Netflix

The list was short because before too long, he forgot about the notebook too.

PROJECT FOR A TRIP TO WESTWORLD

The date of the Father's discharge from the SNF in Oakland was closing in. His insurance was scheduled to lapse in a matter of weeks and it was becoming clear that he couldn't live alone at home anymore. Alice and Amy toured half a dozen assisted living facilities in the area under a cloud of anxiety.

A few of the fancier facilities they visited featured lounge areas tricked out to resemble a 1950s malt shop—a jukebox in the corner, a soda counter, booths lining one wall. Alice wondered what kind of lounge would be constructed for her generation when they got old. A TGI Fridays? A fast-casual burrito bar?

"I think I like the one with the dog," Amy said of the facility where there had been an overweight chocolate Labrador lumbering and panting through the common rooms, a soothing companion to all. The Father loved dogs. "Hey, pooch," he'd say, delighted whenever he passed one in the street.

"Yeah," Alice agreed. "There was that nice vegetable garden in the back." They were grasping for bright spots.

Back at the SNF, the Father had recovered sufficient strength to break the rules. One morning he went missing; later they found him meandering around in the parking lot. He wasn't wandering or lost, the Father insisted. He simply didn't like their rules and had staged a protest by going MIA. A consequence of this incident was that he now had to wear a band around his wrist that triggered an alarm whenever he opened a door.

The Father thrust his arm out under Alice's nose so she could see it. "The fuckers." If he couldn't be Robo-Yul defying the boundaries of the android theme park, he would be Randle McMurphy rattling the cage of the mental ward.

Frankly it was a relief that he wasn't trying to *elope*—the industry's preferred term for demented wandering. He just wanted to leave the place, with its cries, the vacant staring, the fog of apple-scented air freshener, the incessant *ding ding ding* at the nurses' station from people pushing their bedside buttons. But he hadn't managed to leave, or even get farther than the parking lot. Whatever else was going on in his brain, he did not suffer from delusions. He must have understood that the world beyond the perimeter of the facility was beyond his capabilities now. His own diminishment had drawn that border as sure as the transmitter in his wristband.

Alice had read that, in Europe, entire villages are being designed for people with Alzheimer's disease. These built environments come equipped with restaurants, gardens, cafés—even a grocery store and barbershop. The care providers and nurses dress in ordinary street clothes. The idea is that this simulacrum of the outside world, with its familiarizing contours and conveniences for undertaking the chores of daily living, is more likely to catch the stops in a person's memory.

If you stumble, a kind stranger will dart forward to help. It seems the neighborhood is filled with nice people who are always willing to stop and lend a hand, whether it's to hold your bag or extend an arm as you steady yourself. Some of them look a little familiar; they must live around here. At any rate, they certainly know the area very well, which can be useful when you realize you can't quite figure which direction you came from. Sometimes they give you directions on how to get back. Other times, and this is more often the case, they offer to walk with you there, because it turns out they are headed that way themselves.

SOUVENIR

MATTRESS, PILLOW, MIRROR, LIGHT BULB

In the decade after the Artist declared he would no longer make art, he had become even more of a semi-fictive figure, as one art critic described him. Then, about seven years ago, his work began resurfacing in the public eye. The first big thing: The Museum of Modern Art launched a new series on performance art and chose *Cage Piece* as the inaugural exhibition. The simple wooden cage that had once sat in a corner of the Artist's Hudson Street loft was reconstructed in one of the museum's galleries. On the wall label for the installation was an account of every object on display in the cage.

TOOTHBRUSH, BAR OF SOAP, NAIL CLIPPERS, TEA BAGS

These residual objects were the trace evidence of performance works that once were and would never be again. In more recent interviews Alice had read, the Artist had described these relics another way, as *the tip of an iceberg.*

The objects reveal only what is visible above the water. Beneath the water, he said, is where the art is.

How often has Alice read a wall label at a museum only to be further confounded. Knowing which materials an artist used and the artwork's precise dimensions is like reading a sign pointed at a complicated person that says *brain*.

CIGARETTES, ASHTRAY, CIRCULARS

After the Father's fall, Alice dropped in on his house to retrieve a few of his things and pick up his mail. She had slept there the first night when she got in, but the decades of heavy cigarette smoke that clung in the air made her wheeze if she stayed there too long. She'd hardly ever been in the house when the Father wasn't in it. Walking through the empty rooms was like drifting through a sunken galleon on the seafloor. His absence was its own atmosphere.

She once read that Serge Gainsbourg's flat in the Seventh Arrondissement has been preserved, at his daughter's request, exactly as he'd left it when he died of a heart attack in his sleep. His Gitanes, extinguished by his hand, remain scattered in ashtrays across every room. On the nightstand by his bed, his favorite brand of chewing gum and mints. By the bathroom sink, his toothbrush, the bristles bent back by his teeth. Two cans of tomato juice chill in the refrigerator.

Alice tried airing out the house by opening all the windows. She didn't know how long she'd be in Berkeley and needed to make it work. She went through the Father's refrigerator and threw out his milk, baloney, and cheese slices. She left intact, on the little wooden table by his TV chair, his lighter and ashtray and the unfiltered cigarettes he'd lined up in two neat rows like torpedoes in the belly of a bomber.

She equivocated whether to toss the growing stack of Safeway circulars and mail-order catalogues. The misplacement of a single piece of paper could send him off into a rage. She left them alone. Later when she reflected on this decision, she realized she must have been holding out on the slim chance that he'd be coming home one day. Her wishful thinking took the form of devotional items left at an altar.

Because the Father never did live in his house again. His mind and body were too wrecked. He now required a level of care of the kind neither Amy nor Alice felt qualified or prepared to give. Also: They were afraid. It was officially time to bring in the professionals. Now that they had a firmer sense of what the Father could and couldn't do on his own, none of the assisted living facilities they'd toured seemed to make sense, if they ever had. He needed something on a much smaller scale, more intimate and hands-on. Alice and Amy zeroed in on a residential care home on a quiet suburban street in San Jose not far from where Amy lived, a sprawling one-story ranch-style house, worn but clean, run by a Filipino couple. Three other elderly men lived there; the Father would be the fourth. The couple and their children lived in a separate wing of the house.

To be cared for in this new house, the Father's own house would have to be sold. The Father wasn't particularly good with money, yet in the early nineties he'd managed to put a down payment on a modest two-bedroom bungalow in West Berkeley—a decision that would save them all.

In the spring Alice returned to California to take charge of clearing out the Father's belongings so the house could be staged by the realtor. She divided a lifetime's worth of his possessions into three categories: resale value, Goodwill value, and no value:

trash. While she sorted, she scanned for items to skim off the top. *Souvenir* wasn't the right word, but it was the word that kept coming to mind. She wanted something to hold on to, to carry away the memory of the Father in her pocket, even though he hadn't yet died.

HEAD, ARMS, TORSO

After Serge Gainsbourg died, his daughter, his exes, and his amour at the time of his death gathered over his body, which they laid in his bedroom for four days. They couldn't bear to let him go. His body was the souvenir.

In fact, one of the first souvenirs on record, at least in the way we use the term now, *was* a body. Or rather, parts of one. A souvenir wasn't always a thing; prior to the mid–eighteenth century, a souvenir referred more to a memory, an abstract remembrance. But then a Frenchman convicted of high treason named David Tyrie changed all that. He was the last person in France to be hanged and drawn and quartered as punishment for his crime. After Tyrie dangled by the neck for the requisite twenty-two minutes of public shaming, he was lowered so his head could be chopped off. Next, he was sliced open and his heart removed so it could be set on fire. Others of his internal organs were rooted out; his legs and arms were torn from his torso.

After that, all the parts of him were gathered together and placed in a coffin for burial. Tyrie had barely cooled in his grave before he was dug up by a group of sailors who proceeded to slice his body up so that hundreds of pieces of him could be smuggled away as proof of his sensational punishment and their proximity to it. Voilà: the souvenir. Only when a souvenir is removed from its place of origin does it accumulate its talismanic power. The thrill of ownership is inseparable from the scandal of its removal.

COOKBOOKS, GUNS, CAMERAS

The Father was a collector. He collected analog cameras and had amassed an extraordinary number of lenses, enlargers, timers, and other photography equipment, most of which he never used. He also collected blues records and secondhand cookbooks he came across in used book stores, flea markets, and yard sales. When Alice was clearing the Father's shelves she found, between the pages of his books, subscription advertisements for *Guns & Ammo* because he also collected guns, which he stored in his bedroom closet in a safe the size of a refrigerator, the kind you see in movie westerns.

The Father was a melancholic. It is the tendency of the melancholic to be faithless to people, as Sontag wrote of Walter Benjamin, that famous melancholic of history. This faithlessness in humanity correlates to the melancholic's generalized, despondent surrender to catastrophe. What the melancholic is faithful to are *things*: that's what makes him such an enthusiastic collector. (Benjamin was a collector of books, toys, postcards, and other graphic ephemera.) Melancholics, Sontag argues, also make the best addicts, "for the true addictive experience is always a solitary one."

Alice was neither a collector nor an addict, yet felt she could claim affinity to those born under the sign of Saturn. As Benjamin described it, Saturn was "the star of the slowest revolution, the planet of detours and delays," and Benjamin was the patron saint of unfinished projects. For thirteen years he toiled over his masterwork, *The Arcades Project*, which he envisioned as a "primal history" of modernity as seen through the prism of the glass-roofed shopping emporiums of mid-century Paris. His draft manuscript, a panoramic maze of quotations from hundreds of sources ranging from philosophical texts to advertising copy and his own reflections, was left incomplete at the time of his suicide on the Franco-Spanish border in 1940. Fleeing Nazi persecution, Benjamin made the grueling journey across the Pyrenees on foot, only to be denied passage into Spain because his papers weren't in order. He committed suicide with an overdose of morphine. His plan had been to seek asylum in the United States. The published version of *The Arcades Project* was constructed from the more than thirty notebooks he'd left in the care of his friend Georges Bataille, who hid them in the archives of the Bibliothèque Nationale in Paris where Benjamin had gathered much of his research.

Benjamin could have fled Paris earlier, but he couldn't bear to. In the autumn before France surrendered, Benjamin was imprisoned for several months in a concentration camp outside Paris before his French friends intervened and brokered his release. Rather than leave the city as thousands of people were doing at the time ahead of the German invasion, Benjamin chose to renew his library card so he could be near his books and resume working on his projects.

STEAMERS, ROTISSERIE, TEACUP

On Craigslist, Alice posted a listing for a garage sale and spent a day arranging and tagging the Father's things. On the morning of the sale, the mini-fridge and microwave were snatched instantly.

A brooding couple dressed head-to-toe in black bought a small saucepan and the Father's vintage drafting tool set; an Asian woman made off with his record player and Chinese steamers. Late in the day when the crowd had thinned out, a family—a father, a mother, three girls, and their grandmother—entered the house together. The father spent a great deal of time fiddling with a never-used indoor chicken rotisserie, while his daughters looked shyly around them, touching nothing. They touched only with their eyes. The father rotated the spit a few times and consulted with his wife in Spanish. They smiled briefly at Alice, then left. Why hadn't she just given it to them?

The family reminded her of her own family's start in this country. The Father had flown in from Taipei first, landing a job as a security guard and securing a studio apartment near downtown Berkeley. Their mother arrived later with her and her sister and everything they owned in two suitcases. Their first winter was their first Christmas. The Father explained about Santa, their mother thumbtacked a pair of socks to the wall next to a tree they'd cut from cardboard. On Christmas morning, Alice and Amy unwrapped their thrift store gifts: vintage tin teacups; a blue stuffed dog and sleeping cat; a couple of Little Golden picture books with their gilded spines—thrilling proof of this strange new mythology and the miracle of objects that their young parents conjured in secret while they slept.

TABLE, WATERING CAN, TABLE
Alice arranged to have an old family friend take the first piece of Chinese furniture the Father ever made: a narrow rosewood table that wobbled slightly if you pressed down on its long deer

legs. She took a carload of kitchen supplies to a thrift store on Telegraph Avenue and hired a junk company to haul away the rest. The company charged six hundred dollars, which just about amounted to the take from the garage sale.

When she told her friend Nobu about all this *stuff*, he nodded.

A few years ago, Nobu said, he had helped with a similar purge when his mother's older sister moved from the family's ancestral home outside Yokohama. This aunt, who never married, had taken care of Nobu's grandparents until they died. Now that she was older, the house had become too much for her to manage alone. Even so, the aunt hadn't wanted to leave, and was especially aggrieved over the dispossession of her things, which had to be significantly winnowed down to fit inside a small condominium in the city.

During the week of the move, Nobu would find his aunt sitting cross-legged in the middle of a room, very still, with an old watering can in her lap. "Every object has history, every object is a memory," Nobu said. "But now I wonder if it was the things that really mattered or how the things lived in the house. I think the house became like a shrine and she was its only worshipper."

Eventually he managed to persuade his aunt that taking photographs of all her things would suffice as keepsakes. Their materiality, he explained, was not essential.

"Yes, you are so right," she agreed, looking down at her hands with a smile. "I am just being a sentimental old fool." Together they worked on the archive project: the aunt arranged each item—a cracked, beloved teapot, the low tea table where Nobu's grandfather used to enjoy his sweets while watching variety shows—and Nobu snapped their pictures and pasted them into an album.

"Do you know if it helped?" Alice asked. "Did she ever look at the album?"

"I'm not sure," Nobu said. "She died about a year after the house was sold. The pictures were either a perfect idea or a very bad one."

PHOTOS, PHOTOS, PHOTOS

The Father kept all his photos in a single cardboard box. She knew this because he once asked if she wanted to have a few childhood snapshots of herself that he'd kept. The rest—mostly pictures of his family in Alabama—he intended to toss in the trash. The melancholic in him collected things; the depressive wanted to throw everything away. She had insisted he keep all the photos, thinking he might later regret the purge.

Which was how she found herself years later going through the same cardboard box, this time with the dead eyes of an executioner. She used to wonder how personal photographs ended up in junk stores—pictures of friends grinning drunkenly around a kitchen table surrounded by a moat of empties and casino ashtrays; young couples posing shyly with their arms around each other in front of monuments and fountains; children showing off their Christmas spoils. These photos end up in secondhand bins because it's impossible to throw them in the trash. To be *found* meant the photos were lost; the provenance of the moment the shutter was released was joyful, but the fate of the images was unhappy.

Yet the photos the Father would ask for months later wouldn't be of family. They were the pictures he'd taken himself with the cameras in his collection—his own projects. There weren't that many, or at least he hadn't kept that many. Alice had found a few batches of negatives and prints, the kind you used to get back from the drugstore when you got them printed. These were of a solo road trip he'd taken, after he retired, to Bodie, a ghost town up north, but mostly his photos were of things in and around his house, the window blinds, the trees and bushes that grew in his backyard, a hunk of dried ginger on a plate. Alice had thrown nearly all of these prints away in a frenzy of disposal: everything that was not junked would end up cluttering Amy's apartment, which was not really an option. She did keep a few prints to take home to Brooklyn. But part of her also wanted to punish the Father for his nihilism. How could he throw away pictures of his own family? Her revenge was to throw out his art.

LIGHTER, LAMP, TABLE

In the Father's dresser drawer, mingled with loose change and expired health insurance cards, Alice found a cigarette lighter— one of those personally engraved Zippos popular among American soldiers during the war, now sold in Vietnam as knockoff souvenirs for tourists.

The engraving on the Father's Zippo was simple—no winged skulls or nudie girls, no *Death is my business and business has been good* or *When I die bury me facedown so the world can kiss my ass.* Just his name, the name of the city, Phu Bai, where he was deployed, and his years of service.

The lighter was broken: the mechanism that sparked the flame failed to catch. She pocketed it, along with a table lamp in the shape of a pagoda and a battered Modern Library edition of Irving Stone's *Lust for Life*, which had been on the Father's shelves for as long as she could remember. Taped on the inside of the book was a torn receipt (CAVES BOOK CO., CHUNG SHAN RD. TAIPEI TAIWAN CHINA). On her refrigerator at home in Brooklyn, she kept the photograph of the Father's rosewood table pinned under a magnet.

MYRTLE AVENUE

In the fall Alice went to visit the Father at his residential home. The first week had been rocky, according to Amy: On his first night there, the Father, anxious about his new surroundings, had been ornery and belligerent. Kenny, the round-faced man with an open smile who ran the home with his wife, had talked the Father down by promising to get him whatever he wanted for dinner. "A cheeseburger!" the Father shouted. In short order, a cheeseburger with fries appeared before him and a detente was reached. Now he seemed settled in, less on edge, less prone to complain, although Amy, wry, assured Alice he was still filled with plenty of gripes.

The morning after her red-eye home, Alice fed the cat and tried sleeping for a few hours before giving up. When she left her apartment to stock her refrigerator, the street was nearly empty of cars and people. Whenever she came back to Brooklyn, the thing she most looked forward to doing was walking down Myrtle Avenue. It was the routine that restored the rhythm of her own life.

At that hour the brightness and angle of the sun cast the row of storefronts in bold relief—half in shadow, half in light. Hopper's painting of a desolate morning street flashed in her mind. Leonard Michaels wrote that Hopper put the feeling of the hours in his paintings. Hopper understood, as Henri Bergson did, that time existed long before we put it in clocks. Two types of time: the time it takes for sugar to melt in water, indisputable, scientific; and the time Bergson called durée réelle—real duration—time as we actually feel and live it: an old woman lost in a reverie as she sweetens her tea through a sugar cube held between her teeth.

Fact: Bergson married a cousin of Marcel Proust's.

Michaels: What Hopper sees, Bergson means.

Alice was away visiting the Father when she first got the idea to visit the fortune-teller on Myrtle Avenue. For the purposes of the Project, she would consult the future. The fortune-teller did not have a storefront; she ran her operation from the second floor of a brick building above the bodega across the street from where Alice lived. The only way you could tell the fortune-teller was open for business—or that she even existed—was the red neon hand that hung from her window. Alice admired the economy and mystery of that shingle. The glowing hand was the Dr. T. J. Eckleburg of Myrtle Avenue.

She made a mental note to check for a name or a phone number on the building's intercom panel when she got home. She daydreamed about what she might find when she finally made it up those stairs: Would it smell of stale cooking oil or incense? Would there be evidence of small children, or would the room be staged as a proper fortune-teller's lair with heavy drapes and rugs?

For ten days, the red hand glowed in her mind. When she got home, the sign was gone.

A few years ago, she'd gone to see a lecture by Luc Sante at a documentary film space in Williamsburg. The talk was about the history of the New York City tabloid.

Sante said the city dweller's days are measured by the front page of tabloid newspapers. We see their headlines flash by us in news kiosks as we rush onto the subway platform. We scan the headlines from a stack of papers at the bodega while waiting in line for Tylenol, cigarettes. Sante said: Tabloids measure the day. Movie posters measure the week. Storefronts measure a year.

Alice hadn't been convinced by Sante's storefront theory. Yet when she started coming and going more frequently between California and New York, she found that the time away sharpened her sense of changes on the street. Each time she returned she noted the transition between the death of one business and the birth of another, from the shuttering and FOR LEASE sign to the papering of the windows and the colorful flags of the GRAND OPENING banner. Where she lived, the year was the measure of a gentrifying neighborhood. She was part of this ritual: a gentrifier lamenting the waves of gentrification in the wake of her arrival.

At her local Walgreens where she stopped in for toilet paper and hand soap, the arrival of seasons was marked by the rotation of products in aisle six. Now that it was October, the shelves were stacked with witch hats, bunny ears, and devil's horns.

The customer at the register, a heavyset woman leaning on a cane, was clarifying the discounts she was entitled to in the coupon circular.

"Is it a two-for-one? Well, I don't need two."

The coupon issue was resolved. Now there was the matter of counting exact change from her coin purse.

Behind her, the faces in the line hardened. A young mother shifted a bundle of diapers from one arm to the other. Behind her, a man tapped a package of double-A batteries against his thigh. The clerks behind the counter were all young—not one appeared close to breaking thirty. Sometimes, Alice noticed, they were required to recite a script. "Would you be interested in adding M&M's or Snickers to your purchase today?" For a spell they all said, "Be well," in parting as they handed over the receipts. The workers came and went with the seasons; the pay wasn't enough to keep them for long.

Before her time, before she'd become a quasi-permanent subletter of a garden-level studio rental of an actor friend who'd left for Los Angeles and did not appear to be returning anytime soon, Myrtle Avenue was known as Murder Avenue. The trace evidence was a mural of a local man on the side of the liquor store. He was on a wall, which meant he was dead. The mural man looked indomitable, with his broad neck and concrete forehead. A thin mustache teased his upper lip. He was gunned down after he returned to the neighborhood from doing time upstate. The shooters got him in a phone booth. Most people who walked by the mural paid it no mind. But the mural was doing what it was meant to do. The man in the mural was like a modern-day Ozymandias, a fixture and relic of the street. The people who remembered still remembered. At last count there were only four working walk-in phone booths left in New York City.

Alice once had the idea of taking a photograph of every business on her stretch of Myrtle Avenue, in the spirit of Ed Ruscha's *Every Building on the Sunset Strip*, that sun-bleached drive-by of mid-century modern banks, realty offices and motor inns, the Liquor Locker and Sun-Bee Food Mart—a deadpan record of what the artist called "technical data" unraveling like a run-on sentence in California vernacular.

Her motivation for photographing the street wasn't to make art. It was to shore her memory against forgetting, the outsized aggravation she felt when she couldn't remember the name of the glum, antiseptic Polish restaurant that had preceded the gourmet burger spot that was now a Nepalese restaurant. Once, she returned home to discover the sweets shop that sold candy and ice cream was gone. The shop was self-consciously old-fashioned: hard candy was kept in big wooden barrels; jumbo lollipops, swirled and hallucinatory, sat by the register. The business didn't last long. The originating concept, already a nostalgia, prefigured its own death.

But the store she mourned the most was Culture for Life. Owned and operated by a couple in their fifties just around the corner from her apartment, the store was part café, part haberdashery, and part photography studio. What little counter space existed was nearly taken up entirely by hats and natural beauty products—oils, body butters, and fragrances. The couple had gambled that, even in the age of digital cameras and smartphones, people would still want professional portraits to mark special occasions.

Alice used to drop in sometimes for coffee and a cookie. The husband was cheerful, a little frayed and bohemian, his hair shot through with salt-and-pepper like a cast member on *Sesame Street*.

"How's business?" she'd ask him.

"Can't complain, can't complain. Got a little slow there in the winter, but we're coming back up!"

He permitted no cracks in the veneer. He didn't want pity. He wanted business. He and his wife kept trying: a new offering of home-baked cakes and pies; a Santa Claus hired to busk in front of the store over the holidays. It wasn't enough. One day Alice walked by the store on her way to the park and discovered that it had been vacated. No warning, no EVERYTHING MUST GO. Their storefront on Myrtle became a French bakery; when that folded, a pet supply store.

In the end, Alice hadn't taken photographs of the street. Instead, she relied on Google Street View.

Every Building on the Sunset Strip was Google Street View before Google Street View. Ruscha strung together the images in *Sunset Strip* by snapping photos from a Nikon camera mounted on the back of a Ford pickup truck. Every few years, he'd go back to take photographs of the same one-and-a-half-mile stretch of West Hollywood. The evolution of the commercial landscape over time made him unhappy. "I wish time would stand still," he lamented.

Four years after he made *Sunset Strip*, Ruscha published another book of pictures. This time his subject was baldly speculative: The title of the book, a series of photos of vacant lots in and around Los Angeles, was *Real Estate Opportunities*. Visit the lots now, and you'll find the strip malls, gas stations, dingbat apartment buildings, and Christian centers of Los Angeles playing itself.

Annie Ernaux: The sensation of time passing is not inside

us, but outside of us. On Myrtle Avenue, the White Castle drive-through was now a luxury condo. Where there was once a dollar store stood a Starbucks. The coffee shop's corporate homogeneity had somehow turned it into the neighborhood's intergalactic cantina: everyone stopped in— contractors arguing in Russian; art students from China; yoga-sculpted women breezing in for pre-ordered matcha lattes; followed in the afternoon by teenagers splurging on frothy confections. The street changed imperceptibly like the passing of days.

She had in mind to visit the fortune-teller on Myrtle Avenue. Instead of asking about her own fortune, she would ask the fortune-teller to tell the future of the street. She didn't think the future would become the past so soon, that time itself could foreclose.

She stood on the subway platform at Lafayette waiting for the C train. The new season for television shows had begun. Nearly every billboard was taken up by teenage vampires, workplace dramas, undercover spies. There was a new show about a woman who, after a night of partying, wakes up infected with a zombie virus. To satisfy her sordid hunger without having to kill, she finds work at the local morgue. The show whirs to life when she feeds on human brains: memories of the newly dead flash in her mind.

With this knowledge, she begins to solve crimes.

THE RESIDENCY

It had taken Alice a month to catch up on the work assignments she'd neglected while she was in California, and now it was even harder for her to reenter the world of the Project. It was always like this: step away for too long and you lose the path back in. Not that she'd gotten very far. The problem was she'd been trying to dig herself into the Project since the beginning of the year with nothing to show but bookmarks in her browser.

She drew a map of the places and spaces the Artist had inhabited during the making of his performance works. She would go to these sites, take notes, make sketches, manufacture notions and provocations. Scattered across Lower Manhattan, the sites were mostly drawn from the year of *Outdoor Piece*, the parking lots where he sometimes slept between cars that buffered against the wind; the eaves that protected him as he waited out the rain; pizza joints that handed out slices through an open window; doorways and benches where he lingered in a steady accumulation of days.

She found that, even without the map in hand, when she walked the streets of Manhattan, she'd begun to feel his presence. In a city where it could be rare to run into someone you knew, the Artist's imprint made the city feel more grounded, connected to the past and, she supposed, the idea of New York City that continued to draw people here despite the outrageous rents and capitalist grind. Had the Artist been here? Or here? Alice thought this now as she gazed below at the narrow, shadowed streets of the Financial District from her perch on the fifteenth floor. Farther south, she could see a line of cars threaded through the entrance of the Holland Tunnel. The late afternoon sun glanced off the surface of the river with the gleam of a blade.

The view was from Nobu's new art studio on Rector Street, which came with the arts residency he'd landed along with a dozen other artists and writers. Sponsored by an arts organization once housed in one of the Twin Towers, the arts residency had become a roving affair after 9/11: provisional studio space for the artists was secured year to year from landlords that had yet to lease their offices to corporate tenants. This year, the residency was being hosted in a Beaux Arts building that was in the process of being tricked out to attract media and high-tech companies. Constructed at the turn of the century, the building originally belonged to a national freight shipping conglomerate. Alice had applied for the residency, didn't get it, and was trying on a blithe attitude toward the whole thing, which was working, for the most part.

Already Nobu had filled his studio, a divorce attorney's former office, nearly to the ceiling with his projects.

"What's this?" Alice asked him, pointing her toe at a half-dozen empty beer and soda cans on the floor in a corner of the room. The aluminum was dirty and battered; a few of the cans were doubled over as though they'd been punched in the stomach.

Nobu explained that he'd found the cans in the street. To him the cans were wounded. Some of them had been smashed completely flat. He'd been repairing them one by one, restoring them to their original shape. Sometimes he used a pair of pliers, but mostly he used his fingers. He held up his hands, grinning. "Sometimes they wound me back."

Alice was pleased to see two plaster maneki-nekos on the window ledge that she remembered from his previous studio in the Lower East Side. Nobu had arranged the lucky cat talismans so they faced one another. Each cat had a battery-powered paw that seemed to beckon as it swung up and down. He'd tied a string connecting the paws of the two cats and hung a dollar bill between them so they looked to be in an endless tug-of-war for the money.

"Follow me," Nobu said. "I'll take you on a tour."

Allyson, a poet and fellow resident, had been taking photos of her trash every day and posting them on social media, a regular rotation of rinds, Q-tips, coffee filters, and empty yogurt containers. Wojciech showed them his paintings, each canvas the size of a subway platform billboard. Over time he'd painted over the same canvases many times, replicas of the ads themselves—graffiti and all—for banks, whiskey, and commuter colleges. Sometimes he painted the boards in their fallow state, stripped of everything but the zigzag sediment of past posters. He'd been working these paintings off and on, he said, for more than a decade between other projects.

The resident dancers were young, newly married, endowed with enviable musculature. When they weren't at the residency space, they lived in a trailer without running water or electricity parked on a street in Bushwick, forgoing the cost of rent so they could devote as much time as possible to their work. Watching them dance was like watching water rush through a channel of boulders and fallen trees.

Aisha, who had the corner studio next to Nobu's, was meditating on traps—identity traps, spirit traps. She'd been making sculptures from huge cardboard boxes tricked out with eye-popping fabric and big enough for a person to crawl through. Her best fabric, she said, came from a store in the Bronx that specializes in Vlisco, a Dutch brand that made its name reproducing cheaper versions of the batiks from the former Dutch East Indies. The cloths passed through the hands of West African traders and saleswomen who sold them in open markets and gave each pattern its signature name: Kofi Annan's Brains. The Eye of My Rival. Day and Night.

As Alice passed by the windows on the other side of the building, she could see the stolid glass carapace of One World Trade in the near distance, studded with the reflection of clouds. Across the street about five stories below her, a swarm of men in hard hats and neon safety vests moved in a complex choreography as a skyscraper grew beneath their feet.

To the east was a high-rise hotel. Parallel from where she stood, Alice watched a housekeeper through the window of a hotel room making up the bed. After fluffing out the pillows and comforter, the housekeeper dragged her forearm across the top of the bed three times so it would have the appearance of having never been touched. The woman never looked up; Alice looked away.

"Nobu, you've struck gold," she said as they made their way back to his studio. "The gods have given you space and time."

"Yes, nine months." He smiled shyly, rubbing his scruffy beard with the back of his hand. "I better create a super art baby."

ESL

Morning light flooded through the great windows. Alice had secured a good seat on the third floor of the branch library in the Lower East Side to flip through the books she'd checked out on the history of New York's downtown arts and performance scene.

After a time, an old Chinese man, his face freckled like a quail egg, settled into the seat next to her. His white hair peeked from under a baseball cap. On the table he spread copies of *The New York Times, The Wall Street Journal,* a frayed English-language dictionary, and some loose papers. As he read, he raised his pencil, underlining and jabbing the air like the conductor of an orchestra.

A round, middle-aged Indian woman approached him. They knew each other—maybe from the library's ESL conversation class? Alice listened in: Why aren't there free tea and biscuits like the flyers promised? Has the library run out of money?

They clucked their tongues and chuckled incredulously at the latest headlines about same-sex marriage. "Two men are going to have babies?"

After his friend took her leave, the old man turned to Alice and stage-whispered as though in confidence, "The world turn upside down."

After a moment he got up, leaving his reading materials behind. She peered over at the notes he'd written on sheets torn from a notepad branded with the name of a local food bank. Under a dancing pumpkin he'd scribbled out definitions for the words he didn't know:

Hobble: create difficulty for
Ironically: happening in the opposite way as what is expected
Boomer: a large male kangaroo

DICTIONARY

1.

Cleaning out the Father's house, Alice had found three different Chinese-English dictionaries powdered with dust on the bottom row of a bookshelf in his living room. Learning Chinese had released the Father from combat duty in Vietnam and probably saved his life. For years, Alice's mother also kept a Chinese-English dictionary by her bedside with pages thin as a Bible's. Learning English propelled her out of a bad marriage and into her new life—their new lives—in a foreign country speaking a foreign language.

2.

"I am an inmate at P— State Prison. I am doing six-and-a-half years and am at the beginning of my sentence. I am interested in a dictionary. I'm not sure if you are able to send me a specific one, but I'm very interested in the New Oxford American Dictionary Third Edition. I can receive hardback at my custody level."

Alice slipped the letter back into its envelope and scanned the shelves for dictionaries: nothing except a thesaurus and an old *AP Stylebook*. That dictionaries are high on the request list from people in prison was one of the first things Alice learned when she began working with a volunteer collective that fulfilled book requests from prisons across the country. The collective operated in the basement of a used book store on the Brooklyn waterfront. You entered by going down a street-level hatch into a low bunker heaving with bookshelves. Once Alice saw a rat lumber casually from the Native American section and disappear behind a stack of milk crates sagging with business and econ books. Across the street from the bookstore was a chain-link fence, and beyond that, the East River and the lights of Manhattan across the water.

Requests came in for sci-fi, westerns, Aztec and Nordic histories, Machiavelli, Marvel comics, Santeria, authors the Father favored like Michael Connelly and Lee Child. But always there was demand for dictionaries.

"I am currently housed at the L— Unit. I am requesting two dictionaries. First a Merriam-Webster English Dictionary that has more than 150,000 entry words. Second I am requesting a Spanish-English dictionary with more than 150,000 words."

Some letters were written on quarter slips of paper, carefully torn from an 8.5-by-11-inch sheet. Nearly all were handwritten. Some requests were florid: "If you would be so kind as to deliver a few books for my perusal I shall be eternally grateful." Others appear tentative on the page, the words put together like notes on an instrument seldom played. "I am currently incarcerated here in Texas. I'm humbling asking if you could issue me a dictionary. I'm very ambitious to learn more about the written word. This would be an enormous gift I receive."

3.

When asked by a reporter what his alma mater was, Malcolm X famously replied, "Books."

The dictionary was his first love and deepest well. While doing time for a string of robberies, Malcolm X turned, for the first time in his life, to writing letters. He who had prided himself as the "most articulate hustler out there"—able to command attention with the authority of his speech—found himself straining against the limits of his vocabulary. Through the prison library, he gets his hands on a dictionary. (In Spike Lee's biopic, it's a *Webster's Collegiate*, fifth edition.) He spends two days just turning the pages. Finally decides the thing to do is to copy an entire page of definitions by hand. This takes him an entire day. He reads everything back to himself in his own wobbly handwriting, all the words he hadn't known existed. He copies another page, and another one after that.

Ten p.m. is lights-out. He figures out that if he positions himself on the floor just so, the light from the corridor outside his cell shines just brightly enough to read by. The night guards make their rounds at one-hour intervals. When he hears one approach, he leaps back onto his cot and pretends to be asleep. Once the footsteps fade, he's back out on the floor, book in hand. In his autobiography, he wrote: "Months passed without my even thinking about being imprisoned. In fact, up to then, I never had been so truly free in my life." He was twenty-three years old.

4.

A friend of the Artist's once suggested that he use the downtime while he was doing his performance works to improve his English.

"Find some English language books," the friend urged. "Learn."

The Artist told his friend that he didn't want to. He preferred to simply pass the time.

That's why, in so many years, I still haven't learned English well, the Artist said. *I don't have some part of me that is devoted to following civilization.*

In interviews over the years, the Artist has been described as speaking:

—Broken English in a thick Asian accent.

—Thickly accented English.

—Painfully fractured English.

—With a limited but direct vocabulary.

In more recent interviews, after the fashion of the times, his facility with English is not mentioned at all.

According to the Artist's wife, his manner of talking, even in Chinese, falls somewhere between that of an eight-year-old and a philosopher.

5.

The *Oxford English Dictionary* took seventy years to complete with the help of a team of volunteer philologists. Among the most prolific of them was an American named William Chester Minor. A surgeon by training, Minor contributed thousands of quotations to support the definitions of words while imprisoned in an asylum for the criminally insane. The origin of his incipient madness began in the battlefields of the Civil War while treating the Union wounded, and came to a head years later when, under a psychotic delusion, he shot and killed a complete stranger—a young coal stoker—in the streets of a London slum. Minor spent nearly the rest of his life in an upper chamber of the asylum with his collection of rare antiquarian books and his solitude. Food and drink arrived through a slot in the door.

6.

In Spike Lee's biopic, Denzel-Malcolm sits side by side with his jailhouse mentor in the prison library, a dictionary between them. Together, they look up the definition of "black" (the camera zooms in on the page, close enough to see the grain in the paper): *soiled with dirt, foully or outrageously wicked, sullen, hostile, forbidding.* Then "white": *innocent, pure, free from spot or blemish, without evil intent, harmless, square-dealing.* Denzel-Malcolm scowls, all but pushes the book away. "This is written by white folks, right?"

Learn the meaning of words so you can undo them. Read their shade. Learn to read a sentence like an ace poker player reads the table—the weight shifting from one butt cheek to the other, a chin scratch, the hardening of an otherwise blank expression. Read the silences too. Develop a second sense for those who would cage you.

7.

Origin stories of *OED*s: Alice's college ex made peanuts working as a bookseller for a chain bookstore in San Francisco. As a holiday bonus, he received a check for six dollars. On the day he quit, he pulled his ancient Honda hatchback up to the loading area, tossed a stolen *OED* in the trunk, and sped off. Another friend, new to New York City and broke, walked past an *OED* for sale on a street in Morningside Heights. After two blocks, he turned around and bought it with twenty dollars that he should have spent on groceries. Now he's married, lives in Queens, and his son likes playing with the magnifying glass that comes with the *OED*, which fits into a little drawer built into the slipcase.

When Alice asked her mother if she remembered where their family's *OED* came from, her mother said she sent away for it after seeing an ad in *Time* magazine.

"But why?

"For you and your sister, of course!"

Like the massive leather-bound tome with gilded pages of Shakespeare's collected works and the *New Yorker* subscription her mother had given her as birthday gifts, the *OED* is a totem of aspiration, which makes it an archetypal immigrant gift.

For the ESL immigrant, the refugee, for anyone whose English is lacking proficiency, the dictionary is a refuge: the simplest of words can be looked up without judgment. The dictionary understands our private shame, the part of us that cringes with empathy when a preening Elizabeth Berkley pronounces Versace "Versayce" in *Showgirls,* even as the dictionary's pronunciation guide never quite dispels our suspicion that our lack of fluency or sophistication will be exposed.

8.

Post-truth was the Oxford Dictionaries Word of the Year. As in, "relating to or denoting circumstances in which objective facts are less influential in shaping public opinion than appeals to emotion and personal belief." As in, we're all living in a post-truth world now. (James, derisive: "I've had a tent pitched in this world for years. Where you all been?")

9.

When someone is released from prison, what happens to his dictionary? Alice guessed nearly all the dictionaries were left behind where their value is greatest—with a cell mate, a friend, someone serving the sentence. Maybe the original owner of the dictionary figures he'll buy a newer edition once he's set up with a job and a steady paycheck, all in good time.

10.

The digital edition of the next *OED* is expected to drop two decades from now. There will be no print edition and no more serendipity of chance proximity when you search for a word and your eye wanders to its neighbors on the page. But who actually looks for anything inside the two-volume print edition of the *OED*? The print is so small it can't be read without a magnifying glass; the volumes are too heavy and cumbersome to slide easily from their protective slipcase. And yet something of the infinite is lost when a dictionary is not contained between two covers.

WHY A YEAR?

Notes on the Artist's origin story: He was born in 1950 in Nanzhou, a rural township in Pingtung County in southern Taiwan known for its tuna fisheries and wax apples. His father owned a small trucking company. He had five wives. The Artist was the oldest of ten children and must have disappointed the old man, who did not consider art to be a serious occupation, when he dropped out of school to become a painter.

The Artist made hundreds of paintings before abandoning painting and turning to performance art, although he didn't know what performance art was at the time. (The first time someone said the word *performance* to him in New York, he thought the person was referring to high-performance cars.)

Early experiments by the Artist as a young man in Taiwan:

—Stuffing himself with fried rice until he vomited.
—Holding a heap of drywall above his head, the load steadily increased until it reached a half ton, at which point he dove to the ground. (He broke his clavicle.)

—Jumping from a two-story building. (He broke both his ankles.)

The Artist considered all of the above juvenilia. (The hole hadn't yet opened under his work.)

In nearly every interview, the Artist is asked why his performance works take the span of a year.

A: *A year is the largest single unit of how we count time.*
Q: But why a year?
A: *If I had done two years or three years, I would have just been trying to prove I could do something for a long time. That's not my concept. It had to be the circle the earth goes around the sun.*
Q: Why a year?
A: *It is about being human, how we explain time, how we measure our existence.*
Q: Why a year?
A: *One year is a human calculation within a life cycle, so I could say something about life in a circle, repetition in a circle, over and over.*

ONE YEAR PERFORMANCE 1980-1981

April, 1980

STATEMENT

I, **SAM HSIEH**, plan to do a one year performance
piece.

I shall punch a Time Clock in my studio every hour
on the hour for one year.

I shall immediately leave my Time Clock room,
each time after I punch the Time Clock.

The performance shall begin on April 11, 1980 at
7 P.M. and continue until April 11, 1981 at 6 P.M.

Sam Hsieh

MAKING TIME

The Artist made a film of *Time Clock Piece*. It's stitched together from photographs he'd taken of each time he stood in the same spot when he punched the clock every hour on the hour for an entire year—a total of eight thousand six hundred and twenty-seven clock punches. (He missed a hundred and thirty-three of them.)

The film works like time-lapse photography: one hour is collapsed into one second, so the Artist appears to be shuddering slightly in place, the creases and wrinkles in the gray uniform he wore every day rippling as though a parasite were crawling underneath the surface of the cloth. His hair sprouts from his shaved head and grows past his shoulders. Next to him is the punch clock itself, the hour and minute hands spinning wildly around the dial like an out-of-control time machine. From beginning to end the film is about six minutes long.

When life is reduced to its minimum, he said, *time emerges.*

———

Alice at the bodega, deliberating over brands of beer and distracted by the resident cat, gray with yellow eyes, licking furiously between his toes on top of a stack of delivery boxes. Near the register a customer called out his order for a ham sandwich on a roll, pickles, provolone, no onions. She was late for a dinner party at Nobu's. His latest project involved collecting grocery lists that he'd found during his walks through the city. He'd buy the items on the list and take photographs of each arrangement. The dinner party was a way to use up all the perishables he'd accumulated—eggs, nopales, half-and-half, tomatoes—before they went bad.

"I'm making the food up," he warned Alice. "It's too crazy for a real recipe."

Alice told Nobu that the project made her think of the gig economy shoppers she sometimes saw at the grocery store, identified by the cheerful carrot on their polo shirts and the intensity with which they stared at their phones and raced from one display to another.

"Except, of course, you're not getting paid and no one's expecting to receive your groceries on the other end."

"Maybe I do gig shopping if my art doesn't sell," Nobu said. Was he joking? Sometimes it was hard to tell with him; his aspect was generally absurdist, which both charmed and mystified her. Alice wasn't sure how Nobu made a living. She knew he sometimes taught art classes to children and earned a commission here and there. The children, he once told her with good-natured resignation, made fun of his English.

She'd first met him years ago at an after-party for a mutual friend's art opening. At the time she was working on a photo project (since abandoned) of chairs discarded in the streets of the city. They talked for a long time about their shared admiration for the artist Yuji Agematsu's miniature trash dioramas—exquisite mucks of hair, gum, candy wrappers, and dead bugs that the artist, a pack-a-day smoker, found on his daily perambulations, then arranged in the cellophane sleeves of cigarette packs.

Earlier that morning, Alice had read a news item about a New Jersey woman who'd been found dead in her car in a convenience store parking lot. There was no foul play: at the time of her death, the woman was working three part-time shifts for a donut conglomerate—mornings at the Newark train station, overnights in Linden, and weekends in Harrison. She bagged crullers, mixed ice macchiatos, warmed up chicken biscuits and ham and cheese flatbreads for something like $8.25 an hour. On the day she died, the woman did what she often did—crank her car seat back so she could catch a short nap between shifts, keeping the engine running for the heat. Except this time a gas can overturned in the cargo hold of her SUV.

The article didn't say whether the donut company used workforce efficiency software to configure the woman's schedule, but Alice couldn't help but wonder if hers was a death by algorithm.

For the purposes of the Project, Alice had been researching the effects of sleep deprivation. As a method of torture, sleep deprivation goes way back, at least to the sixteenth century. The Scots found it useful to shake out the witches among them. It was standard operating procedure in Stalin's gulag. In Guantánamo, it went by the code name Operation Sandman.

———

Three days into *Time Clock Piece*, the Artist would have begun feeling the effects of lack of sleep. First, a fog descends. As his brain mulched, the slightest irritant would set him on edge. Next, delirium seeps in like gas in a windowless room. As the months wore on, the Artist would have found it harder and harder to keep his eyes open, and when they were open, his dulled brain would barely be able to process the sensory information his eyes took in.

Which was why he eventually had to rig a system of twelve alarm clocks to go off all at once. Still, that was not enough. He set the alarm on his wristwatch next to a microphone and attached that to a loudspeaker. Even then he managed to sleep through more than a hundred clock-ins.

When we sleep, we can't work, we can't shop, we can't eat or drink, we can't download, surf, or stream; our movements can't be tracked by a global positioning system; the movement of our eyeballs can't be mined for data. Human beings used to sleep an average of eight hours a night; now it's down to six and a half.

The punch clock was invented in 1888 by an American, a jeweler who lived in Auburn, a town off the tip of the Finger Lakes. From her volunteer gig, Alice recognized Auburn from the return addresses on the envelopes sent by people in prison.

When the clock was invented, time was too.

Although the Artist's dreams were constantly being interrupted, his dream life was where he experienced the greatest freedom from the project, even when the dreams were bad. *I dreamt I didn't want to be an artist anymore. Many times my dreams were about my illegality and the immigration authorities trying to catch me. Or sending me back to Taiwan, and I would try to cross the Mexican border to come back again.*

Punch clocks aren't necessarily punched anymore. The new systems are biometric: you clock in by submitting your fingerprint, finger vein, palm vein, iris, or retina. Sometimes it's your entire face.

Time monitoring with *a human touch* is how one manufacturer puts it. Which is some bullshit. With biometric time clocks, you can't, for example, punch in for a friend who is running late because of a child's doctor's appointment or who is hungover with his head over a toilet.

The punch clock did not invent time but its surveillance.

You could be friends with someone in New York for years and never see the inside of their apartment. The dinner party was the first time Alice had been to Nobu's. It was a dark one-bedroom railroad that he shared with a roommate in Ridgewood. The guests were piled around the aluminum table in the kitchen. Yusef Lateef's light-footed *Eastern Sounds* blew from a laptop. Alice sat nearly in the lap of a woman in a scalloped white dress that reminded her of cake frosting. The woman was showing Alice her favorite app against wasting time.

"First, you set a timer," she explained in a vaguely Slavic accent, displaying her phone. "Then, look, you can see, this tree sprouts on your screen. What is so cool," the woman continued, "is that the app is connected to a real-life tree farm—in Chile, I believe. The more time you spend on your activity, the more trees get planted."

"What happens if you get distracted?" Alice asked.

"The tree, it gets sick and dies until there is nothing but a dead stump." The woman shrugged. "I maybe kill an entire forest shopping for shoes and doing Tinder."

"Is there a version with a garden?" Nobu asked. His glasses were fogged up from the pot boiling on the stove, which made him look like a mad scientist. "I'd rather grow vegetables."

The same year the punch clock inventor filed a patent, a Buffalo man became the first person to be legally executed by electric chair. The theory was that being shocked with a high-voltage electrical current would be less painful and more humane than death from hanging. But it took two tries and eight minutes for the man to die.

The first execution by electric chair took place in 1890 at Auburn State Prison, the second oldest state prison in New York. Auburn was also the first penal institution in the world to profit from prison labor. Historically, the men imprisoned at Auburn made clothes, shoes, boots, nails, carpets, buttons, carpentry tools, combs, harnesses, brooms, and buckets. They manufactured steam engines and boilers.

They also made clocks.

The vast majority of people on death row are denied educational and vocational programs. This is because they're understood to have no future, the argument goes, so such programs would be a waste of taxpayer money.

But at San Quentin, the men on death row are permitted one type of program: art.

The Artist is often asked how much he suffered to make the piece. He replied that he didn't suffer. *I have pleasure to do the piece.* Some who have written about *Time Clock Piece* point out how exhausted the Artist looks. Yet when Alice looks closely at the Artist's face—in the film, in the photo stills—she doesn't see it. What she sees is the will of a man stitching himself into time. Only after the piece was completed was the Artist disconsolate. He felt that way after all his pieces ended, he said, because it meant returning to the life of an ordinary man.

KEEPING TIME

At the hospital, after his fall, the Father had become obsessed with time.

"What time is it?" he'd ask, again and again. He had to have his cell phone within sight at all times so he could consult its clock face. He became deeply anxious if the phone momentarily disappeared before it was retrieved from the folds of his bedsheets or between the mattress and the steel frame of his hospital bed.

Why did it matter what time it was? It wasn't like he had someplace to be. Later Alice and Amy learned that losing sense of time is one of the first signs of dementia. Lose your sense of time and you lose yourself. When were you?

At night the Father required an overnight sitter because he would wake up at two in the morning disoriented and start screaming.

When she was a girl, Alice used to dial POPCORN on the phone so she could hear the recorded voice of a lady on the other end of the line say, "At the tone, the time is"—followed by the hour, the minute, and, most cosmically, the second of the exact moment Alice stood in time. She did this sometimes when she felt bored or lonely. When phones began telling time, the number was disconnected.

Now that she thought about it, the Father's preoccupation with keeping time had begun well before he landed in the hospital.

Alice recalled how he used to carry a wristwatch in his hand as he shuffled from room to room. (He no longer had the dexterity to affix the band around his wrist.) By then the Father no longer drove. His universe had shrunk to a three-block radius: Safeway, his bank, the post office, and a tobacco store on Shattuck Avenue where he stocked up on cartons of cigarettes. (At his request, Alice had bought cartons for him from that store in the past, which triggered a car crash of feelings—getting good value on a bulk purchase while accelerating her father's death. The shape of the cartons reminded her of an infant's casket.)

Without work and routines and places where his presence was expected, the skein of the Father's days detached from others. He was a satellite orbiting earth, touching down for the occasional podiatrist appointment, a Meals on Wheels delivery, a visit from a daughter.

He fussed continually over the digital alarm clock by his bed, which was set to wake him, inexplicably, at three in the morning. When the clock stopped working, he asked Alice for a replacement. She knew, because of his bad hands, that windup clocks wouldn't do. New clocks wouldn't work, either, with all their complicated features. She spent hours rooting through the thrift stores on University Avenue for an old-fashioned digital clock with minimal functions.

Savers, which sprawled across the footprint of a former supermarket, was her favorite thrift. Along a long wall nearly the length of the entire store hung rows of clear plastic baggies organized by categories of utility: boxes of birthday candles packed with party decorations; cookie cutters with frosting tips; bundles of office supplies—Post-its and half-used boxes of staples and paper clips. Her family's life in this country had begun in stores like these, with their ramshackle racks of silverware, paperweight globes, table lamps, coffee makers. Once they became solidly middle-class, her mother disdained anything used, however gently. As a girl in Taiwan, she'd worn too-big shoes that had to be stuffed with newspaper until she grew into them. She already knew what it was to be poor. Now that she could afford new things, she wanted only new things. But the Father, and Alice, still enjoyed scouring garage sales and flea markets for old things and the mild exhilaration of discovering something you didn't know you wanted and at steep discount.

The Chinese believe gifting a clock or watch is bad luck because "giving a clock" in Chinese is a homonym for "attending a funeral." Alice read this on the internet. But the clocks she bought for the Father were not gifts, exactly, nor was she a superstitious person. And how strongly rooted could a superstition be if you first encountered it on the internet? Some years ago, Alice had given a watch to Ezra on his birthday. The watch was solar-powered and glowed Hulk-green. Ezra loved it. He'd strap it on and run around in circles outside, shouting and lifting his arm high in the air to intensify the power of the sun rays. Then he'd hold it close to his face as though receiving intel for some secret commando operation.

Amy told Alice that Ezra reminded her of *Ultraman*, the tokusatsu TV show they watched as children. They chuckled, recalling the pendant in Ultraman's chest that glowed different colors, emitting an alarm that sounded like an air raid and that escalated per beat depending on the energy Ultraman had expended battling rubber-suited monsters. And yet Alice remembered the twinge she felt—anxiety knotted with regret—whenever she saw the watch wrapped around her nephew's twig-like wrist, unable to undo her knowledge of the bad omen despite her disavowal of it. She was relieved when Ezra inevitably lost interest in the watch and its solar properties, and, indeed, in telling time altogether, which he had no real need to do, being a little boy.

In the end Alice bought several clocks for the Father in case one of them proved too complicated. She walked him through the steps he'd need to operate it; preset one of them as per his preferences; and left a sheet of paper with step-by-step instructions on his nightstand. Later he complained that none of the clocks worked, meaning he was broken.

Another find from the purge of the Father's house: on a high shelf in the coat closet, a digital alarm clock still in its original packaging. The clock, which came with a feature that could project the time on the ceiling, could also play a selection of "nature sounds"—ocean waves, tropical forest, rainstorm. Maybe the clock had been state-of-the-art back in the day, but when she turned it on, the speaker quality sounded tinny, distant, like AM on a car radio. She liked cueing up the effects anyway, her bedside souvenir. It was like listening to the sound of her father's whimsy.

ZOMBIES

 onths after the Father's fall, Alice was archiving photos from her phone when she came across one she'd taken at the hospital while he was recovering. The photo was of a black dot the size of an Eisenhower dollar floating against the background of the Father's pale back. The doctor explained that it was an old bedsore, most likely incubated by too many hours spent sitting. The skin appeared to have rotted and died some time ago, leaving necrotic tissue.

"It doesn't hurt," the Father insisted.

"Do you want to see it?" Alice asked.

He nodded. "Sure."

That's when she'd snapped the picture with her smartphone. Together they looked at his backside, marveling at how horrible and weird it was.

The Father did get a little better at the hospital. Alice could get him to laugh, and she saw his old self emerge in the way he clearly favored a certain nurse who made him feel less like a patient and more like a man. They shot the shit about vintage cars and beer, and he even offered her a sincere invitation to his house once he got out. She laughed. It wasn't her first invitation. On good days, even his grumbling felt more good-natured and familiar. Yet there was damage—cognitive, motor control—that seemed permanent and most likely had been set in motion even before the fall. The doctors offered different diagnoses: Vascular dementia. A stroke. A series of small strokes. Wernicke-Korsakoff syndrome, from drinking. There was no way of knowing for sure without more tests, and more tests, they were told, wouldn't change anything anyway. The Father wanted to know, but then he didn't care, and then he definitely didn't want to be bothered with brain scans and the like. Over time there would be so many different doctors, each with their own speculations. Alice Goo- gled each of these diagnoses exhaustively. The type of dementia she finally settled on—based on the Father's behavior and how the suspension cables in his brain were snapping—was fronto- temporal dementia, or FTD. Did his alcoholism have a hand in it? She remembered an offhand comment he'd made about being drunk and losing his footing and how he'd hit his head against a metal beam left on the floor of his living room meant for the darkroom he'd never gotten around to constructing.

When nerve cells die in the frontal lobes, Alice learned, it's not memory that falls away. It's your control over language, motor skills, your emotions, and your judgment. The Father could no longer dress himself anymore. He could hold a cup, he could still grasp a pen and write his name, but with great difficulty. He for- got more words and scrambled the ones he could remember. His bad tempers remained uncensored: to talk with him was to be called an asshole and told to shut the hell up as part of the natural flow of conversation. There was no talk of cures.

In her book-length essay *The Art of Death,* Edwidge Danticat comes to grips with her mother's death from cancer by summoning other writers who have grappled with death and mourning. At one point she describes Zora Neale Hurston's encounter with a zombie when Hurston was in Haiti conducting anthropological research. From Hurston's account:

"I listened to the broken noises in its throat . . . The sight was dreadful. That blank face with the dead eyes. There was nothing you could say to her or get from her except by looking at her, and the sight of this wreckage was too much to endure for long."

It. Her. Person. Thing. Hurston finished her interviews, took a few photographs, and then got the hell out of there.

Danticat insisted that, if her mother were to turn into a zombie, she wouldn't hesitate for a second to embrace her, to take her in fully. She wouldn't want to let go, no matter what her mother's state or condition.

When Alice read this, she thought: Here is someone whose parent did not suffer from dementia. She knew how this sounded, yet how swiftly and inexorably thoughts devolve to the incorrect when dealing with a loved one with dementia. The demented person is also incorrect—they're the same person but wrong—wrong because you know this isn't the life they wanted: you end up being all wrong together.

It feels wrong to laugh, but we laugh when the zombies on the zombie show bumble into the sharp end of their own deaths. So is laughing to manage the pain of living grief. One of the funniest memories she had of the Father involved his preoccupation with assisted suicide. The Father lived in dread of his own father's fate: dying slowly from Alzheimer's disease. The Father wanted Alice to look into Oregon's assisted suicide law. This was last year, when he was still managing more or less on his own. Looking back, Alice realized that the dementia clouds must have been gathering in his mind thicker than he was letting on. He must have been terrified. She knew the Oregon law only kicked in if you could prove you had a terminal illness that would kill you inside of six months. She also knew about the Father's gun collection, so she tried a different tack.

"Okay, I'll look into it, but I better not come over one day and find you with your brains blown out."

"Oh no, I would never do that to you and your sister," the Father said, offended. But if he were to shoot himself, he admitted, well, he *had* thought this through. What he would do is shoot himself in the bathtub. This method would leave the least amount of mess, or rather, contain the mess in the best way possible.

"That thing is cast iron!" This he said admiringly, ever the craftsman attuned to the quality of materials.

"Oh *Je*-sus," Alice groaned, and they laughed. Then she told him a story about a dark period in her early twenties when she too experienced a brief, shallow period of suicidal ideation. Her plan had been to throw herself off the Golden Gate Bridge, but whenever she thought too deeply about it, she would get bogged down in logistics. She didn't own a car and was a terrible driver anyway. She'd have to get on the right bus, several buses, in fact, or hail a taxi. This was before ride-sharing apps. Where exactly should she ask the taxi driver to let her off? Then there were those new suicide prevention barriers on the bridge that would have to be hurdled, and next thing she knew, she was still alive.

The Father thought on this. "I could never throw myself off a bridge."

"Why not?"

"Don't laugh," he said, sinking his neck into his shirt collar. "But it's because I can't swim."

Theories abounded about why the zombie show, now staggering through its eighth season, was past its prime. Too many fan favorites killed off. The unrelenting grimness of the material; the repetitive arcs; not enough screen time for the zombies. But what Alice missed most were the story lines that explored the rough, emotional terrain of loving and letting go of the undead.

There was the old farmer who kept his zombie wife and zombie neighbors padlocked in an old barn on his property. And the Jim Jones–like cult leader who chained his little zombie daughter in a secret chamber, letting her out on occasion—seething and snapping at him with her jaws—to tenderly brush her hair. As the seasons progressed, these types of mournful attachments evaporated. The zombies became less the people they once were and more props to be deployed in battle strategy, like falling boulders or a pool of sharks.

On the show much pathos was wrung from the pacts people made with one another to "do what needs to be done" if they should become infected. Someone had to be entrusted to drive a knife through your head if you'd been bit—the only surefire way to make sure you didn't rise from the dead and hurt other people.

The Father did not want to end up like his father, demented

and confined in a nursing home. The Father had stopped visiting his daddy because he couldn't deal with the shadow of the man he used to go deer hunting and watch wrestling on TV with; who taught him how to make peach ice cream with rock salt and a hand-crank machine. When the Father told Alice this, he hung his head, ashamed. Alice had met her grandparents only once, on a trip out to Alabama when she was a girl. They were white-haired and impossibly old, she had thought, although they were likely only in their sixties at the time. On her birthday they sent her store-bought cards with checks for five or ten dollars. After her parents divorced, the cards stopped.

Alice's friend Julia had a grandfather whose strokes had left him mostly paralyzed and unable to speak except to say in Chinese: Fuck your mother's pussy. Sometimes the grandfather burst out laughing for no reason; most of the time his face looked unhappy. Shitting was agony. Did he know them anymore? Did he want to be alive? Should he be alive? Julia wasn't sure. In the meantime, the family hired a full-time caregiver who lived with them in the house.

"It feels weird to take measures to prolong his life," she said. "But doing nothing would feel crazy too."

In the TV world of the zombie apocalypse, enough time had passed that no one got sentimental anymore about keeping loved ones who were undead around. They'd had to learn to let go, to adapt to a new reality. Every time Alice visited the Father, she saw that he lost a little bit more—his speech, his acuity, his wit, his laughter. Modern medicine has made it so we get to live longer. Our lungs expand, our hearts pump, our stomachs churn their efficient acids. We're wheeled out for bingo and holiday cookies wearing chain-pharmacy Santa hats. As we age, we reassess what makes life worth living, so say the experts who study such things. At the age of eighty, we may find that playing gin rummy followed by a hot lunch and a bowl of ice cream are enough to keep us going. But dementia complicates this, Alice thought, and dying is getting harder.

THE RUM CAKE

It was Sunday night and Alice was on the phone with her mother. It had been almost six years since her mother had moved to a suburb outside Seattle to live with her boyfriend, whom she'd met on an educational travel tour of British Columbia. The boyfriend seemed fine, a reedy birder who worked in college admissions and who covered his mouth and shook silently when he laughed. Alice wanted for her mother what she suspected all grown children want for their parents: a safe, easy life largely purged of incident.

What kind of cake, she asked her mother, had she made for her monthly mah-jongg game? A rum cake, her mother said. She'd been meaning to use up a bottle of rum that had been sitting in her cupboard for ages, and this recipe called for an entire cup.

The problem was that it was a Bundt cake, and she no longer owned a Bundt pan. She used to own a Bundt pan but she'd lent it to someone back in California and never got it back. Luckily, a neighbor let her borrow her Bundt pan so she didn't have to buy a new one. At her age, Alice's mother figured, although she didn't say any of this out loud, she wouldn't be able to recoup the full value of a brand-new Bundt pan to justify the cost of purchasing one. At most, she must have calculated, she'd likely use the pan only a handful more times. The maneuvering of a loaner cake pan, a little barter against her mortality, seemed to please her immensely.

CRASH

It had been two weeks since James was laid off from his transcribing job. The company had transitioned mostly to AI, although they'd retained, for the premium rate, an elite squad of human transcribers capable of delivering greater accuracy. James did not meet the cut.

"It's okay. I'm fine," he assured Alice. "Relieved, frankly."

They'd walked north from Chinatown and were now in the neighborhood where she'd first lived when she moved to New York. In real estate parlance, the neighborhood was known as Nolita, as in north of Little Italy, as in No-lee-ta: *the tip of the tongue taking a trip of three steps down.* Even then the neighborhood was overrun by useless luxury boutiques. Still, there was a little supermarket, a bookstore, a Chinese-run Laundromat. In September the annual San Gennaro Festival flooded the streets with the smell of frying sausages and onions; despite the noise and the crowds trampling on foot-tall plastic cocktail cups and masticated corncobs, the festival still managed to charm her. Her sublet had been a dark box lit by two windows that overlooked a remorseless air shaft. Across the street was a small concrete park where she used to sit sometimes to console herself when she was desperate for sunlight and the weather was nice. This was where she'd taken James. The two friends sat on a bench and ate their pork buns while watching two boys wage an imaginary turf war on a play structure.

James said the work had been wearing him down. The work involved transcribing videotaped speeches, mostly of corporate events. The company allotted time for each transcription, and he'd been finding it harder and harder to marshal the necessary focus to keep pace. Lately he'd been having dreams; the last one involved words that had somehow morphed into raw hot dogs and it was his job to shove these pink, fisty bouquets into flimsy pre-assembled boxes.

Alice and James had met through a temp job during the recession. They entered data side by side on the tenth floor of a building in Midtown with mismatched office furniture and stains Rorschaching the low drop ceiling. It was a friendship forged over ten-minute smoke breaks and happy hours at nearby watering holes that got sexual, mildly romantic, and then fizzled out, a temporary thing between two temporary people. Why had they let it go? She couldn't remember anymore, or preferred not to. What had endured was friendship. That, they could do. In her experience, friendships stood the chance of lasting longer. You could keep parts of yourself—the peevish, ugly, lazy, needy parts—mostly out of it.

James crumpled the paper bag that had held their buns and squeezed it into a ball. He had counted on the vapidity of the speeches he was transcribing—businessmen doing their best TED talk impersonations, *opening the kimono* on this and *blue-*

sky thinking on that—to provide a certain protective coating around his brain for real work. What he hadn't anticipated was how much the frantic tedium of transcription left little energy for anything else.

After the layoff came the second stroke of bad luck: James lost his apartment in Flatbush. His roommate, an oafish redhead and the sole leaseholder, had not paid the landlord for nearly six months. Instead, he'd pocketed the rent money and fled to South Korea.

In what now struck James as an instance of thunderous foreshadowing, his roommate had, for close to an entire year, been talking up Seoul as a site of future conquest. His Americanness all but assured his success. He would get himself a Korean girlfriend because Korean women, in his estimation, were the ultimate in Asian beauty (Chinese women tended to have rougher skin and flatter noses, and he was not into the Japanese crooked-teeth, bowlegged thing); he felt certain that, with his gift for beats and the right connections, he'd break into the K-pop industry no problem once he made the right connections. James had heard variations of this story many times waiting for the roommate to finish microwaving his leftover burrito.

"Eye roll," Alice said.

"I didn't have the heart to tell him no woman was going to give him the time of day unless he showed them the money."

"Wait, what are you saying about Asian women?"

"I said *all* women. Equal opportunity offender."

James turned to face her, serious. He thanked her for letting him crash at her place for the past few days. He knew how small apartments were in this town. No one had said no to a crash, but he could tell not everyone was pleased with the arrangement, however temporary.

"It's like they smell failure or something," he said. "Like I stepped in bad-luck dog shit and they don't want me tracking it into their house."

"Everybody hits a hump. You'll be back on your feet before you know it," she assured him, although privately she was looking forward to his departure date. She hadn't watched bad TV, jerked off, or munched on Cheetos in days, trying to keep up appearances. She wasn't used to having another person around with whom she had to negotiate space or coordinate time.

Maybe, she suggested, he could take advantage of the interval between jobs to do something different, something he'd always wanted to do.

James sighed and looked away. "How come free time never feels free?"

Three nights later James was gone, headed for a cat-sitting gig on the Upper West Side. He'd left a slightly overwrought thank-you note on the back of an envelope propped up against the saltshaker, and, in Alice's refrigerator, an aggregate of mysterious plastic-wrapped leftovers the shape of ears. At first she was pleased to have her life back. But after a day of being alone in the apartment, she found herself having imaginary conversations with James—about the purported side effects of ingesting datura and other flowering nightshades; *Solaris*: Tarkovsky vs. Soderbergh; whether Diet Coke was, in fact, bad for you. She picked up her phone and started tapping out a text to James, then changed her mind and erased what she'd begun, letter by letter like a vanishing ellipsis.

ALMANAC

This was no regular chicken. Not the kind you find in a learn-your-alphabet picture book under C, all white feathers and red wattles. Alice was within a block of the bookstore in Red Hook when she came across the bird, which had tucked itself onto the narrow ledge of a doorway inches from the sidewalk. The sky was slate, drizzly, and the cold made the chicken appear even more disoriented and forlorn. A tiny head attached to a plump body, densely speckled with black polka dots, gave it the look of an overinflated balloon. The chicken blinked; nothing else moved. Holding absolutely still was its strategy for preventing a total mental breakdown. Alice looked up and down the street. Where had the chicken come from? It must have escaped from somewhere. A backyard coop? A live poultry market? A fugitive chicken in the city struck her as nothing but doomed.

When she reached the bookstore, Alice snapped her umbrella shut and clambered down the hatch that led to the basement. The rain had cut down the usual number of volunteers, yet she recognized a few regulars—a Paul Dano look-alike in combat boots and Dickies and a high school teacher in her forties with a wide rubbery mouth who liked talking politics, especially Palestine and the BDS movement. Not today. The group worked mostly in silence, punctuated by the gutting tear of packing tape and the occasional call-out for certain requests. Anyone seen a book on guitar lessons? Do we have *Statistics for Dummies?*

Alice slid a letter open from an envelope: a request for an almanac. This wasn't the first such request she'd come across. Why this abiding interest in long-range weather forecasts? As usual, there were no almanacs on the shelves, but she did find a few other requests from the same letter writer—a joke book and a novel by Stephen King—and wrapped those in a paper grocery bag.

A week later, when Alice found herself not far from the Barnes & Noble in downtown Brooklyn, she ducked into the store on a whim and bought a copy of *The Old Farmer's Almanac,* thinking to satisfy her curiosity before donating the book.

Signature features of the almanac: a pale yellow cover, filigreed with grapevines and wheat stalks, the kind of design you might find garlanding certificates. A hole that bores through the entire book from front to back so the almanac can be hung—say, from a nail in the barn or the outhouse—the pages doubling as toilet paper.

The *almanac* reminded Alice of the Hickory Farms holiday baskets that used to arrive in the mail every winter when she was a girl, Christmas gifts from the Father's side of the family. Summer-sausage logs and *party spreads* nestled in cellophane grass, soft strawberry candies that doubled as decorative filler. She and Amy had never seen—or eaten—anything so extravagantly American. They spread the whipped cheese on crackers, topping them off with a shiny wheel of meat with the assiduousness of tourists.

The gift baskets, like *The Old Farmer's Almanac*, were exhibits of Americana. So was the secondhand couch upholstered with fox-hunting scenes that sagged in her family's living room, the wallpaper with its repeating pattern of dasher-style butter churns in the rental where she lived with her mother and sister after her parents' divorce. In the doctor's office, *Highlights* was Americana; *Reader's Digest* was Americana. Or maybe they weren't Americana but Middle America? The distinction wasn't clear to her. Was Americana the more self-consciously antiquated, idealized, and expensive version of Middle America, or simply its cultural distillation?

Even though it was still 2016, the bookstore where she'd bought *The Old Farmer's Almanac* was already stocking the commemorative 225th anniversary edition. Alice was boggled at the idea that the year the almanac was first printed, George Washington established the U.S. Postal Service, Kentucky became the fifteenth state, and indigenous warriors were still winning battles in the Northwest Territories.

Some years ago, the publisher of the almanac had tried doing away with the hole in the upper left-hand corner—a production element that cost thousands of dollars. Readers responded with outrage. They demanded that the hole be restored. Make the almanac hole again. It wasn't the hole so much as the past they didn't want to lose. That was Americana too.

When Alice first began volunteering with the collective, she recognized a few of the return addresses, storied prisons like Sing Sing, Attica, and Pelican Bay, but there were many prisons she'd never heard of. These were prisons built during the incarceration boom of the last thirty years, mostly in rural areas and near former manufacturing towns. Alabama's largest maximum-security prison was built a half-hour drive from where the Father was born and raised, a former coal-mining town of under five thousand people. Today there are more people in prison and jail in this country than there are farmers.

In the old days the almanac functioned as newspaper, magazine, weather report, and mail-order catalogue all rolled into one. In other words, an analog internet. It follows that the natural constituents for the almanac today are those with poor to zero internet access: people in prison and people who live in rural areas.

The edition Alice bought included a long feature on the history of beer-making by the Founding Fathers (Sally Hemings's younger brother Robert brewed for Monticello); a section devoted to social trends (cat cafés and casual carpools); and pages and pages of ads for hernia briefs, weed whackers and rodent insurance, special offers on three-month supplies of nonperishables for preppers and onetime deals on silver eagle dollars. The almanac's trademark weather charts were still in there, alongside specialized forecasting for the best days to undertake certain activities, from pickling and planting to losing weight and ending projects(!).

After Alice was finished leafing through its pages, she brought the almanac to the basement of the bookstore and slipped it on the shelf above the row of résumé-writing guidebooks. Only later would she realize her own foolishness: It wasn't *The Old Farmer's Almanac* with its homespun miscellany and predictions of the future that the men in prison wanted, but *The World Almanac and Book of Facts,* a wrap-up of the year's current events that could, in theory, catch them up on all they had been missing in the time they'd been away.

WITNESS

"Oh no, I can't watch that."

Alice stood next to two women chatting on a crowded subway train. The train swayed and rolled. "Ever since I became a mother, I just can't watch things like that."

Alice turned her head to get a better look at them. They were slim and stylish, one South Asian, the other white. Buttery leather handbags hung from their shoulders.

Were they talking about a movie, a TV show? The noise of the train made it difficult to hear. Alice was doubly annoyed—by the young mother's refusal to be distressed and by her own thwarted eavesdropping. The train shot aboveground onto the Manhattan Bridge. Below them the East River glimmered in the afternoon light. A few passengers looked up to take in the view, but most continued to stare down into their phones.

Another thing that annoyed Alice: her hypocrisy. Because for weeks she'd been unable to bring herself to watch a video of a starving polar bear that had been pinging around the internet. She'd seen a still of it, enough to know the polar bear was painfully, mortally thin. What more was there to know? Maybe there was nothing, but still she felt pulled to watch it. When she got home later that evening, she powered up her laptop, typed *starving polar bear*, and clicked on *video*.

Across a yellow, haggard plain once covered with sea ice, the emaciated bear, its muscles atrophied, drags itself along on its knees in the manner of a religious penitent. The camera tracks the bear as it musters the strength to rummage through a trash barrel, gnawing hopelessly on the carcass of a snowmobile seat before slumping to the ground.

The video was less than two minutes long. After it played out, the usual prompt appeared onscreen: *Watch again.* Alice leaned against the back of her chair, feeling about as awful as she thought she would. She hadn't looked away. She wouldn't be one of those people who looked away. But what exactly had she accomplished? She folded the laptop shut.

LAST TIME

It was Amy who worked with the realtor on selling the Father's house, which was snatched up fairly quickly by a family with small children that had been renting in San Francisco. But before that, before Alice had emptied the place of nearly any trace evidence of the Father, he did manage to visit his home one last time.

By then the Father had settled into the care home in San Jose. In the weeks leading up to the visit, there was some fretting over what might happen if his emotions overtook him. Their mother didn't want Amy driving alone with him. What if he got distressed and accidentally caused her to run off the road? Alice, who had flown in earlier and was already at the house, was more concerned that the Father would enter his familiar sanctuary, bunker down, and refuse to leave. In her mind's eye she saw him hunched in a chair with his arms folded tightly over his chest, his head pointed down like a bull's. What would they do? Wait him out? Call his bluff and leave him there?

When the day came, Alice, still on East Coast time, had risen early and gotten a coffee at the French Hotel Café on Shattuck, already full as it always was with white-haired men bent over their newspapers. There were certain days in New York in April around this time when the silkiness of the air would transport her back to Berkeley. She missed the thin fog that rolled in from the Bay at dawn, burning off by midmorning like curtains rising over the day.

When the Father entered the door of his home of more than twenty years, he was calm. He barely cast an eye around him. Sunlight glared through the dusty blinds drawn over the windows. The house still smelled of stale tobacco. The first thing the Father did was shuffle into the living room to check if he'd left any cigarettes. Amy and Alice stood aside, silent and observing. He never said what it was he wanted from his house, just that he needed to go back there. Who wouldn't want at least one backward glance?

To their bafflement, he lumbered over to the medicine cabinet in the bathroom and began packing half-used tubes of toothpaste, dental floss, and aspirin.

It wasn't only the cigarettes and toiletries he was after. Once he was finished with the bathroom, he made a beeline for the kitchen, where Alice knew he kept an open bottle of Jim Beam stored in the pantry, and poured himself a shot. Amy was distracted, flipping through his mail, but Alice had seen him, and some combination of chickenshit and empathy for all that the Father had been through stopped her from stopping him. Amy had more guts than Alice did. When she saw what he was up to, she gripped the whiskey bottle by the neck and poured the contents down the sink right in front of him.

"I don't care," she said over his protests. "If you want to ride back with me, you can't drink."

The Father grumbled but he didn't make a fuss. That surprised Alice too. He reminded her at that moment of a bear in a circus, capable of ripping a man's face off with one swipe yet who sullenly accepted the order of things. He didn't even bother taking a final look at all the rooms in the house. Maybe he had long ago stopped caring about the things that had gathered there, the books and cameras, the cooking implements and all the other objects that had once occupied his time and had since lost their purpose, the house no more than a series of trip wires and land mines he'd learned to avoid for fear of falling. Alice felt grateful and more than a little sad for his lack of sentiment. It wasn't until much later that she understood that this estrangement was, in fact, another symptom of his dementia.

WHY A YEAR?

A: *To me, we all have time, and we fill it with content.*

Q: Why a year?

A: *What is important for me is passing time, not how to pass time. I do it my way and you receive what you want. I don't change anything. I just unfold, bring it to life. Other people could find out what's inside of the work philosophically because I feel that's not my concern.*

Q: Why a year?

A: *Answering your own questions gets you closer to the fundamental question.*

ONE YEAR PERFORMANCE 1981–1982

September 26, 1981

STATEMENT

I, Tehching Hsieh, plan to do a one year performance piece.

I shall stay OUTDOORS for one year, never go inside.

I shall not go in to a building, subway, train, car, airplane, ship, cave, tent.

I shall have a sleeping bag.

The performance shall begin on September 26, 1981 at 2 P.M. and continue until September 26, 1982 at 2 P.M.

Tehching Hsieh

ENTERING AND EXITING
OUTDOOR PIECE

1.

Start with the Artist, his hair newly shaved down to his scalp, a rucksack across his shoulders, about to cross the threshold from his loft to the street. For the purposes of this project, he would go against the clock; he would waste time.

2.

Or go gonzo: Spend at least a day entirely outdoors in Lower Manhattan. Loiter for a while around Hudson Street, near the Artist's old loft. Make note of the silver mannequins wrapped in deconstructed cocoons in the window of a designer clothing boutique. Observe, through the glass front of a luxury spa, two men with their trousers rolled up having their calves plastic-wrapped in some kind of revitalizing pap by two Asian women in face masks. On the street ponytailed women in Lycra come and go, sipping from bottles of pressed juice. You last out there—this is embarrassing—all of four hours.

3.

Cut across to the corner of Beach and Greenwich, where, according to the Artist's maps, he often went to shit. The corner, probably an abandoned lot in his day, was now occupied by a glass building. Head north to a favorite sleeping spot: the public swimming pool on Thompson Street, drained and derelict, the bottom of which protected him from the wind and other people. Then down and east to the pizza joint that still hands slices through a window to customers on the sidewalk, and onward to Greene Street, another of the Artist's regular resting spots next to a designer shoe and handbag store where a security guard, hands clasped behind his back, peers out at you.

4.

Now roll the 16mm archival footage you found online of the Artist throwing a ball over and over against the wall of a handball court. Over the duration of the performance piece, various filmmaker and photographer friends captured moments like this. When you first watched the footage, you thought he was tossing the ball out of sheer boredom. Then you noticed that he was pacing back and forth in the handball court at a rapid clip and swinging his arms: he must have been trying to keep his blood circulating to stay warm.

5.

Note that, in the year the Artist lived outdoors, there was a boom in the number of New Yorkers living and sleeping in the streets, on church steps, in subway stations and public parks. It was a record year for robberies—a hundred and twenty thousand—and a record year for Wall Street: for the first time ever, a hundred-million-plus shares were traded in a single day on the New York Stock Exchange.

6.

Play up the fact that the winter that year in New York City was one of the coldest on record. Cut to archival photographs of the Artist rubbing his hands over an open fire on the bank of the East River. Zoom in on the ice floes bobbing on the surface of the river behind him.

7.

Conjure the silence of the reference room on the third floor of the New York Public Library, where you filled out a request card for the exhibition catalogue of *Outdoor Piece*. The librarian, a sunless man in glasses the shape of goat pupils, reemerged with the slim book in his hands. From its pages poured the seasons—the gush of water from a fire hydrant in summer; a scatter of snow dusting the Artist's coat and knit hat; the stark morning light on a stretch of the East River Parkway, smokestacks rising in the distance like cigarettes shaken from a pack. Remember how you left California for these seasons, for a city that had seasons, afraid that if you kept living on the West Coast you'd lose all sense of time, turn into that frog in the science experiment, hapless, boiled alive as the temperature of the water is cranked up bit by bit.

8.

Or don't start with the Artist or his project at all but with a scene you witnessed the other day on a subway platform. A little boy, clutching his stomach in a knot of unhappiness, cries, "I'm hungry! I'm hungry!" as his young mother looks at him, a little cross.

"Don't be so dramatic," she says. "I can't be spending any more money outside. I left with thirty dollars and now I have one dollar."

She tries placating the boy with a piece of gum. When he turns his face away, she stares down at him dispassionately. "You are acting exaggerated."

9.

Throw in the Artist's response to the question: What was the hardest thing about that year? *Staying clean*. By the end of winter, his hands looked like the hands of a miner, blackened up to his wrists with dirt. Find a place for this quote from Julien Green: "The soul of a big city was not to be grasped so easily. In order to make contact with it, you have to have been bored, you have to have suffered a bit in those places that contain it."

10.

Or try on this idea: All projects are a shift from an inside to an outside. Nothing is risked, nothing takes form, until you cross that threshold.

11.

Note, by the end of *Outdoor Piece*, Reaganomics had a name. AIDS had a name. *The New York Times* revised its style guide to indicate that, from this point forward, the population previously described as *vagrants* and *transients* would henceforth be referred to as *homeless*.

FIFTEEN HOURS

It should be noted that, of the eight thousand seven hundred and sixty hours that the Artist performed *Outdoor Piece*, fifteen hours were spent indoors against his will.

What happened was this: He was south of Houston Street sitting in a doorway sipping a hot cup of tea when a man emerged from the building and yelled at him to beat it. The Artist could have slunk away, but this time, for whatever reason, he didn't. The man didn't back down, either. He disappeared for a minute, then came back swinging a metal rod. The Artist stood his ground, ready to defend himself with the pair of nunchucks he kept in his rucksack. That's when the police stepped in.

A friend happened to be filming that day, which is why there's video of the Artist being hauled away by two cops to the police station. By the time of this incident, the Artist had been living outdoors for many months and his hair had grown long, which made him look a little wild. *I can't go inside*, you can hear him plead in the film footage. At the moment the cops begin dragging him forward, the Artist released an uncanny high-pitched wail. He wailed because he didn't want to break the piece. These weren't the only stakes. He was still undocumented: any encounter with law enforcement could result in his being deported. (Did the Artist know then that the city had classified nunchucks as an illegal weapon? A bullshit law cooked up in the seventies in response to the kung fu craze incited by Bruce Lee movies.)

The Artist was held in jail until he was called into court. He caught a lucky break: The judge overseeing the Artist's case recognized him from a story he'd read in *The Wall Street Journal*. (How the *Journal* story came to be: At the time of publication, the Artist was supporting himself by working construction. His boss, who was dating the *Journal* reporter at the time, tipped her off about the Chinese guy who was working the job with a sideline as a performance artist.) *Who's to say what passes for art these days?* was the judge's position. He released the Artist in exchange for a guilty plea on a charge of disorderly conduct and sentenced him to time served. When the piece is broken, the whole emerges.

THE TICKET

The last time Alice had seen James was at their favorite diner on Twenty-Third Street. They sat in a two-seater booth across from the counter. The notes in her journal said they tried guessing the flavors of the pies under their clouds of meringue and whipped cream in the mirrored display case. Her notes said "Free Fallin' " was playing over the sound system, followed by Huey Lewis and the News, a band she'd hated as a kid but that now made her melancholic for dumber, gentler times.

A few months ago, a homemade bomb had detonated a few blocks away, sending a dumpster flying into the air and shattering glass all around. In the days following, the staff at the diner had taken it upon themselves to make deliveries to their regulars, many of whom lived nearby in an apartment building for the blind. Once, out of curiosity, Alice had asked for the diner's Braille menu. The menu, spiral-bound like an old college reader, was surprisingly heavy, the pages as white as the walls of a new rental apartment. Alice ran her fingers across the bumps to feel her illiteracy. Few of the blind customers used it; it was easier to tell the waiter what you wanted. Voice technology was making Braille increasingly obsolete.

James had been on edge that day. He scraped the contents of a sugar packet back and forth on his saucer like he was preparing to do lines.

The update was that he'd recently checked into a homeless shelter. He knew he could have easily hit up friends for a couch or stayed with his sister in Long Island. But he couldn't bring himself to do it. Maybe part of him wanted to touch rock bottom, like how you can't help sniffing a carton of milk you know has expired. "I already feel like I'm not part of this world, so why not try the underworld?" He wasn't sure. He rubbed his chin. He wasn't sure about lot of things right now.

At the shelter he met with a social worker, a lady with glorious Toni Morrison dreads, who was not without sympathy. She leaned across the table and told him that the city would buy him a one-way bus ticket to any destination in the country he wanted to go. She said this in a low voice as though what she was offering were a special deal. Maybe he had family somewhere?

"I said sure, I'll take that ticket," James said, then he remembered how much he hated buses; they made him carsick. And he couldn't actually think of where else to go. He had relatives in North Carolina and a childhood friend and ex in Chicago, but none of that seemed enough to go on.

"What did you do?" Alice asked. "Did you take the ticket?"

James was evasive. He said he was still thinking on it. Then he changed the topic and they spent the next hour talking about their fathers. James's seemed to be doing okay now at home, although his short-term memory was not what it used to be.

They gossiped about a mutual friend's newish boyfriend whom no one liked but felt guilty about not liking because his only fault was lacking a discernible personality.

A few weeks later James sent a text to say he'd moved, for now anyway, upstate to Troy.

U did what? Howzit? More important—how are u? She texted back. Then nothing.

THE MONK

Rushing out of her apartment, Alice was stopped in the street by a monk in saffron robes and sneakers. He bowed his shaved head slightly and extended his arm, revealing a Buddhist fetish the size of a domino tile on his open palm. She was confused. Did he want her to take it? Was he selling it? She shook her head; he nodded as if to bid her good day and moved on.

Only after she'd nearly reached the subway station did she realize he must have been a fake monk, one of a loose confederation of grifters who fleeced tourists in Times Square with their false piety. The performance artist as scam artist. She was crestfallen that she'd let him go. There was so much she wanted to ask him about his wickedness!

HUDSON STREET LOFT RENTAL LISTING

Spectacular one-bedroom (convertible 2) loft in a key-locked elevator condo building in the heart of Tribeca.

This spacious apartment has been fully renovated and boasts an array of exquisite details including black oak floors, a state-of-the-art home control system, and high ceilings.

The bright and airy living room features original Corinthian columns and oversized windows that offer sweeping architectural views facing east.

The adjoining kitchen is complete with Viking stainless steel appliances as well as white Calcutta Gold marble counter-tops and backsplash.

The brand-new bathroom continues with the same marble finishes all over, and also includes a steam shower. From here, French doors lead to the bedroom which has two closets in addition to overhead storage.

Other stunning highlights of this unit include a new washer/ dryer, overhead fans, eco-friendly LED lighting, and multiple storage areas throughout.

Located in the most desirable section of Tribeca, near the corner of N Moore Street, this loft is the perfect place to make a home.

ONE YEAR PERFORMANCE 1983-1984

July 4, 1983

<u>STATEMENT</u>

We, Linda Montano and Tehching Hsieh, plan to do a
one year performance.

We will stay together for one year and never be
alone.

We will be in the same room at the same time, when we
are inside.

We will be tied together at waist with an 8 foot rope.

We will never touch each other during the year.

The performance will begin on July 4, 1983 at 6 P.M.
and continue until July 4, 1984 at 6 P.M.

Linda Montano
Tehching Hsieh

WHAT WAS *ROPE PIECE*

WHAT YOU DID

You take the subway together. You ride bicycles, separately, side by side, you shop for groceries and walk home holding the heavy bag between you. You go jogging, you knock back drinks at an East Village drinking hole. You withdraw money side-by-side from tellers at the bank, play pinball at the local arcade, walk the dog. You wait on the other side of the shower curtain while one of you bathes; the other side of the bathroom door while one of you shits. You see visitors and pose for photos, have a Coke at a nearby diner with Ai Weiwei. You trudge through snow, you take naps, do light construction, read tarot cards. You feed the cat. You fry eggs sunny side up, wait in line at the Murray Hill Cinema for *Greystoke: The Legend of Tarzan*. For money you do work for other artists—hanging shows, cleaning lofts, updating mailing lists. You read newspapers together, one in English, one in Chinese. You give a friend a haircut, take a bus to Philadelphia, watch a lot of television, and drink many cups of tea. You cross the Brooklyn Bridge by foot. You have your photo taken with visitors and in front of the massive orb of the World Fair's Unisphere in Flushing Meadows Corona Park in Queens. You take turns.

Early on you discover that walking around SoHo, where you were more likely to be recognized and whispered about, makes you both uncomfortable, so you avoid the area. You can't help but be a spectacle. You turn down requests from *That's Incredible!, Entertainment Tonight,* and *Ripley's Believe It or Not.* You keep yourselves mostly to Tribeca and Chinatown, where you hit up the Chinese restaurants and watch kung fu flicks at the Pagoda Theater or Music Palace on the Bowery where watermelon seeds crack under your feet and the aroma of citrus from peeled tangerines blooms in the dark.

To curious passersby you explain that what you are doing is an *experiment.* You've learned from experience that if you call it *art* the reaction is sometimes hostile. An experiment is more humble. An experiment suggests you wanted to learn something—about human nature, say, or our capacity for coexistence. Calling the project art confounds people (*Why do you do such performances?*), or, worse, comes off as self-indulgent, as though your behavior is mocking people's efforts to live their lives without illusions.

One night you take the three-minute walk from your Hudson Street loft to Area, the buzzy, newly unveiled nightclub near the Holland Tunnel. Every six weeks, the club reinvents itself with a new theme. Basquiat is spinning records. Grace Jones strides by on the arm of Dolph Lundgren. There's Malcolm Forbes, his nipples peeking through a mesh shirt. Amid the eye-popping theatrics, the vamping, the bustiers and latex, the tank of live sharks, the two of you still attract stares. Not because of the rope—that's nothing. It is the terribly unfashionable clothes you're wearing.

WHAT THE PROJECT IS AND ISN'T

The Artist insisted the piece was not about two people or about marriage.

He said: *As individuals, we each have our own ideas of what it is we want to do. We struggle because we want our freedom. Yet we can't go on in life without other people. So we become each other's cage.*

Linda Montano saw the project as an opportunity to practice paying attention. To stay in the moment. To explore ego and power. Because of the project, she believed everything you did together— fighting, eating, sleeping—was "raised to the dignity of art."

The project made Montano think of meditation retreats.

The project made the Artist think of his three years of compulsory military service in Taiwan.

To him, the project was not about dignity. The project was a mirror that reflected back your nakedness, your weakness and limitations. The project revealed you to be an animal—craven, abject, undignified.

WHY STRANGERS

The idea for the project, the Artist said, grew out of his struggle to communicate with other people. This was why he chose a stranger to be his partner for the piece. Performing the piece would have put such enormous pressure on a romantic partner that the only outcome, he believed, would have been to split apart.

HOW THE PROJECT BREAKS DOWN

In the beginning there is so much to know. The two of you talk for nearly six hours a day. Then talk becomes exhausting. It takes hours to negotiate what it is you will do. Your arguments escalate until a new rule is set: any action of one can be vetoed by the other.

You spend most of the winter indoors in the loft vetoing each other's proposed activities. Montano hates going to Chinatown, which is where the Artist prefers to have his meals. He resents having to walk her dog. Sometimes the vetoes come in such rapid, aggressive succession that the two of them are immobilized for hours.

Montano said she fantasized about killing him thousands of times. Twice in rage he threw pieces of furniture that crashed to the floor near her feet.

Marina Abramović drops in during this time and remembers being puzzled by the scratches she saw above your two separate twin beds. Later she heard the two of you did not get along and scratched the walls out of frustration.

Gradually, like monkeys, you nearly cease speaking altogether, relying instead on a series of simple gestures—pointing to the bathroom when you need to relieve yourself, the kitchen when you want to eat. You grunt and make moaning sounds to signal your impatience or displeasure.

WHAT IT LOOKED LIKE

None of this anguish is legible in the photographic record of the piece. What's striking about the pictures—once you get past the peculiar circumstance of two people tied together—is how mundane your lives look.

How would *Rope Piece* be performed today? Would there

be a live twenty-four-hour webcam so anyone anywhere in the world could tune in, as they would to a squirming litter of Shiba Inu puppies? A daily Instagram of your every meal? His-and-her live tweets, *Rashomon*-style? Would you release weekly Spotify playlists based on your mood or harness any number of other digital platforms that may not exist by the time these words are read, platforms that will appear as hopelessly dated as the glowing red digital time stamps in the right-hand corner of the photographs you took in 1984?

WHEN YOU DREAMED
was the only time either of you had any privacy.

WHY YOU MADE RECORDINGS
Every day you made sound recordings of the project on ninety-minute audiocassette tapes. Each tape—about seven hundred in total—was marked with the date and labeled "TALKING."

The Walkman you used to make these recordings is visible in many photos from this time, the tape whirring as you talk, bang dishes in the sink, clatter on the typewriter, laugh, shout, hum, cough, hiccup, snore, burp, fart, yell.

You disagreed on the purpose of the tapes. She said knowing her actions were being recorded made her behave with greater intentionality. He said the tapes were strictly conceptual, nothing more than a symbol of "talking." What was actually said didn't matter.

The two of you agreed on this: The tape recordings were never meant to be heard. The tapes make privacy.

HOW IT WAS DANGEROUS

Montano recalled an incident when he sped ahead of her to catch an elevator. She was still on the other side as the doors began sliding shut.

The piece was dangerous emotionally, she added.

She said, "I think raising a child is dangerous. And being married is dangerous. And having early-onset dementia is dangerous. I've been allowed this open area of research to do my studies. And maybe aestheticized danger is a luxury item because it is chosen and it ends. I can't do the other: I can't do the marriage, I can't do the relationship, I can't do the children, I do what I can do."

WHAT OF IT

Later, reflecting on the project, the Artist said the year he'd spent in self-imposed imprisonment was much easier. Alone in his cage, he could focus on art. Being tied to another human being, he said, was *too much life*.

CASSETTE TAPES

For the purposes of the Project, Alice learned the average life span of an audiocassette tape is thirty years. This doesn't mean the tape, when it reaches the thirty-year mark, spontaneously combusts or unravels. The sound quality just won't be as sharp, like the potency of expired pills or the flavor of an old can of soup. The sound will be distorted around the edges, like memory.

It holds that if the thirty-year rule is true, the tapes from *Rope Piece* have been compromised. Then again, no one was ever meant to hear them.

The Artist once compared these tapes to the black box aboard aircrafts. Never retrieving the box from the bottom of the ocean, he said, makes a question.

At the same time the Artist and Linda Montano were making tape recordings of *Rope Piece*, Andy Warhol was downtown making audio recordings of his own.

Television was Warhol's first love. But when he got his first tape recorder in 1964, he claimed he met his wife. In all he made more than four thousand tape recordings. Warhol brought his Sony recorder everywhere—Studio 54, the Waldorf, the Four

Seasons, P. J. Clarke's. ("I would go to the opening of anything, including a toilet seat," he once said.) You can spot it in photographs, peeking out from under his arm as he hobnobs from one nightspot to another. It's there at his waist as he chats backstage with Raquel Welch after a performance of *Woman of the Year*; it's clutched in his hand as he enters a building with Bianca Jagger, a long fur flung across her shoulders; it's balanced on his lap as he forks a plate of food at a party.

Warhol, tongue-struck son of Slovakian immigrants, specter, master of banality, po-mo genius of his times, said that having the tape recorder always at his side had the effect of preempting any emotional life he might otherwise have had. He didn't miss having these emotions. When he pressed play, bad emotions—awkwardness, pain, envy—didn't have to stay bad. A problem just meant a good tape. And when a problem transformed itself into a good tape, well, then it wasn't a problem anymore. It could be turned into something more useful.

In Samuel Beckett's *Krapp's Last Tape*, it's Krapp's sixty-ninth birthday. He clomps around in too-big shoes and too-short trousers. He chews a banana. He turns on a reel-to-reel player and listens to an old recording of himself, a birthday ritual.

In the recording of the play Alice watched on YouTube (file under: *Famous Tapes in Art*), John Hurt plays Krapp. With his lanky frame and hair sticking straight up like a thicket, he looks not unlike Beckett. Krapp also reminded Alice a little of the Father. They were two old men who had abandoned nearly all human relationships in exchange for a few small pleasures, the eating of a banana, the uncorking of a bottle of spirits. Krapp also reminded her a little of herself—the type of person who, in the middle of reflecting on his mother's death, pauses like an asshole to look up *viduity* in the dictionary.

Onstage, Krapp plays his last tape. We learn about his disappointments, past loves, resentments, a fleeting rapture—all the moments that make up a life. The play ends with a disavowal. Krapp: "Perhaps my best years are gone. When there was a chance of happiness. But I wouldn't want them back. Not with the fire in me now. No, I wouldn't want them back."

Celebrities of a certain age are often asked in interviews: If you could do it all over again, would you change anything? Sometimes you can see a shadow cross their face before they deliver the emphatic, inevitable no. They wouldn't change a thing. Not. One. Thing. Regret is something you're meant to do in private.

Alice watched the fire in the Father go out. It happened at the rehab facility in Oakland. It was late in the afternoon when most of the other residents were dozing or waking up from their naps; dinner was still an hour away. The winter light had ceded to darkness. She was preparing to leave, already looking forward to the long bus ride to the Father's house in Berkeley so she could clear her head.

The Father was in bed, lying on his back. Tears streaked from the corners of his eyes. He wanted to go home. He shouted this, his mouth a gash of anguish. He'd made a goddamned mess of his life. He knew that! And now all he wanted to do was go home.

This was not the same man who had been calling her every night for weeks at two or three in the morning in a raging delirium, cussing her out, yelling for his car keys, his wallet. He was lucid, clear as he would ever be. She listened and told him she was sorry. Did she lie to him then? She can't remember. Maybe a little: She told him he had to get better first. The truth was he was free to go; no one had the legal authority to keep him there, not the doctor, not his daughters. Maybe some part of him knew this, and that what was at stake wasn't whether he could leave, but how he would live. This reckoning made his fire go out.

In her second year in New York, Alice had a boyfriend with a coke habit and who drove a Honda Civic hatchback. The car was old, with more than two hundred thousand miles on it. In the two years Alice had been with this man, the car was beset by a series of minor injuries—a broken windshield wiper, timing belt trouble, a coolant leak. Nothing catastrophic, just enough to signal that the vehicle was well past its prime, each repair more patch than resurrection.

The boyfriend joked that he held on to the car because it was the last contraption he had that still played cassette tapes. Alice adored the feature that allowed you, with a press of a button, to flip from side A to side B. A dozen old tapes were jammed in the glove compartment, the door of which fell open if you looked at it sideways, disgorging cassettes onto the floor of the car. She was constantly crushing their clear plastic cases underfoot. She'd been mortified the first time she'd broken one, but he'd laughed it off. She remembered this as something she admired about him, how little stock he put in things, in objects.

Eventually the boyfriend did sell the car, and soon after, they broke up. "Try spending some time outside of your own head," was one of his parting shots. She could see their disintegration coming before it actually happened and, as was her way, prepared for it. A few weeks before the breakup, he left her sitting on the passenger side of the car while he went into a gas station mini-mart to buy cigarettes. She opened the glove compartment and slipped a few cassette tapes into her backpack, selected at random. These she kept in a shoebox on a shelf in her closet along with mix tapes from other ex-boyfriends and no machine to play them.

NOT TALKING

Some have asked Alice if she intends to interview the Artist. "Yes, yes, I should do that," she'd say, nodding agreeably. In the beginning, she half believed she would. Yet as more time passed, she knew she wouldn't.

"The author can never, by definition, be quite the one we love." Pico Iyer wrote this to differentiate the feelings he had about Graham Greene the man and Graham Greene the writer. Iyer identified ardently with Greene (the "patron saint of the foreigner alone") as his fellow restless traveler. Yet he wrote an entire book about his obsession with Greene—*The Man Within My Head*—without once speaking with his subject.

For Iyer, engaging with Greene off the page was neither here nor there; the Greene inside his head was the one who mattered. *That* was the Greene Iyer talked to, wrestled with. The Greene who was not in his head would have inevitably disappointed because that Greene would have been a polite stranger, forced to look away from his desk and put on the public face he assumed to greet the world.

As an artist, you meet many different kinds of people, the Artist once said in an interview. *Some people are plainspoken, and that makes talking easier. But sometimes you can tell the communication won't happen. You feel badly about this because you want to respond to everything with consideration and seriousness. But that means answering this, this, and this. All the responses are different and they make you feel fragile.*

Alice wondered if the Artist's resistance to improving his English was a way to recuse himself from having to explain or talk too much, like how old people sometimes pretend they're hard of hearing so they can ignore you without qualms. She'd read enough interviews with the Artist, the ones in English anyway, to know that he was so often asked the same questions that he'd developed, over time, a number of fallback responses.

Here, for example, was his stock response when pressed for the meaning of his work: *Life is a life sentence. Life is passing time. Life is free thinking.* That was usually enough to satisfy his interlocutors.

It wasn't that Alice didn't have her own questions for him; she did. For example, questions that would satisfy her puerile curiosity about his private life. He had two previous wives before his current one. Who were they? She was curious if he went to the movies, what he did to unwind or indulge, who he counted among his closest comrades. If only there were a tell-all tabloid about avant-garde performance artists! As for the other questions, the bigger questions—

Why do you do such performances?

(Do I have what it takes to—?)

Answering your own questions gets you closer to the fundamental question.

THE POSSIBILITY OF LOVE AND PROJECTS

Because Alice had no data on the Artist's first two wives, she didn't know, for instance, if the Artist was married during the making of his projects.

The odds were likely, because he was forty-nine years old the year he declared that he would no longer be making any new projects. True, he could have been married multiple times since then, or, for that matter, when he was a very young man in Taiwan. These marriages might have dissolved for all the usual reasons—bad communication, disagreeable habits, arguments over money and how to spend it, children and whether to have them. Yet it was not hard to imagine that the projects themselves exerted uncommon pressure, as they would have on the union of any two people, if not broken them in half.

In her twenties, like many hetero women in their twenties, Alice had had her share of bad men and good reasons to be rid of them. They were bad because, like her, they were callow, thoughtless, and young, or because she had limited experience navigating the neuroses of bad older men who were more experienced at being bad and convincing her they were good. Or, as was more likely the case, they were better at making her believe that she was the bad one. In the case of good men who were somehow not the right men—the reasons being more complicated and harder to explain—she found herself thinking that what she really ought to be doing was focusing more on projects.

Once, to break up with a man, she used projects as the reason. The end of the relationship was not unlike the end of a project: She no longer knew how to go further. There seemed to be no more words or actions that could produce different feelings. She needed to give everything to her projects, she explained, which meant she couldn't give him what he wanted or deserved. He was silent for a while. Then he said, "I need a drink," and left, and that was that. She was sure he didn't believe her, but he didn't call her out on it, either. All saved face with the deus ex machina of the project.

Some people, it should be said, are better at projects than they are at love. How often had she thought in her loneliness, especially on a Friday or Saturday night when the world just outside her door seemed to be blazing with music, laughter, chance, and possibility: But at least there is the project.

A GOOD WORD

In an interview Linda Montano was asked how she felt after she and the Artist were separated after a year of living together in such intimate conditions.

"Were you bereft?" the reporter asked.

"Yes, we were. I was," she said. "Not having had children and not having been . . . yes, I was bereft. That is a good word."

THE PROTEST

When Alice arrived at the protest, Julia was already there, shivering in her too-thin vintage leopardskin coat. Julia opened her fist to reveal a little blue pill. Alice smiled and shook her head.

Julia shrugged and popped the Xanax in her mouth, swallowed hard. Alice knew how Julia felt about protests—the claustrophobic marching; the rallying chants she could never quite juice herself to join full-heartedly; the lonely-in-the-crowd melancholy. Alice felt all these things too but for the purposes of the protest, that was beside the point.

It was an overcast evening and darkness had already set in, the ink of it even thicker in this under-lit industrial area of the Brooklyn waterfront where about twenty other protesters had gathered. Looming above them was the federal jail, a twelve-story monolith that was only a short walk away from a Bed Bath & Beyond and Saks Fifth Avenue outlet store on Third Avenue.

A national prison strike had been called on the forty-fifth anniversary of the Attica uprising. Prosecutors had charged corrections officers at the Brooklyn jail with sexual assault; reports of rotten food and lack of heat were rampant. The protesters on the ground yelled and pumped their cardboard signs up and down while a man in a black hoodie and torn jeans banged against the steel door of a warehouse with a baseball bat. Above them on every floor of the jail they could see lights flashing on and off through the windows of the holding cells, narrow slits of frosted glass. Cell phones were not allowed; the lights were most likely miniature flashlights that were sold for eight dollars apiece at the commissary.

She wished she could describe the scene better to you than this—how twenty people screamed, clapped, and banged on pots from below as the lights above them flickered on and off in an improvisatory duet of flash and sound.

After a while, the protesters were on the move. Alice and Julia fell in line, following the crowd as it made its way around the perimeter of the jail. It had begun drizzling. A few umbrellas opened; people pulled up the hoods of their jackets. Their rallying cries rose and fell as the group circled the block-long jail building and spilled out onto the street under the shadow of the Brooklyn-Queens Expressway. There were no cars in sight. Some protesters flung a few garbage cans in the air and rolled them into the street; a flag was set on fire—or what Alice thought was a flag, it was too dark to tell and the material had gone up in flames quickly. No one spoke, which made their actions seem almost ceremonial.

After a few blocks, Julia leaned in close to Alice and said she was splitting off. Okay, see you later. Alice stayed on for a few more blocks until the small group turned into a handful of people who no longer had cause to walk together in the same direction. She held her collar up to her neck as she made her way to the subway. The drizzle lashed into rain.

THE ENCOUNTER

You should know Alice did not set out to speak to the Artist, but she did stalk him.

She learned from a news article, dated by several years, that the Artist owned a loft above a dollar store in a Brooklyn neighborhood not far from her studio apartment. The parameters of the neighborhood were not extensive; surely the building wouldn't be hard to find?

After several passes in the area on her bike, she zeroed in on a dollar store wedged between a Thai restaurant and a fried chicken place not far from the local police station and a big housing project. The building didn't sit right: there were two floors of apartments above the street-level retail. She had assumed what she was looking for was more of a stand-alone—a live/work unit above a commercial unit—because that's what the Artist would likely have been able to afford. She found a dollar store, but it was only one story tall. She was about to call it a day when she passed a boarded-off storefront that she'd ridden by before and slowed down. The building was under renovation and the old signage had been removed, cloaking its former identity. Could it be? On a hunch she searched for a name on the mailbox outside a metal grate that blocked off a dark stairwell. In faded handwriting in all caps was the Artist's name.

For the next few months, she kept occasional tabs on the place. She peered through an opening in the plywood planks that shielded the street from the construction but never saw anyone working inside. She scrutinized a lamp with a torn lampshade pressed against the window in the unit on the second floor overlooking the street. Once she saw a dark-haired figure hunched over the kitchen sink. A man? A woman? It was impossible to tell.

Then, on a spring day months later, she passed by the storefront and saw that all the scaffolding had been removed and that the ground-floor business was open. She pushed through the heavy glass door into what appeared to be a cross between a café and a restaurant. The interior was unadorned, the walls bare except for a chalkboard menu featuring the usual coffee drinks as well as a selection of Taiwanese dishes like lu rou fan. Near the entrance was a simple wooden booth where an older Chinese woman in a baseball cap stood folding dumplings.

Did the store belong to the Artist? Alice guessed yes. The Artist, she knew, had worked in construction; he'd once owned a building in Williamsburg, bought with the sales of his early paintings to a Taiwanese collector, which he converted into artist studios.

As she scanned the seating area in the back of the shop, she thought she recognized the man perched on a tall stool, deep in conversation with two Chinese women. His hair was silver and shaved close to his skull. There were deep lines carved into his face, but his build—compact and wired to spring on a moment's notice—seemed to have changed very little from thirty years ago.

It was the Artist.

The surprise at seeing him in the flesh for the first time without preamble, without the scrim of the screen or the page, thrust herself into her body: she didn't know what to do with her hands and face, where to direct her eyes. For a few seconds she imagined she'd walked into a gallery installation (*Small Business Piece?*) and that everything around her was prop and performance, from the refrigerator units banked along one wall to the young barista with pink hair slouching at the register.

Alice stood rooted to the floor. She had no reason to stay but she couldn't make herself leave, either. Buying food or drink, which would have been the normal thing to do, struck her as farcical. It was the giddy paralysis of finding yourself in close proximity to someone famous who you have no intention of speaking to—indeed, you are pretending that you haven't noticed them at all, along with everyone else around you caught in a quivering, suspended hive that no one can leave because anything can happen, and to leave would risk missing something, whatever that something was.

Nothing happened. Alice forced herself to lift her feet off the floor. At that moment the Artist also rose—the conversation he'd been having must have ended—and Alice and the Artist locked eyes. "Thank you," he said reflexively to her, the anonymous customer. She nodded, smiled, then looked away, slightly embarrassed, as though she'd been caught doing something rude or unseemly, and made her way to the exit. She wasn't ready. For what? To talk to him. To play her hand. For her subject to slip his moorings and cease being, to some degree, a figment.

Pico Iyer has imagined meeting Graham Greene, the meeting that never happened. Greene lived a famously reclusive life in the Mediterranean resort town of Antibes. Iyer would have had to fly into the airport in Nice and, after a short drive or train ride, arrive at Greene's fourth-floor flat overlooking the port of Côte d'Azur. Once he stepped across the threshold, he would have paused to admire a dramatic oil painting that hung on the wall, a gift from Fidel Castro. Then, as Greene fixed him a drink, Iyer pictured himself settling into a bamboo chair, all smiles and charm, his nerves on edge with the thirst to extract from Greene an anecdote, a story, some telling nugget or impression that had not yet been revealed to all the other strangers who'd come knocking at Greene's door.

"I'd come away, of course, with a souvenir—the illusion that I 'knew' him a little," Iyer wrote. "But the cost would be tremendous." Alice thought she knew what the cost was. That you could know too much or not enough and either way end up stranded at the mouth of the hole.

PROJECT FOR A TRIP TO CHINA

In Sontag's short story "Project for a Trip to China" the unnamed narrator is invited to China on a junket by the Chinese government. The project unfolds as a loose association of daydreams, impressions, epigrams, facts, and memories triggered by the planning for this future trip. She expects to board a train for Canton. She wants to walk across the Luhu Bridge. The specter in the story is the narrator's father, who, like Sontag's, died in China when she was a girl. The mystery of the father is as vast as China.

Alice has always been partial to this story. Like the narrator in Sontag's story, she has always imagined she would go to China one day.

Doesn't every Chinese person not from China have a project for a trip to China? Alice's mother, even as a little girl in Tainan, yearned to see the Three Gorges. Before he got sick, the Father used to talk about his dream of traveling the Silk Road.

Visual synecdoches of modern-day China: rows of young women on the assembly line, their black hair tucked in shower caps, faces hidden by surgical masks. Farmers squatting by pyramids of rubble, cigarettes burning down to their fingers. Concrete buildings erupting out of the rice fields. Figures blurred by a bad air day.

Years ago, Alice had a project for a trip to China. The project involved seeing her biological father—whom she had not seen in more than twenty years—into the afterlife.

Sontag did once accept an invitation to travel with a delegation to China sponsored by the Chinese government. In her journal, she describes her intention to write a book about China. The book would most emphatically not be an account of her travels there. (The tour, as she predicted, was a stultifying parade of speeches and stage-managed visits to factories, schools, and municipal buildings.) No, the book would be about something much more than that. It would, she hoped, be the "everything book I've been trying to write."

Sontag the critic, the novelist, the playwright. Yet it's Sontag the journal keeper—those torrential lists of books and films and exhibitions she means to devour, the conceptual enjambments whose jotted swiftness even typeface manages to convey—who is, for Alice, the essential Sontag, the reason why young women will always read Sontag. Reading the journals is like being inside a metabolizing intellect so extreme the threat of death could not register as anything but a shock. But there isn't any *time* to die, Sontag must have thought, dying.

It turns out not everything can be turned into a book. But just about everything can be meat for a project. Everything? Sontag's journal offers the thrill of standing on the scaffolding of her project to China. She makes notes to herself to read Wittfogel's book on China, Barthes on Japan, Pound on Chinese calligraphy, the Sinologists Granet and Needham. Maybe the book will be titled *Notes Toward a Definition of Cultural Revolution*. An examination of China as an alternative to consumer society? Perhaps the book could be collaged, like John Cage's *A Year from Monday*.

"I can put my whole life into this book," Sontag wrote. "It's about everything, and yet it's about the moon—the most exotic place—about nothing at all."

Chinese internet rumor: A corrupt individual has been caught stealing cadavers, slicing off the fat and meat from the buttocks and the backs of the legs to sell as dumpling meat. The indecipherable mash at the center of the dumpling is the locus of national anxiety. Alice's mother once described to her a favorite dish of the empress dowager's: First, individual bean sprouts are split down their length with a copper wire. Each narrow trough is filled with seasoned minced pork and then steamed just enough so the meat cooks but the sprouts retain a slight crispness. It took a team of ten court cooks and assistants to prepare this one delicacy.

Sontag's would-be traveler to China thrills in her uncommon fondness for thousand-year-old eggs, ordering them in restaurants over the protests of Chinese waiters and the horror of her friends. "Everyone I know finds the sight of them disgusting."

Alice shouldn't scoff. Some years ago, she bought a jade bracelet in San Francisco Chinatown. She wanted to feel more—what? Well, Chinese. She chose a bracelet that was not too green, swirled with white smoke. She couldn't remove the bracelet unless she slicked her wrist with a gob of lotion. The bracelet clanged against dishes, stairwell railings, car windows. Her mother took one glance and proclaimed it a fake. The natural skepticism of the Chinese: wary of imposters, of being cheated and overcharged, taken for fools.

When Ezra was six, Alice asked him what he imagined Disneyland was like. The boy thought on this.

"It's a world . . . a pretend world where everything you can't see, *are*."

Once we visit a place in person, our imaginary of it breaks apart like a melting strip of film reel. We're shocked to discover that, directly across the street from the storied, centuries-old fountain, squats a Burger King, that the ground is filthy with cheese-crusted hamburger wrappers, trampled napkins, the sundials of plastic cup lids pierced with straws. As with the tourists who came before us, we wait patiently for people in their brightly colored leisure wear to bumble out of the frame so we can reproduce with our cameras the same illusion of an authentic past that brought us here in the first place.

"Nothing is more beautiful than Peking unless it is the memory of Peking," says the narrator of *Dimanche à Pekin*, a short, whimsical documentary about China by Chris Marker, maker of wounded time machines. Since he was a child, Marker had yearned to visit Peking, a city he was only able to glimpse through books.

In the film, the roving camera is delighted by quotidian scenes of passing rickshaws and vegetable carts, young lovers at a lake. A street acrobat prances with swords. An old woman, a baby strapped to her back, teeters by on bound feet. Had the utter foreignness of China turned the filmmaker into just another tourist hitting *record* on his smartphone? The result is a film that skates the surface of meaning, superficial, and not that interesting—even if his outsider's impressions are the point. The first time Alice saw the film, she was reminded of the 1930 German silent *People on Sunday*, which, apart from also having *Sunday* in its title, was, like Marker's film, an ephemerality shot over a period of weeks and edited so events appear to unfold mostly over a single leisurely day with little plot to speak of. *People on Sunday* follows a group of friends on their day off from work. (The weekend had only recently been invented.) They listen to a portable record player, enjoy a picnic, flirt, and ride pedal boats in the park. It is Berlin in the twilight of the Weimar Republic; in the Beijing of *Dimanche à Pekin,* the Great Leap Forward is barely visible on the horizon. The two films are haunted by the prophecy of cataclysmic events that have yet to happen.

A few years ago, China's state censors issued new guidelines meant to crack down on depictions of time travel in TV dramas and movies. Government officials denounced these resurrections of feudalism, superstitions, and other retrograde fantasias as "frivolous" and lacking in "positive thoughts and meaning."

Silly Chinese bureaucrats, we say, laughing and shaking our heads. And yet our own country has elected a president whose campaign slogan—*Make America Great Again*—was built on a perverse desire for time travel.

Sontag's father died in China of tuberculosis. He was a furrier, an occupation from another century. One pictures a man in a bearish overcoat that hangs down to his ankles, trudging along in snowshoes to honor his transactions. In "Project," the narrator imagines if she goes to the land where her father died, she will finally be able to bury him. ("By visiting my father's death, I make him heavier.")

One morning Alice woke to three voice mail messages from her mother. It had been an unseasonably warm winter in New York City; she remembered hardly any snow on the ground that year. Her father—her biological father—had died.

How? In his sleep. A good death.

Where? In China.

Alice and Amy had not even known he had been living in Shanghai, his hometown, since they fell out of each other's lives. Like Sontag's furrier father, their biological father had become vapor. Which is why most people she knows, sensing his absence, never ask about him. If someone had asked, she might have replied that he was *not a good person*—code in polite company for something much worse.

The Shanghainese are known for their preoccupation with mianzi, her mother once told her. They have a weakness for superficial displays and keeping face. Their biological father was proud, easily slighted, and quick to anger. Every woman knows a man like this. Alice's family fled all the way across the ocean from Taipei to California to escape him.

They learned about his death from a Mr. Wong, an emissary from their bio-father's past and the executor of his wishes. The two men had met through mutual friends when Mr. Wong was struggling to open a dry-cleaner's in Los Angeles where both men lived. Over the years Alice's father had mentored the younger man on business matters. In his seventies, their father's eyesight had begun to fail, and soon after, said Mr. Wong, he moved back to China and married for a third time.

Now there was to be a funeral. Would Alice and Amy be going? An old-school Chinese man like him would have wanted a formal send-off into the afterlife. Paying their respects seemed like the least they could do, so they said yes. Make him heavier. Mr. Wong assured them that their father in heaven would be very happy.

What Alice knew of Chinese funerals: People in white, trailing the body through the streets, beating their chests and wailing. The spicy, medicinal smell of joss sticks, burning joss paper hell money so the dead can spend lavishly in the afterlife. Kneeling, bowing, and more bowing. Pyramids of tangerines, platters of food.

The last time Alice and Amy had seen him was decades ago, when they were teenagers in high school. It was a reunification effort of sorts. They flew out from California to a hamlet in Connecticut where he ran a small grocery in town. At the airport when he first spotted them, he was so engulfed by emotion that his hands shook.

He took them to Bloomingdale's; he took them to a matinee of *Cats* on Broadway.

One night he drove them through the shimmering boulevards of Flushing, Queens, to a friend's seafood restaurant.

They performed the rituals of divorced fathers and their children, a carousel ride of entertainment, dining, and window-shopping designed to canter over their estrangement. By the end of the trip, he had started to crack. He complained bitterly about how he'd been wronged all these years, how none of it was his fault. It was all he wanted to talk about. Afterward, there were phone calls, and then there weren't. That was the last time they saw him.

In her journal Sontag considered dedicating her "everything" book to her father. Later she changed her mind: She would dedicate it to her son. The book was never written. Instead Sontag wrote an ecstatic ode to projects—the harnessing of the intellect and soul in preparation for, not the next, but this unfettered life. Alice was not a believer in the afterlife, yet after her bio-father died, she found her thoughts turning to the netherworld. In his case, the afterlife possessed a certain logic. Why wouldn't he continue to exist, as he had when he was alive, in a world utterly foreign and unknown to her?

What Alice knew of Chinese hell: a bureaucracy of judicial control under a totalitarian regime. As in eighteen levels, ten courts, and sixteen wards, a byzantine system that metes out punishment in exquisite correspondence to the sins committed in life. (Some speculate Dante's nine concentric rings of torment may have been inspired by his seeing a Buddhist rendering of the underworld.)

There appeared to be a place in this hell for everyone in Alice's family: her mother belonged with the other *wives who are a worry to their husbands,* suspended upside down, their hearts and livers plucked out, faces scraped by iron instruments, knees crushed, fingers, toes, and feet sawed off. After being forced to drink their own blood, they are devoured by maggots and vermin. As for Alice and Amy, *children who neglect to feed, serve, and bury their parents,* they would be dispatched to the Eighth Court of Hell, where their bodies would be crushed beneath carriage wheels, suffocated in ovens, sliced to pieces, their tongues cut out, nails driven into their skulls. In the coup de grâce, their dismembered torsos, like slabs of meat, would be hung for display on steel forks.

There were punishments for wasters of food, tax evaders, sellers of inferior silk, drunkards, busybodies, destroyers of books. There were bespoke tortures for corrupt officials, cheating accountants, bail runners, the overly litigious, rich people who never give alms, rumormongers, arsonists, pornographers, cannibals, lazy and neglectful teachers who ruin the futures of their pupils, medical quacks and charlatans, matchmakers who lie about the shortcomings of their prospects. But there didn't seem to be a court to oversee men who abused and terrorized their wives.

Instead of getting sucked into Chinese hell, Alice should have been researching Chinese funeral rites: guidelines for estranged daughters. Not to worry, Mr. Wong assured them. There will be someone there to show you what to do. Alice tried to imagine interacting with Third Wife's family. Alice's Mandarin was nearly nonexistent, a hapless hodgepodge of words for fart, sanitary napkin, phlegm, and the names of Chinese dishes mostly involving pork. She would probably end up standing around with a blank look on her face while people talked over her. Some unfortunate young relative, singled out for her relative command of English, would no doubt be enlisted to be their minder.

Through Mr. Wong, they learned that the Shanghai family insisted they not stay at a hotel but at an apartment of a niece of theirs. The niece would even pick them up from the airport.

Mr. Wong forwarded the address. Amy, who hadn't been sleeping well, entered the address into a search engine. Despite the graininess of the satellite image, there could be no mistaking what she was looking at: an empty field. She tried blowing up the image, striking + + + on the keyboard. The field was not a field. It was a raw open pit, a gulping abyss. She freaked. Who were these people anyway, this new family? In fact, they learned that their father had insinuated to Mr. Wong that he didn't trust his third wife, but they knew it was also his way to be untrusting. Either way, Alice and Amy didn't know a single thing about them.

A likely explanation for the online abyss: Google Street Views can be outdated by as much as five years before new images are captured and loaded to stand in for the present. For most places, this outlay in time would be negligible, but not necessarily in China, where entire city blocks and mountain villages were being plowed under faster than the pace of history. In the end the answer to the mystery coordinates turned out to be even more prosaic: Amy realized she'd typed in the wrong address in a sleep-deprived fugue state.

Alice bought her tickets, arranged for a cat-sitter, and expedited her passport. Then, with a few days to go, Amy backed out. She said she didn't have the stomach to go through with it. Alice didn't have the nerve to go without her.

Another crime punishable in Chinese hell: holding up funerals.

Alice couldn't blame her sister: Amy would surely have had to bear the burden of being the official family representative because she was older and her Mandarin was better, which would have meant more talking and more social pressure. And she didn't have what Alice had, what Alice always had when confronted with an ordeal: the possibility that the experience would prove useful for a project. She could endure anything as long as it could be bent, in recollection, to her design, the mercenary impulse as coping mechanism.

Did Marco Polo invent his trip to China? Some claim he sailed no farther than the Black Sea and that his account had been ripped whole cloth from a Persian seaman's travelogue. These skeptics point to gaping holes in his records of chopsticks, tea-drinking, or the logographic nature of Chinese ideograms. The most glaring omission of all: no mention of the Great Wall of China. Polo did report on coal and porcelain. He took great pains to detail the look, weight, feel, and value of Chinese currency; he did the same with the minutiae of salt production. In other words, he saw China through the calculating eyes of a Venetian merchant. But if Marco Polo did invent China, he wouldn't be the first. China is always being invented. It has existed for too long and is too big for this not to be so.

Alice's project for her trip to China devolved into a project for the procurement of a tasteful condolence card for Third Wife and her family. She hit the stationery stores on Smith Street. By then the days had gotten colder; she had to remove her gloves to handle the cards. Cards with written sentiments (*Sorry for your loss; Our thoughts are with you*) had to be eliminated outright because of the English. She pondered whether a bird or a winter scene or a pumpkin signified the same thing to Mainland Chinese as it did for Americans. She also dismissed cards made of inferior paper stock. Recycled pulp was unacceptable. The paper had to be thick, substantive. Mianzi and all.

At the third shop she visited, she found a card with a screen print of a koi rippling through a pond. It looked like the cover to a collection of dull lyric poems by an Asian American poet. This would do. She wrote a short, respectful message and had a friend translate it into Mandarin. She got the family's address from Mr. Wong and then never got around to sending it. Who are these people? the family back in China must have thought.

Alice wondered if Sontag ever learned Chinese or climbed the Matterhorn like she wanted to, before she died. Probably not. All our lives we imagine the places we'll go. For most of Alice's childhood, her family was too anxious about money to travel abroad. By the time they had it, they'd nearly lost their nerve to spend it. Already she was mourning the trip down the Yangtze River with her mother that would never happen. Let Peking be Peking a bit longer. Try not to mourn the future too quickly. It's too dangerous a form of time travel.

LINDA MONTANO

The Artist said of Linda Montano that she was one of the most honest people he'd ever known. They fought during the year they'd spent tied to one another, but that was to be expected. In another interview, however, he bristled, unhappy that she'd tried to take too much credit for *Rope Piece*. She was the better-known artist at the time.

At first Alice reflexively took the Artist's side, the side of the POC, the immigrant, the art world outsider. Maybe that was unfair. And it was true she also found Montano's work—the performance where she lived locked in a room with her five different personalities; the one in which she impersonated Mother Teresa in the streets; her fourteen-year project wearing a different color each year to match the qualities of a specific chakra; the energy healing, the New Age voodoo, the appropriation of Eastern spiritual practice—kind of goofy.

On YouTube Alice watched a short documentary about the chakras piece (*14 Years Of Living Art 1984–1998*), which was restaged a few years ago in Montreal. In one sequence, Montano is stretched out on a divan (her "Sacramental Chakra Chaise") in a large open gallery, dispensing spiritual guru advice to a young woman at her side. Linda Montano presses a rose against the woman's abdomen like a wand, murmuring, "Embrace your courageous girl, inner child."

In another scene, she presides over an all-female sleepover in a gallery space where everyone is dressed in chakras-inspired monochrome clothing. She activates their vibrating chakras by laughing out loud, coughing emphatically, blessing them. Then they give each other head massages and eat snacks arranged by color.

Watching all this, Alice felt herself getting impatient. But then, O shit. She discovered *Dad Art*.

Dad Art was the name of a seven-year project that Montano began in 1998 after leaving her university teaching job in Texas and moving back to her hometown in upstate New York where her father still lived.

As Montano described, the move home was a reckoning. Teaching performance art at an institute of higher learning had made her feel accomplished. Even though she'd been turned down for tenure twice, which was wounding, she kept teaching with the belief that she was living the life she ought to be living because teaching was a gig, and she was, if nothing else, a gigger. She certainly was not a stayer and she was not a caregiver. All her life she hadn't stayed anywhere long enough to create a family or care for one. She didn't consider herself a part of a community, she said, or even as a real professor with a permanent office, and this suited her.

Back in her hometown she began taking her elderly father to doctor's appointments. She started going to church and sharing meals with him, all while documenting their lives with a video camera. Father and daughter became friends for the first time in their lives. They also became a project.

Midway through the *Dad Art* project, her father had a stroke, after which he required around-the-clock care. Montano fed him, bathed him, transferred him from wheelchair to toilet to bed. It pained her to see him fallen. Still, she kept filming. She looked through the lens of her camera because she had to get behind something. Otherwise, she couldn't bear to look at what was happening. She filmed her father on his deathbed and through his funeral.

All this film became the backdrop for a two-hour *Interactive Performance about Life and Death and Love* in which Montano sings a number of her father's favorite songs and invites people from the audience onstage for a glass of water or to talk to a grief counselor—to deal with death "performatively" and to be present with impermanence. Life is short, she explained. "Art makes it spacious and long for a minute."

Alice clicked to a more recent video of Montano taking part in a panel on aging sponsored by the Museum of Modern Art. Montano shakes a little in her chair from Parkinson's. When it's her turn to speak, she talks about her latest project, inspired, she says, by the caregivers who took care of her father in his final years. She needed them—society needs them!—yet how little they are paid. She vows to do her part: when the time comes when she'll require the help of an overworked, underpaid home health aide, she'll do her best to be as least burdensome as possible.

And so, she says, she's been rehearsing for her future role as a lady who lives in a nursing home. She's learning to position her body so she can be lifted by others with the least amount of strain. She shares a short video clip of this work in progress: she's flopped in an armchair rotating her arms and legs, occasionally blurting out certain words loudly before slipping back into regular speech. These verbal outbursts, she explains, are also part of her self-training. She's shouting to release rage so her anger won't boil over and end up being directed at her future caregiver.

Like all her projects, Alice thought, there was something too much and not enough about the work. And yet they had ended up in the same place: making projects about their sick fathers. She imagined Linda Montano could give a shit about her critique or anyone else's. She was beyond fashion, beyond cool. She was doing her thing and swaggering in her projects freely.

"I am most authentic when I am performing," Montano once said. "I am really one hundred percent there. I can't say that about any other aspect of my life."

~~ONE YEAR PERFORMANCE 1985–1986~~

ORGANIZED by **TEHCHING HSIEH**

PERFORMED by OTHER PEOPLE

STATEMENT

I, **TEHCHING HSIEH,** plan to do a one year
performance.

I will find people to hold/carry a Torch for one
year.

The Fire will never go out.

Each person will set their own Time for how long
they will hold and then carry the Torch to the next
person's space.

I will not hold/carry the Torch, but I will Witness
the piece for the whole year.

The piece will happen in New York City.

The performance will begin on ? ? 1985 and continue
until ? ? 1986.

THE PROJECT THAT WASN'T

*T*orch Piece, as it surely would have been called, was not to be.
The torch, which weighed three and a half pounds, was never lit
by a butane gas cartridge. The two thousand volunteers the Artist had intended to recruit to perform the piece did not materi-
alize; nothing was documented with Polaroids as the Artist had
originally hoped.

The year before *Torch Piece* would have been performed,
Los Angeles hosted the Olympic Games. That year, thousands
of people carried the torch from New York to L.A. (A buoyant O. J. Simpson jogged the torch up the final stretch along
the Pacific Coast Highway.) It was the year of the boycott
from the Eastern Bloc countries, and the year the closing
ceremony featured a flying saucer that descended into the
open mouth of Memorial Coliseum, from which emerged an
eight-foot-tall alien. The alien lumbered forward, raised its
arm—did this really happen?—and saluted humanity in perfect English.

Questions:

1. Did the Artist get swept up in Olympic fever? Was he beguiled by the ephemeral properties of a lit torch?
2. Did he feel pressure to raise the stakes on his next performance by delivering more spectacle with a literal cast of thousands?
3. Was *Torch Piece* intended to rectify the ineluctable loneliness of the project?

When Alice described the *Torch Piece* to Nobu, he said he was kind of glad it never came to be. He preferred to think of the Artist as Sisyphus, a man alone.

At a picnic in Prospect Park sprawling with faded bedsheets, spilled olive juice, and greasy samosas, Alice met an experimental filmmaker who said he'd known the Artist back in the day. The filmmaker had been part of a loose affiliation of downtown artists who frequented the same watering holes and faithfully showed up to each other's gallery shows, performances, and readings; some shared the same drug dealers.

This was what Alice wanted to know: Was the Artist really as isolated as he said he was?

The filmmaker recalled that the Artist didn't talk much. "He often had a sad look on his face. But I wouldn't say he didn't have friends." He remembered seeing the Artist hanging out at Puffy's Tavern, a dive bar in Tribeca popular with artists. He couldn't recall if the Artist also hung out at Club 57, the no-budget, campy performance space that operated out of the basement of a Polish church in St. Marks Place. The space hosted a Monster Movie Night on Tuesdays and featured a rotation of onstage acts: Keith Haring performing inside a busted television set; Klaus Nomi singing falsetto in his iconic, sharp-shouldered plastic suit. (Alice found it impossible to imagine the Artist in the thick of this scene.)

When the Artist was performing *Outdoor Piece*, the filmmaker said he invited the Artist to sleep on the roof of his building if he ever found the streets to be too rough or dangerous. The Artist never took him up on it. When winter hit, he even brought the Artist a pair of boots, which were politely turned down. The filmmaker wasn't the only one looking out for the Artist in this way. "The winter he was out there was real bad, record-setting bad," the filmmaker said. "I don't know how he survived it."

So the Artist was alone and not alone. In an interview, Alice had read the Artist describe himself as a caveman who was missing an adaptor that would allow him to connect with the rest of civilization. Yet Alice suspected if the Artist ever found such an adaptor, he would bury it under a pile of rocks. He may not have amassed the two thousand volunteers that he envisioned for *Torch Piece*, but more than a hundred people did sign up for the project. Managing them, however, was a whole other thing. In the end, the Artist sent each would-be participant a letter informing them that the project wouldn't be moving forward after all. *I have found, after experimentation, that this is too much for me to do alone as I had planned.*

One of Warhol's unrealized projects was a paean to aloneness: he envisioned a chain of neighborhood restaurants designed specifically for single diners. Customers at these restaurants, which he called "Andy-mats," would take their individual tray of food to a booth outfitted for one, where they could watch television while they ate.

The writer and artist Édouard Levé wrote an entire book devoted to unrealized projects called *Oeuvres.* In the book, he describes five hundred and thirty-three such projects, some ridiculous—"Fifty people go on a protest march in silence bearing placards and banners with nothing written on them"; and some sublime—"A building's architecture mimes its explosion."

Alice had an idea about what to do with her own accumulation of unrealized projects. The idea was, admittedly, utterly derivative of Levé: she would inject the conceptual descriptions of all these projects into the overall Project. It would be a meta-statement about projects as compost heap and regenerative organism. The thought that her failed projects would finally have a home was surprisingly gratifying; it was as though she'd found a perfectly affordable storage space after decades of lugging them around in black plastic trash bags. But when she shared her list of unrealized projects with Nobu, he tapped his fingertips together and suggested, gently, that she look at them again, very hard. "Maybe it is better to leave out?"

A PARTIAL LIST OF VOLUNTEERS

Among the volunteers who signed up for *Torch Piece* were Dick Bellamy, art dealer and owner of the Green Gallery, one of the first galleries to show Yayoi Kusama's polka-dotted frenzies and Claes Oldenburg's lumpy, oversized sculptures of ice-cream cones and french fries (Bellamy died in his sleep, age seventy, in 1998); Robert Attanasio, who made a short film of himself spinning in circles outside the Guggenheim to mimic the building's spiral structure (died after a brief illness in 2015, age sixty-three); the mail artist Buster Cleveland, who sold Dadaist collages the size of postage stamps from the back of a rented limo on the corner of Spring Street and West Broadway (died of cardiac arrest, age fifty-five, in 1998); a couple of sound artists, acolytes of John Cage; Barbara Held, an experimental flutist who now lives and teaches in Barcelona; Rip Hayman, who still manages the Ear Inn on the West Side; Jeanette Ingberman (died of cancer at fifty-nine in 2011), daughter of Polish Holocaust survivors and cofounder with her partner the artist Papo Colo of the pioneering nonprofit arts space Exit Art—an early champion of the Artist as well as of Wojnarowicz, Adrian Piper, and Martin Wong;

"Cowboy" Ray Kelly of the Rivington School, an arts movement of welders, street painters, and performance artists that turned abandoned lots in the Lower East Side into towering metal sculpture gardens (represented by Saatchi, he now makes perfunctory cowboy hats from steel and rebar); the feminist artist Vernita Nemec, a.k.a. N'Cognita, who's still curating group shows featuring art made from detritus and trash; Pauline Oliveros, the experimental composer and "deep listening" electronic music pioneer (died in 2016 at age eighty-four); Kyong Park, who was, at the time, directing the Storefront for Art and Architecture and now teaches urban ecology at UC San Diego; Carlo Pittore, mail artist and painter of boxers and nudes (died of cancer, 2005); Pola Rapaport, who would go on to make documentaries about Nadia Comăneci and *Hair*, the musical; artist and activist Nina Kuo of Basement Workshop on St. Marks and Godzilla, the Asian American arts collective; Ai Weiwei, who'd dropped out of art school and haunted the East Village taking pictures of the neighborhood and of his fellow expats, the "torched flowers of China." There were others on the list whose online trails and connection to the art scene are less clear—a woman who now works as a clinical social worker and therapist; another who may have studied dance and performance but now lives in Santa Cruz with her husband—women difficult to trace because they took their husbands' names and all the other ways women with or without projects become unsearchable.

THE LIFE AND DEATH OF PROJECTS

Once—this was when the Father was still recovering at the skilled nursing facility in Oakland—Alice walked in on him as he lay in bed, staring at the ceiling in a ruminative mood. He told her that he had been up late the night before. Unable to sleep, he'd gotten out of bed to investigate the world outside his room.

At night the facility was a very different place, quiet as a mountain town sunk in snow. The corridors were empty of the usual wanderers; there were no nurses rushing to and fro. All the rooms were dark. He heard a voice in the distance and followed it. As he got closer to the source and the voice grew louder and louder, he realized the voice was not speaking but crying softly. The Father entered a room and found a man crouched in the corner with his head bowed and resting against his knees. The Father shook his head slowly at the memory of it.

Alice listened. She thought this story was a good sign. The Father, whose concerns had become nearly entirely solipsistic, was registering the pain of another human being, taking in some of the world outside himself, yet part of her couldn't help but wonder if the encounter was made up, given his recent history of hallucinations.

This morning after his nighttime wandering, the Father said, he asked a nurse whether he was allowed to take photographs of the facility and the people who lived there. Real or imagined, the incident had resurrected his interest in projects. Years had passed since he'd handled a camera. His brain could no longer trigger the motor skills needed to work one, especially the manual models he favored. Still, he knew a subject when he saw one. He didn't need a camera for that, just the meat of his eyes. The nurse told him in no uncertain terms would that be possible—privacy laws and all.

The other complication was that Alice had, at the Father's own request, sold all his camera equipment, nearly all of which was from the analog era and not worth very much. She didn't remind him of this; she didn't need to. After he told her this story about the crying man, he never brought up taking pictures again.

When she first grasped the full extent of the Father's camera collection and gear—including more than a dozen cameras and hundreds of lenses, lens hoods, tripods, light meters, timers, filters, and other items he'd acquired mostly through eBay auctions and local flea markets, some of them not even removed from their boxes—Alice was aggrieved by how much time and money he'd wasted on things he'd barely even used. Such were the dreams of the project, the arid talk about opening a bar or gallery-café space; the late-night tinkering on a doomed automobile; the movie treatments, the list of possible band names—all those larval, mewling things like newborn kittens, their eyes still gummed shut and their ears not even properly sprouted, vulnerable to being drowned in a sack or left in a shoebox beneath a freeway underpass—and how, despite and because of all this, nothing quite gleams like a future project, forever the unspoiled crush-object seen from across the room.

THE RETURN

James was back. He'd been back. Troy was okay, until it wasn't. He had a younger cousin who got him a part-time gig at the medical billing office where she worked. But he never did quite sync with the rhythm of the place, he told Alice. On the surface the city was calm as Sunday morning, yet he couldn't shake the feeling that he was being watched even when he knew no one was looking.

New York City was different. He had a third eye for the place. Since his return, he'd been sleeping in bank kiosks and sometimes on the second floor of a twenty-four-hour McDonald's in Midtown. He'd figured out the best branch libraries across town to get clean and change his clothes. He'd learned the soup kitchen circuit, which ones were most vegan-friendly and which ones insisted on prayer before you were permitted to lift a fork.

James said he'd never felt freer in his life. He didn't want to oversell it: being broke was hard; not having a place to live was hard. Yes, he knew he could've strung together at least a few months of couch-surfing and other friendly handouts. But he'd discovered something liberating and unexpectedly light from living outside civilization's regulating systems. He was learning to master a more elemental way of living that came with its own registers of triumph, absurdity, and defeat, and he could feel himself becoming addicted to it. He said he had the Artist to thank for giving him the idea of living on his own terms in the urban wild.

Alice was worried about him, but she tried not to show it too much. That was how they maintained: by keeping it cool. James looked the same except that his hair and beard had grown out, which, with his sleepy eyes, gave him the indolent, insouciant air of a retired scoundrel. They were sitting at a table on the second floor of the Whole Foods on the Bowery. At that late morning hour, the sun was nearly blinding through the floor-to-ceiling windows. In a few hours the place would be overrun with people and their quinoa bowls on lunch break. When Alice lived nearby, she used to come there sometimes on the weekends to work on projects. She noticed that a seating area made up of a couch and comfortable armchairs had been removed since she'd been there last, no doubt to discourage homeless people from lingering.

James said he knew he couldn't live this life forever. It was hard on the body and he wasn't a kid in his twenties anymore. It wasn't doing his love life any favors, either. The vagabond mystique wore off right quick.

He shrugged. "Who knows, maybe I wouldn't be getting any action even if I did have a roof over my head."

"I mean, look at me," Alice said. "I have a whole apartment to myself and no love!"

James shot her a look. He seemed to be working a thought into words before reconsidering. Instead, he made a chortling sound from the back of his throat. "Probably I should be in therapy. But I'm worried I'd like it too much."

"Except for the part where each session costs hundreds of dollars."

"Exactly. I'll just hold out for the AI therapist," James said. "By then they'll have come up with some kind of combination Taco-Bell-Pizza-Hut-type service—a robo-therapist who'll tool us around in a driverless car while we get our chores done and cry."

James said he'd been keeping notes on his new life. Maybe, sometime, not now, he'd have enough for some kind of survival manual for newly down-and-out New Yorkers. Not sure what form it'd take. He could show people the best places to dumpster-dive; what time Starbucks purges its daily stash of unsold Cheese and Fruit Bistro Boxes; how to keep your belongings to a minimum; where to score free hygiene products and the like. Whatever form it took, the project had to feel free, be free. That's what all the best projects are, he said. Then he leaned back in his chair and rubbed his eyes. For the first time, Alice saw how tired he was.

CAMEO

By the time Alice reached Chinatown, it was late in the afternoon and the crowd of shoppers on Mott Street had begun thinning out. Buskers at the sidewalk vegetable stands seemed to shout louder and with greater urgency, eager to sell their picked-over offerings before calling it a day. Gutters bled with runoff from the fish markets. Alice ducked under the red awning of her favorite grocery, which was laid out like a bowling alley, with entrances on opposite sides of two parallel streets. At peak hours, you risked getting trapped in the middle, wedged between the butcher counter and the hot buffet that was never without a line of people jostling to get a better look at the food.

That was when Alice spotted the Artist. He was sitting on a stack of milk crates next to a display freezer of frozen dumplings and fish balls reading a Chinese newspaper. The sight of him stopped her cold. Outside of that one time she'd seen him at his restaurant café, she'd never seen the Artist anywhere else out in the world living the life of an ordinary man. Now here he was, materialized like a cameo in the stream of her day. Or was

Alice the one with the walk-on part in his life? Who was on and who was off?

The question triggered her memory of a case that had been written about in a psychiatry journal of a man who suffered from the delusion that he was always on—the unwitting star of the TV show that was his life. Like the titular character Jim Carrey plays in *The Truman Show*, the man suspected everyone around him was an actor and that the places he went to were elaborately built sets. To put his conviction to the test, he traveled across the country to New York City. His mission was to confirm with his own eyes whether the Twin Towers were leveled or still standing. If the towers remained intact, he would take that as incontrovertible proof that the cataclysm of 9/11 was nothing more than a plot twist to entertain the millions of viewers watching the show that was being filmed by cameras implanted in his eyes.

Alice was jolted out of her thoughts by a woman hefting a hand basket, who threw her an indignant look as she executed a pinball maneuver to get past her in the narrow aisle where they stood. The Artist continued flipping the pages of his newspaper. He was dressed in cargo shorts, sneakers, and a plain T-shirt. Like Alice, he was just going about his daily business, his mundane chores (*Performance Artists: They're Just Like Us!*), probably waiting on an order for his restaurant. He didn't expect to be seen. When his reading glasses slipped to the tip of his nose, her heart fluttered a little.

Before Linda Montano met the Artist in person, she said she saw a picture of him and thought, Oh, that fabulous, boy-man face: so passionately innocent and expressive.

Boy-man!

In all the photographs Alice had seen of the Artist, he's rarely smiling, and yet he doesn't appear unhappy. Well, maybe in a few pictures. Mostly he looks serious. The look on his face reminded her of another famously serious face: Buster Keaton's. Like the Artist, Keaton never smiled in his films. Early in his career, he was asked why. He said he hadn't realized he wasn't smiling; he was simply focused on the work.

"One of the most beautiful men I ever saw on the screen," was how Orson Welles described Keaton. He meant Keaton's face, but there was beauty, too, in the unalloyed fluidity of his movement, filmed in uninterrupted takes so there could be no mistaking that it's Buster crashing through three awnings on his fall down the side of a building, and Buster clinging to a roadblock gate as it drops two stories and deposits him into the backseat of a speeding car. Using a stunt double would have broken the covenant with his audience. His fiction was all fact. The Artist, too, joined his work with the solder of truth. He had the proofs—the signed affidavits, the attorneys and witnesses attesting to his fidelity to the rules of each project—to show for it. Look, no invisible wires, no trap doors.

Asked about his influences, the Artist often cites Camus's *The Myth of Sisyphus*, a book he first read when he was eighteen. What intrigued him most about Sisyphus's interminable labors, he said, was the possibility of happiness.

Sisyphus makes a cameo appearance in Ovid's story of Orpheus and Eurydice. Orpheus plucks his lyre in Hades, hoping his music will charm Death into releasing his wife from the Underworld. As Ovid tells it, Orpheus's song is so sweet, even Sisyphus sets his rock aside for a minute to have a listen.

Many years past his prime, Keaton landed a cameo role

in *Sunset Boulevard*. He's one of three silent-era has-beens that Norma Desmond invites over for a game of bridge. Her mansion, lightless as a tomb, overflows with bric-a-brac mementos and ashtrays the size of dinner plates choked with spent cigarettes. Keaton isn't given much to do except to say, "Pass," with a doleful expression. He's there to confirm Norma's irrelevance by the feeble light of his own eclipsed star.

At the Chinese grocery, Alice inched her way past the Artist, looking at him from the corner of her eye as he chatted with a store employee. She bought a few things and made her way to the exit on the opposite side of the store. Exit, cameo.

Dementia, she supposed, generated its own weird variation on the cameo. As you're losing your mind, the Old You might make a brief cameo appearance, surprising those around you who have become accustomed to the New You, the demented you. The Old You might sit up in your chair and declare something bracingly lucid; for example, that you're perfectly aware that your own mother, whom you've been pleading to see for weeks, is dead, and has been dead for decades. Of course you know that! Then, just as quickly, the Old You recedes until its next unpredictable appearance.

Dreams are the natural habitat of the cameo, which derives its power from the dissonance of its arrival. The other night in Alice's dreams, the Father made a brief appearance. Nothing much happened. It wasn't the sick father but a younger father, the one she'd known for most of her life. This father rose from a chair, strode across the room in his steel-toed Red Wing boots with the ordinary, thoughtless grace of a healthy man, the lie of which, when she awoke, made her weep.

THE PROJECT THAT WAS THE FATHER

At the Father's bedroom at the residential care home, Alice raised the blinds and peered out through the window that overlooked a ring of rosebushes in the backyard.

This was a solo visit. Alice and Amy hardly ever went to see the Father together; each visit counted and could be maximized in frequency if they went separately. Like the nurses they'd overheard at the hospital trading shifts, they'd become skilled at passing pertinent information between them—what to check in on, which supplies to bring, what the Father needed or was frustrated about. This was Alice's time to offer Amy a bit of a furlough, although she was acutely aware of the imbalance.

What did the Father make of his new life? Did he miss Berkeley? He didn't, to Alice's surprise. He seemed genuinely contented, and it was true, he spent most of his time as he always had—in front of the television. Smoking was allowed on the front porch, and he was eating better. He was also less isolated; there were people in the house always, and Amy's instinct that he would do better with Kenny than a female caregiver seemed to be bearing out. On this visit, Alice chatted with him and they took a short, slow walk around the block, the Father using his cane. When they got back, she scratched up and down his back with both hands while he groaned with pleasure. Then she left. She knew if she stayed past a certain point, his attention would drift to the TV and he'd fall silent. Too much human interaction overtaxed his brain. The world inside the television was the antidote.

An early fall chill had clung to her last days in the Bay Area; the sun was a bleary glow through the clouds. Now that the Father was stabilized, this would be Alice's last trip out here for the year. To mark the occasion, she'd splurged on a flight that would arrive at JFK so she could sleep in her own bed that same night, a courtesy, or concession, to middle age.

Amy drove her to the airport while Ezra, asleep, drooled on his shirt in the backseat. They managed to talk about things unrelated to the Father—the upcoming elections, other people's divorces, Ezra's obsession with Minions. (Alice still couldn't comprehend what those gibbering yellow pill capsules were, exactly.) They egged each other to do online dating and enumerated all the reasons they would not be doing so.

On the plane, she buckled in and pressed her head back while the other passengers searched for their seats and trawled for overhead storage space. She reflected idly on the total number of hours she'd gained and lost crossing time zones that year and how many tons of carbon dioxide she was responsible for releasing into the air, her modest contribution to the end of the world. The cabin felt like a space vessel being readied for a deep sleep. A young man in low-riding jeans and an enormous muff of Bose headphones slotted his duffel bag in the overhead compartment above her and slid into the aisle seat. He immediately turned his attention to his phone.

She closed her eyes. How close was she to her father? a friend once asked. Close, she thought. Then she remembered the months that went by without their speaking or writing each other; the years when she was aware of his drinking but did nothing to intervene except to nudge him toward AA and cheer him on when he'd announce he was on the wagon. In return, he never worried at her, lectured, or advised, like a father. He was, in his own way, a performance artist: he performed sobriety in the company of others. She wondered if all their lives they'd been too polite with each other, stepfather and stepdaughter, always careful to give the space they believed the other was owed. Was theirs a pact of mutual convenience? With her mother there could be no such distance. Alice could be driven to teeth-grinding derangement by her mother and their complicated love. The Father was not cunning like them. In the deployment and dudgeons of passive aggression, he was utterly lacking. He was more transparent, like a child, and he could be as self-centered as a child, unfatherly, more so as his dementia worsened. It was her mother who fretted, raged, and accounted for Alice's survival. In a way this made loving the Father easier.

Which wasn't to say there weren't times over the past year that dealing with the Father made Alice want nothing more than to escape home to Brooklyn—and yet when she returned to Brooklyn, she'd feel the life she had hungered to reclaim fall slack. She surprised herself at how much she missed the all-consuming project that was the Father, which made all other projects feel inconsequential by comparison. (Simone de Beauvoir at her mother's sickbed, deathbed: "The world had shrunk to the size of her room: when I crossed Paris in a taxi I saw nothing more than a stage with extras walking about it. My real life took place at her side.") But eventually time would intervene, and she'd become preoccupied and absorbed by her own life, until it was time to go back to California again.

She could hear a faint bleating from the headphones of the man sitting next to her. When she glanced over at his phone, she saw he was playing some kind of mobile game. His avatar was a yellow cat with a big round head attached to a tiny body. The cat darted and scrambled at great speed across green vales, rings of fire, stone fortresses, and icebergs—toward what end, she couldn't tell. Player and avatar were wrapped up in their own private world of adventure. She turned her attention to the in-flight screen in front of her and began scrolling through the entertainment channels for an equal oblivion.

By the time the plane landed at JFK, it was near midnight. Alice, frowzy, pulled at the collar of her light jacket as she waited in line in the cold for a taxi. Before the cab had even entered the river of traffic—backed up from late-night construction on the Kosciuszko Bridge—the taxi driver was already irritable.

"So many idiots out tonight," he muttered. She couldn't see much of him except for the gray hair curling from under the band of his newsboy hat. The trunk of him was one with his seat, the car's perfume a blend of stale cigarettes and pine-scented air freshener from the little tree dangling from the rearview mirror.

Against her request he'd insisted on taking the BQE and now they were idling in a long, staggering row of vehicles. Mildly carsick, she zipped her window down and peered out across the grounds of the massive cemetery below her. On the graves, visitors had left battery-operated LED candles, so the cemetery looked like a mostly empty stadium lit by the scattered light of mobile phones cued to the saddest ballad in the world.

Might the taxi driver be feeling the slightest bit guilty for stranding them in traffic? Alice used the possibility to get him to talk. Always it was necessary to feed the Project.

Where was he from?

"Uzbekistan. Do you know?"

"Yes, but I don't know much. Wasn't it once an important stop on the Silk Road?"

"Very beautiful country. Good people mostly."

"And how long have you been here?"

"Twenty years I've been driving taxi." The cabbie let that hang in the air. She thought that was it, that he was done chit-chatting, but hearing his own words must have stirred something in him, because he went on, his voice gaining heat.

"The people back home, they are thinking I am big success, making good money. I buy things only they could dream of!"

Then he rolled his shoulders and snorted. "But hey, this is what I tell them: here in America you can get anything you want in life but life itself."

WHY A YEAR?

A: *It doesn't really matter how I spend time: time is still passing. Wasting time is my basic attitude to life; it is a gesture of dealing with the absurdity between life and time.*

Q: But why a year?

A: *I want to talk about life, the intersection between life and universe. One year relates closely to this intersection.*

Q: Why a year?

A: *For me, I think it's a beautiful rhythm to art and life. It's a repetition. But it's also different—every second, every hour is different. There's no going back. But paradoxically, we are doing the same thing over and over again.*

2017

I pace when I give interviews. . . . They always start the same way: Do you think of yourself as an artist or a black artist? Lately I've been answering: I think of myself as a virus.

—WILLIAM POPE.L

ONE YEAR PERFORMANCE 1985-1986

July 1, 1985

STATEMENT

I, **TEHCHING HSIEH**, plan to do a one year
performance.

I ▓▓ not do **ART**, not talk **ART**, not see **ART**,
not read **ART**, not go to **ART** gallery and **ART** museum
for one year.

I ▓▓ just go in life.

The performance ▓▓ begin on July 1, 1985 and
continue until July 1, 1986.

Tehching Hsieh

QUALITY OF LIFE

For three days the cat had refused to eat. He'd taken to hiding in the closet with his head bowed and his paws tucked in. Even human-grade tuna fish failed to entice.

After consulting her vet, Alice had packed the cat in his carrier and taken a taxi to the twenty-four-hour pet ER. The winter sun had sunk hours earlier and Fourth Avenue had felt desolate despite the steady flow and honk of traffic. At the animal hospital, the ceiling lights bore down in a way that seemed reserved for the sick. She had waited in the front office area with an anxious young couple and their shivering pug, its face blanched with age, and stared at the mounted television set without watching.

The cat had been kept overnight for tests and fluids. Now Alice was back at the hospital. The consulting vet, a woman with a high forehead, a no-nonsense ponytail, and the imperturbable demeanor of someone accustomed to delivering wretched news, gave her the breakdown: the preliminary tests showed that the cat's liver and spleen were enlarged and his pancreas inflamed. The cause was likely one of two possibilities—he either had cancer or some kind of inflammatory bowel disorder. If the cat had cancer, then he would probably live four, maybe up to six more months. If his bowels were inflamed, he could live much longer. Only more tests would reveal the truth, and no matter which ailment it was, the treatment would be the same: a daily dose of steroids.

Alice okayed the steroids. Her armpits felt damp. Already she was dreading the bill waiting for her at the reception desk. She'd have to do monthly installments. The vet left them alone in the exam room so Alice could try coaxing the cat to eat. The cat wasn't having it. He weaved between her legs, sniffing abstractedly at the little paper plates she'd arranged on the floor dolloped with different flavored cat foods. Her phone dinged. It was a text from James: *Headed over to JFK protest . . . U going?*

No I can't, she texted back.

The exam room was windowless, antiseptic. The walls were decorated with thank-you cards to the staff from pet owners— mostly, it seemed, from people mourning their dead animals. Her cat's life, his little fate that already felt very small, felt even smaller. She was the only person in the world who cared what happened to him, she thought with maudlin indulgence. No human catastrophe mattered as much to her in that moment as that damn cat.

Not that she'd stopped scrolling on her phone for updates. Over the next hour she tracked social media reports on the hundreds of people who had gathered at the airport to protest the President's Muslim travel ban. She read the updates from friends who were there, watched short videos of the crowds waiting to ascend from the subway station to join the protest. The crowd grew to thousands. The chants started up:

"No hate. No fear. Immigrants are welcome here!"

"No ban. No registry. Fuck. White. Supremacy!"

And what if it ended up being cancer? Alice wanted to prepare for the worst. How would she know, she asked the vet, when it was time to put her cat to sleep?

The vet nodded. "Keep track of the four to five activities that are his favorites—eating, playing with a favorite toy, scratching a particular spot," she said. "If he stops half of those, then his quality of life is affected. Look for focused breathing. If it looks like he's having to make an effort just to breathe, then you'll know he's struggling."

In the airless room Alice and the cat stared at each other surrounded by the gloomy buffet.

LIVES OF MONSTER STARS

The subway cars opened and Alice stepped in, squeezing herself between a man in a security uniform going to or from work and an older woman reading her Bible. Once settled, Alice clicked on the link Nobu had sent her. *Only if you have time*, he winked.

The link took her to a news story about the discovery of a lost generation of monster stars. In their prime, these stars were once hundreds of thousands of times as massive as the sun, according to the article. They burned brightly, then died in a flash. This happened some hundreds of million years after the universe began.

What astronomers had detected with their state-of-the-art telescopes was trace evidence that the stars once existed: their explosive deaths vomited elements into space that then birthed other stars, other planets. Scientists measure the age of stars through a phenomenon known as red-shifting: the farther back in time these celestial implosions occurred, the longer the wavelength of light is stretched, shifting toward the red part of the spectrum, like how the wail of a siren sounds lower as the ambulance recedes. The light from these exploded stars has been traveling toward earth for more than twelve billion years.

Alice looked up from her phone at the mother and son seated across from her. The boy, wearing a striped shirt she'd probably picked out for him, was still young enough to lean against her side without embarrassment. Next to them, two young construction workers in dusty boots and richly pomaded hair; a woman wearing a joke T-shirt, the punch line obscured by her jacket but having something to do with nails drying. Nearly everyone was looking down at a phone or gadget or had earbuds squinched in their ears, the commuter's detachment from time and space.

The Artist once described his durational works as a form of art that he could *live, think freely and pass time within.* Alice, too, had wanted a project she could be within. The more she immersed herself in the Artist's work, the more she found herself inhabiting his zone, metabolizing its logic and rhythms; this zone where everything she encountered, everything she experienced and witnessed, was about time.

TRAVEL BAN

The skin-cracking cold of February. The hot radiator breath of February. The unincorporated area of February, miles inland from March's coast.

It was past seven by the time Alice stepped off the bus and rushed to the courthouse steps in downtown Brooklyn. Four days had passed since protesters descended on JFK Airport. She felt her shoulders release after spending hours hunched in front of two monitors editing the latest installment of *Bring On the Feels*. She didn't have much original video to work with for the episode, a feature on pets saving their owners' lives, and had had to stretch things out by repurposing the same content with silly effects. All the feline-related stories seemed to involve cats sitting on people's chests while they slept and swatting at their noses as carbon monoxide or smoke filled their homes. The former classmate who'd first recruited her for the gig had left the marketing firm some months ago for a start-up. He hadn't bothered to drop Alice a note; she'd come across the announcement on a professional networking site. He was now a VP at some kind of mail-order club for non-hypoallergenic coniferous-scented grooming products for men.

Hours earlier, across the city's boroughs, Yemeni business owners began shutting down their bodegas, restaurants, and coffee shops. One bodega owner in the Bronx had had to run out and buy a lock for his door: his store had never been open for less than twenty-hours.

The protest now gathered in front of Brooklyn's Borough Hall had begun hours earlier, but the square and the marble stairs that led into the government building were still electric with a crowd of at least a hundred people. Every inch of the stairs was filled with protesters. The mood was euphoric. Men smiled broadly at each other and thrust their chests out for selfies. A skinny guy in his twenties clambered onto the shoulders of his bearish friend, shouting and waving the red, white, and black colors of the Yemeni flag. Alice peered at the faces around her, curious if she could pick out the undercover cops.

The event's last official speaker, a community organizer, took the mic. Alice could barely glimpse the top of her hijab through the crush of bodies. There was a screech of audio feedback from the sound system. The organizer began by denouncing the President's actions. She praised the protesters for exercising their right to free speech and for all the contributions they'd made to their adopted country: they were the ones who had made America great!

The crowd roared its approval. Buoyed, the organizer tried to get a chant going: "No racism, no bigo-try. No Muslim registry!" After a few half-hearted rounds, the chant collapsed. Some minutes passed before another chant—this one spontaneous, irrepressible—erupted from the crowd:

"U-S-A! U-S-A! U-S-A!"

Alice could feel the cold creeping through her shoes and through the collar and sleeves of her coat. By then a stream of protesters had begun splitting off from the crowd. Forearms gripped in farewell; more beaming smartphone photos. She watched a few men cut away with their phones pressed to their ears. She imagined most of them were probably on their way back to their shops. The strike had been called for eight hours, not the entire day. There was still income to be made and bills that needed paying.

TRANSLATION

The Father's mind was going. How fast would it go? was the question. Which was how Alice found herself at the Father's care home with a list of questions she'd always meant to ask.

The Father sat in his recliner with his legs sticking out, pale and thin, from his shorts. It was unseasonably warm for early spring. A rotating standing fan spun its head, recycling the air around them. Alice sat on the edge of his twin bed. The room was undecorated except for a print of a painting of sailboats in a harbor that had been mounted above the Father's bed when he moved in, and a kitten calendar that a visiting nurse had hung by the light switch to track his vitals on.

Alice could hear the faint roar of a baseball stadium crowd from the big-screen TV in the living room down the hall. On her way in, she'd waved as she passed by two other residents who were watching the game, old men who never spoke but followed her with their eyes. She guessed they'd probably suffered strokes. When the Father first arrived, there was talk about outings he could take to the local senior center or the barbershop—even shopping, if he was up for it. But it turned out he wasn't much interested in any of these things and no one pushed him. Kenny became his barber, cutting his hair and shaving him.

The Father and Alice had dispatched with their routine chitchat—what he'd had for lunch; what he was watching on TV; how they felt, respectively, about the heat; and could she buy him a new CD player because his didn't seem to work. She used the pause in conversation to launch the first of her questions. She wanted to know more about his time in the Army, in Vietnam. What he did do, exactly, in Phu Bai? She knew he worked as a translator. What was he translating?

The Father cleared his throat. His face took on a distant expression. This time he didn't have to struggle to find the words he wanted. He explained that military linguists were assigned to separate divisions, each responsible for tapping and intercepting different military channels via radio transmissions. His assignment was civilian communiqués. Most of the conversations he listened in on were between Viet Cong soldiers and the families they left behind.

What did they say? Alice pressed.

He paused, then gave her a wry look. Once, he said, he transcribed an angry conversation between a Viet Cong commander and an African madam. The madam was taking the commander to the mat because his soldiers had "beaten the shit" out of her girls, and she wanted more money to compensate for her trouble.

Alice had no words for this. She looked out the window at the roses exploding on their canes.

PROJECT FOR A TRIP TO THE ROCKAWAYS

As Alice stepped off the bus near an abandoned military fort, she wondered if she'd made a mistake coming so late in the afternoon. On the far edge of the Rockaways there were no tall buildings or trees to block the strong winds blowing in from the Atlantic. The sky was so immense it seemed to swallow sound.

But here she was. Somewhere nearby they were once here, too, the Chinese migrants of the *Golden Venture*. Twenty-four years ago, a few hours after midnight, the rusty freighter ran aground off the long finger of the Rockaway Peninsula and more than two hundred and eighty people who'd been smuggled in the ship's cargo hold leapt into the churning, freezing surf below. Or maybe they were not so near here? There was never any official record or marker of the exact location. All Alice had to go on were a few vague references she'd read in news articles and a tip she'd gotten that the freighter had ended its journey somewhere close to the Silver Gull Beach Club, a private cabana complex built on a strip of public beach.

The area was deserted in the off-season. To her dismay, she discovered the entrance gate to Fort Tilden, which would've given her quicker access to the beach, was closed. She'd have to take a detour alongside two lanes of traffic on the long boulevard farther inland that ran parallel to the shore. She pulled the strings of her hoodie tight and started walking.

Alice was here, of course, for the purposes of the Project. How this expedition would fit in its overall architecture she wasn't sure, except that it had something to do with the documentation of undocumented artists and with being Chinese in New York City. Whenever she felt uncertain about the Project, she often thought enviously of the Artist's project statements with their arrow-like set of rules and constraints: whatever happened within the year of the performance piece did not have to be explained or refined; everything simply became absorbed into the work. There was another reason she was out here, and that was to get out of her own head. She'd been in there too much, so she'd been told. Why not take her head to a new place, bombard it with new sights and sensations? The Project, too, could use a change of scenery.

Most of the migrants on the *Golden Venture* ended up getting transported off the beach and deposited at a county prison in southern Pennsylvania. After spending four months cramped in the ship's hold as they sailed from Thailand (where they arrived traveling on foot from China through Myanmar) to Kenya and around the Cape of Good Hope, they found themselves confined again, this time by U.S. immigration authorities.

The first migrant to make a paper sculpture while locked up in York County Prison made a pineapple.

After finishing a magazine he'd been looking at—one that he'd probably flipped through many times before—he began ripping out the pages, folding them into tiny triangles, and nesting the triangles together until they resembled the spiky skin of a pineapple. Impressed by his handiwork, a number of other detainees began making their own. As the men's ambition and skill level grew, they transitioned from pineapples to birds and bowls; dragons and pagodas and miniaturized models of the ship they had come in on.

For materials, they used magazines discarded by prison guards and legal pads from their pro bono attorneys. They made clever use of Styrofoam cups and instant noodle packaging. They fashioned papier-mâché from toothpaste, water, and toilet paper. They made Chinese lanterns from manila folders, loosened the thread from orange prison-issued bath towels for the dangling tassels. The work was painstaking and time-consuming, but the one thing the men had in excess was time.

As Alice trudged along the boulevard, the wind whipping furiously around her, her plan was seeming less and less like a plan. The sun was sagging lower in the sky and the temperature was sinking with it. She passed the desiccated carcass of a raccoon that must have been struck by a car and flung to the shoulder by the impact, the white wedge of its jawbone a grinning rictus. The road ran along the shore, yet was cut off from it by a long barbed-wire fence with few turnoff points. She started to worry: if the entrance to the Silver Gull were off-limits, she'd have to find some other way onto the beach, a workaround that would involve more walking. But it was too late to turn back.

———

The paper sculptures, which were, at first, a way to kill time, soon served another purpose. The migrants began offering them as gifts to their attorneys and to their supporters, a mix of activists and church people who wrote impassioned letters to elected officials appealing for their release. A number of these supporters became the migrants' de facto art dealers, selling the sculptures to raise money for their legal defense.

By then the migrants had done their market research. They abandoned pineapples in favor of bald eagles and American flags, which they modeled after the porcelain figurines and other Americana tchotchkes they'd seen advertised in the back pages of magazines. Two guards, overheard having a conversation about a weekend hunting trip, were gifted a pair of papier-mâché deer with delicately twirled antlers.

A few weeks ago, Alice had seen about forty of these paper sculptures at a museum exhibit. At the show she learned that, at the height of the paper-folding production at the prison, there were two competing "factories" of makers, each with its own school and methods. As she paused to admire the meticulous scales on a dancing dragon, she wondered if the migrants had imagined it might be possible to craft their way out of their own fate.

In Kazuo Ishiguro's *Never Let Me Go,* two young clones come to ponder the same question. The novel begins at a boarding school for clone children. In this world, clones exist and are allowed to grow up—up to a certain point—so their organs can be harvested and implanted in humans. Until their bodies give out, the clones can live a semblance of an ordinary, if brief, life. The young clones at the boarding school are even encouraged to draw, paint, and make sculptures.

When the two young clones at the center of the story fall in love, they get wind of a rumor: that clones who are able to prove the sincerity of their love can obtain a "deferral"—a temporary reprieve from the multiple organ removal procedures that will inevitably kill them.

But how to prove such a thing? The clone boy and girl recall a ritual from their days at the boarding school: Every quarter the best artworks were culled and taken away. Perhaps these exceptional works—windows into the minds of the young people who made them—were stored in an archive and consulted at a later date to determine whether two people were truly soul mates? At school the boy hadn't had any of his work selected; art wasn't his thing then. To make up for this shortfall, he starts making pencil and charcoal drawings at a feverish pace. He's already been cut open for three organ donations. Hardly anyone survives a fourth.

The clones have too little time; the men detained in York County Prison, too much of it. Before the arrival of the *Golden Venture*, asylum seekers in this country were processed, given a future court date, and told they were free to go. This was before the first bombing of the World Trade Center, before waves of Haitian refugees began arriving on the Florida coast. The spectacle of more than two hundred Chinese people jumping off a boat in Queens and swimming madly to shore was, as they say, very bad optics, a vivid manifestation of the xenophobe's worst fear—a horde of desperate foreigners arriving with nothing but the wet clothes on their backs. No wonder they were locked up. Nearly a quarter of a century later, the legacy is this: this country is home to the largest immigration detention system in the world.

In Ishiguro's novel the young clone lovers track down their former headmistress to make a personal, last-ditch appeal even though the school had long since shuttered. They've brought an entire portfolio of artwork to show her. She agrees to talk but is distracted by the presence of moving men at her flat, there to pick up an armoire.

The deferral, the headmistress informs them, was just a rumor. As for the paintings and drawings, "We didn't have the gallery in order to look into your souls," she explains. "We had the gallery to see if you had souls at all."

Ishiguro has said in interviews that the overtly sci-fi aspects of his story were never of much interest to him. There was never any possibility of a clone revolt. What interested him was love and friendship and why it was that most people unquestioningly go along with the terms of their own fate. He was also interested in how our decisions and actions are shaped by the brutal fact that our bodies last only so long.

When Alice reached the long driveway that led to the entrance to the Silver Gull Beach Club, she walked past the unmanned security booth and onto the grounds of the compound, which was closed for the season. She climbed a short flight of stairs to the second floor of the long row of cabanas. From where she stood on the open-air deck overlooking the ocean, she tried to imagine, based on the handful of news photographs she'd gleaned from the internet, the spot where the *Golden Venture* might have grounded on a sandbar.

It was past five in the afternoon. The sun dazzled off the

water. No one else was around. She watched a seagull drop a clam from on high over and over, doggedly trying to crack the shell with the force of gravity as the tide swept the shoreline. The ocean kept its secrets beneath its cresting skirts. Later, walking along the beach toward Fort Tilden, she came across an abandoned concrete bunker. The walls were covered in graffiti and an old mattress lay on the floor surrounded by empties. Had migrants, hiding from the authorities, taken shelter here?

Were the people staying overnight in the Silver Gull cabanas close enough to see the roving spotlights from the rescue boats? Did the shriek of ambulance sirens wake them? (On some nights when the wind blew a certain direction, it was said the men incarcerated on Alcatraz Island could hear revelers at a yacht club from across the bay, laughing and clinking their glasses.)

The same year the Artist was living in the streets for *Outdoor Piece*, one of his artworks was featured in a group show at a downtown gallery. The piece, *Wanted by the US Immigration Service,* was a mock "wanted" poster that featured the Artist's passport photo alongside his vital statistics (eyes: black; height: 5'3"; weight: 115 lbs.; ethnicity: Oriental), occupation (seaman), and copies of his fingerprints. For the first time, the Artist used his real name. He was done hiding. To be free meant risking the loss of freedom itself.

The Artist, too, had arrived in this country on a ship. But it was a different time. He managed to live in New York for two decades without papers and might have done so indefinitely if it hadn't been for a new amnesty law that made it possible for people who'd entered the country before January 1, 1982, to naturalize. The Artist filed the necessary paperwork. He'd paid his taxes and proved he didn't have a criminal history. He demonstrated basic knowledge about U.S. history and government as well as proficiency in English. He agreed to sign an official document confessing his guilt as an illegal alien. Then he was good.

After her trip to the Rockaways, Alice contacted the photographer whose pictures were featured in the museum exhibit, including a photo of a barren strip of beach where the *Golden Venture* migrants presumably stood that June morning, shivering under their blue emergency blankets.

The photographer emailed back: She, too, had been fuzzy on the exact location. She wrote, *Let me know what you find out?* Alice emailed the exhibit's curator, who said he didn't know the specifics, either, but mentioned an aerial photo he'd consulted in his own research. Aha. She used his tip to dig deeper into the online archives and emerged with what must have been the photograph in question, a black-and-white picture that seemed to show, between the Silver Gull's low-lying buildings and the beached freighter, a distance of just under half a mile, or a world away.

In 1996 five *Golden Venture* detainees were reclassified as "aliens of extraordinary ability in the arts" and granted asylum. One year later, so the story goes, a Republican congressman who had gotten swept up in the migrants' cause managed to press a paper sculpture of a bald eagle in President Clinton's hands. The President, a collector of all things bald eagle, was suitably impressed.

Soon after, he paroled the remaining fifty-three detainees still in custody. Ironically, by that time, sculpture-making at the county prison had petered out. After nearly four years in legal limbo behind bars with no end in sight, the remaining detainees had become cynical and despairing. What good were their paper animals?

Back at the headmistress's house, the young clones have overstayed their welcome. The furniture movers are preparing to leave and the headmistress, too, is eager to be on her way.

"There was a certain climate and now it's gone," she tells her former charges. "You have to accept that sometimes that's how things happen in this world. People's opinions, their feelings, they go one way, then the other. It just so happens you grew up at a certain point in this process."

The girl clone has never been one to make waves. She has, until now, accepted her lot with exemplary forbearance, yet she can't bring herself to let this one go.

"It might have been just some trend that came and went," she says quietly. "But for us, it's our life."

All migrants arrive at a certain point in a process. Of those who arrived on the *Golden Venture*, ten died after leaping into the ocean after the ship had grounded. Four escaped from the hospital where they were treated for hypothermia. A few were granted asylum; a hundred and eleven were deported. Fifteen remain in this country in uneasy purgatory, their status indeterminate. Six ran for the dunes that cold early morning in June and were never heard from again.

INCIDENT

In May, a few months after Alice's last visit, the Father had an incident at his care home. It wasn't a fall this time. What happened was he tried to get up from his recliner to have a smoke. This was his routine at least several times a day. Only this time he couldn't stand up.

The paramedics were called and he was taken to a nearby hospital. Amy reported that the only thing that showed up on the tests was a mild fever. Yet the Father seemed to have entered a new phase of decline. He couldn't walk and had become completely incontinent. The problem with his hands, or rather, his brain telling his hands what to do, was also much worse.

Alice spent the next three weeks in California to be with him and to figure out the next steps with Amy.

Since moving to New York, Alice had let her driver's license expire. It took about an hour by bus each way from Amy's condo to the skilled nursing facility where the Father was transferred after being discharged from the hospital. Hardly anyone in the suburbs rode the bus, apart from a handful of teenagers after school let out; a few weather-beaten men in 49ers jackets and caps who didn't have cars or maybe had DUIs; and Asian grand-mothers in floppy sun hats dragging wheeled shopping carts behind them.

The bus Alice was riding that morning was stalled in traf-fic. She'd ridden it enough times to know that the slowdown was routine whenever the bus turned onto Stevens Creek Boule-vard where the road narrowed to one lane. Beyond the eruption of traffic barriers and chain-link fencing, the new Apple mega-headquarters—a sleek five-billion-dollar building in the shape of a ring—was under construction.

How goes it? Julia texted. *I'm in a faculty meeting, dying slowly.* Julia had recently started teaching language arts at a cult-like char-ter school in Brownsville with high test scores and low morale.

Alice wrote that she was stuck in traffic. She mentioned her trip to the Rockaways and the *Golden Venture.*

That's crazy, Julia wrote back. *Kismet!* She reported her mother had visited her in New York recently from Chicago. When they'd taken a cab, her mother, in that blunt, openly curi-ous way of Chinese people, had asked the driver, who was also Chinese, whether he was illegal.

The cabbie said he was here illegally, and much to Julia's surprise, he continued to chatter away. He said he'd come to America by sea, on a boat that was right behind the *Golden Ven-ture*, in fact. A crew member on his boat got wise that some-thing was wrong and steered their vessel away from Queens and toward Mexico. The cabdriver chuckled without bitterness, incredulous at his fortune at having escaped imprisonment—and his misfortune at having to cross Mexico by foot to get to where he was now.

Now THAT's crazy! Alice replied, and set her phone aside. Alice had arrived in this country on an airplane with her sister, mother, and two suitcases. The Father had flown out from Taiwan ahead of them and rented a studio apartment in Berkeley. He got a job as a night-shift security guard. They had hardly any money for furniture. Both her parents enrolled at a community college in Oakland: he had a dream to make and sell Chinese furniture; she would quickly figure out that the classes she took to find work as a bookkeeper or keypunch operator were an utter bore but that her computer class unlocked her aptitude for problem-solving. Everything was struggle, everything was hope. The difficulty of those early years required a united front. What Alice hadn't realized at the time was that the front was crumbling. Six years in, their marriage was through.

Alice gazed out the window to see if any part of the Apple ring was visible. It wasn't. The ring was being built on the site of the company where her mother, now retired, had worked for most of her adult life. As a teenager, Alice had visited her mother's office a handful of times. The vast outlay of cubicles and the free sodas and breakfast Danishes impressed her. Nothing of that building remained; the entire compound had been razed.

The last time Alice and her mother had stayed with Amy for the holidays, Alice and her mother had taken a drive past the new construction to pick up lunch at their favorite beef noodle restaurant and Alice had asked her if she felt sad to see her old workplace disappeared. Her mother shrugged. "Not really." She wasn't sentimental about those old buildings. Earlier in the week Alice had gone with her mother to visit the Father in his residential care home. They seemed genuinely glad to see each other—it had been years—but their conversation did not rise above pleasantries and seemed to echo from a grave distance. Alice tried to imagine her future self visiting an ailing old flame from decades ago. What feeling would remain? Would the intervening years absolve her of responsibility? What if there were no one else? And yet most people in the end do have someone else. The older you get, Alice supposed, the clearer it becomes who they are.

As she and her mother drove past the familiar shopping plazas populated by unfamiliar businesses (Kumon seemed to have sprouted multiple heads overnight), Alice thought how sentimentality didn't seem to compute in this industry town, an outlook she envied at times, but mostly she was relieved to have left the area, although she had to admit the restaurant scene was incredible thanks to the critical mass of Asian tech workers who now lived there.

TELEVISION

The Father had refused to eat his breakfast, but he did take a sip of vanilla-flavored Ensure. That was the report from the morning nurse when Alice arrived at the skilled nursing facility, which was tucked away in a cul-de-sac called Solace Place, part of a sprawling archipelago of hospitals, dialysis and radiology imaging centers, and other facilities for the sick and dying floating in a sea of manicured grass and parking lots.

Alice took a deep breath before walking into the Father's room. He was lying in bed, tears leaking from his eyes. He turned his head when she walked in and told her he wanted to kill himself. What is it that he had to do to make that happen?

She assured him that he was scheduled to leave this place in a week or two; she and Amy had been trying to find a suitable place for him to live. Then she broke the news that he wouldn't be returning to his old residential care home; Kenny and his wife were only equipped to handle people who could walk and go to the bathroom on their own.

The Father listened quietly. He stopped crying. Had the care home become *home* to him? It must have, on some level. He felt safe there. She knew he liked the couple and chatting with the wife about her roses. Once, he told her, his eyes soft, he walked in on them dancing together in the kitchen to a song on the radio.

The television was positioned at a poor angle from his bed. Alice dragged the TV and the low, heavy dresser it sat on a few feet so he could watch more easily. *Dirty Harry* was playing on the movie channel. She distracted the Father with Clint Eastwood trivia, which seemed to cheer him up. They talked about .44 Magnum guns. The Father said he was once a pretty decent one-handed shooter of the Magnum he owned, but the recoil was a bitch and was probably responsible for permanently messing up his shoulder. He explained how newer guns were made with gas gauge releases that reduced the shock of the recoil.

Another topic of conversation: Which movies have great brain-dead endings? *Thunderbolt and Lightfoot. One Flew Over the Cuckoo's Nest. Thunderball.* The Father's face lit up with recognition at each. This felt familiar. This felt good. All those nights when her mother was studying at the campus computer lab or waitressing, the Father would make Jiffy Pop and he and the girls would watch old movies on TV, spaghetti westerns, Marx Brothers, those weird orangutan movies with Clint Eastwood, even the John Wayne war flicks that bored her. The Father had a knack for finding small pleasures in life and for wasting time. Some of the best times she'd wasted, Alice thought, had been in the company of the Father.

You can't waste time with someone for whom it doesn't come naturally. There was an art to it. Wasting time was not something Alice's mother did well or could abide by. She was always after some measure of self-improvement—calisthenics and tai chi for heart health, puzzles and games to strengthen her mind. Whether this was something innate in her personality or immigrant imperative was hard to say; Alice was hardly immune to its pull. She sometimes wondered if projects were an antidote to wasting time, an elaborate manifestation of it, or both.

Silence fell over the room. Alice shot a furtive text to James. No response. What was going on with him? She began flipping through the TV channels. It had been so long since she'd watched actual television that she found the rhythm and randomness of it beguiling. Then something weird happened: On one channel, Shelley Winters was swimming underwater and heroically lifting a door off Gene Hackman's trapped leg in *The Poseidon Adventure*. Click. On another channel, Shelley Winters was guest-starring on an episode of *Roseanne*, playing the family's brash, wisecracking grandma in a trucker hat. Watching television is like memory. Old shows and movies pop up at random and you are thrust into them, midstream. Click. Everything gets scrambled—one minute it's a life-and-death hospital scene; in another, you're dropped into a truck-stop diner with a laugh track. In between, a jingle for chewing gum, a talking lizard shilling car insurance. Channel surfing is like riding the choppy waves of the past and present, which is not unlike grief, Alice would learn. Grief is like watching television.

THE WAR

Another time, in his room at Solace Place while *Saving Private Ryan* played on the TV, the Father said—half to Alice, half to himself—"Sometimes I think maybe I shouldn't have gone to Vietnam."

Alice should have asked him why. Instead, she said, "Even if you hadn't volunteered, you probably would've been drafted."

She thought and didn't say: *If you hadn't gone to Vietnam, you wouldn't have ended up in Taipei and we wouldn't be here now, together.* What if, what if, what if. Her birth did not depend on the Father being born. But without him she wouldn't have had her life.

Did the Father think that, if he hadn't gone to Vietnam, he wouldn't be here now, in this terrible place? Probably he wasn't being quite so literal or linear, just ruminating more generally about how the war had both made and undone him in some chasmal, inexpressible way. In any case, he said no more, lost in his thoughts about the trajectory of his own life—not hers, or theirs.

APTITUDE

The Father was not oblivious to the changes in his brain. More than once in the long empty hours he and Alice spent together in this or that institution, he asked her whether it would be possible to be tested for Alzheimer's.

Okay, she said, but she didn't mean it. There was nothing to be done about his dementia that wasn't already being done, and what could be done was not enough to make a difference.

One morning the attending doctor at Solace Place dropped in on her rounds, smiling and distant in her white coat.

"Good morning," she said.

"Good morning to *you*," he said, slipping automatically into his Southern manners.

The doctor asked him how he was feeling. He said he'd felt better. She asked him if he knew what year it was. He said he didn't know. Then she asked him if he knew where he was.

The Father looked up at the doctor who stood over him in his wheelchair, his eyes wide and trusting, and said he didn't know the answer to that one, either. How Alice wanted to smack that look off his face!

He didn't have to look for his dementia. He was already in it.

TOTAL ASSIST

The Father's physical therapist at Solace Place was a woman with a conclusive center of gravity and a brisk, no-nonsense manner, which had the effect of kicking the Father, who sometimes had to be coaxed into getting up out of bed, into gear.

One morning during the Father's therapy session, she told Alice and Amy: "You're going to need to find a place for him that can handle total assist."

They were standing in the hallway just outside the Father's room. The Father was there, too, but he wasn't paying them any mind. With one hand, the therapist gripped the harness the Father wore around his waist during his movement therapy while he stared off into space, breathing heavily from his exertions. Twice a week the therapist got him out of bed to practice walking with a walker while he muttered curses under his breath. While she egged him on, Alice or Amy would trail behind him with the wheelchair in case the Father fell backward.

The physical therapist explained that, while it might look as though their father was on his feet and walking, he wasn't doing much balancing on his own. She was holding him up. This was unlikely to improve, she said. Ah. Like the other therapists who'd worked with him, it was their job to predict his future.

Total assist. Nothing terrified the sisters as much as those two words. It meant the Father would eventually need someone to dress him, bathe him, feed him, change him, shave him, and move him from chair to bed, room to room. Which, three months later, was what happened.

BASKET CASE

Afriend might ask, "How's your dad doing?" and Alice would picture in her mind the Father's frantic, mumbling sadness as she quashed the impulse to say, *He's a basket case.*

This was wicked speech, spastic, involuntary. It was the poltergeist of the Father's hidden life behind the doors of the memory care unit as she lived her life—shopping online, laughing at cat videos, eating and drinking the things he couldn't. On the radio she'd heard the President call someone a basket case, a favorite put-down of his—ugly like her ugly feelings.

Basket case was coined during World War I to describe soldiers—like the narrator in Dalton Trumbo's anti-war novel *Johnny Got His Gun*—who'd lost all his arms and legs in battle and had to be transported from place to place in baskets, although whether this actually happened is heavily disputed. A rumor began circulating that the military was hiding and playing down the actual number of quadruple amputees because they were a bad look for the war effort. The rumor kept metastasizing to the point that the military had to issue a formal statement assuring the public that not a single basket case had turned up after a thorough investigation. Which didn't stop the same rumor from surfacing again in World War II.

How was her father? He's doing okay, was Alice's reply when asked. She might draw out *okay* with the slightest lilt of uncertainty to indicate that he was not, in fact, okay and she felt helpless and ashamed but they were not obliged to talk about it.

DARKNESS

Life is a life sentence. Life is passing time. Life is free thinking.

Q: But what do you mean by "free thinking"?

A: *Rebellion, betrayal, crime, punishment, suffering, then freedom . . . it is a circle. Freedom is just a tiny reward after all the pain you've experienced throughout the process. And you have to keep fighting for it. It's elusive.*

The project went in search of a bird—

PROJECT FOR A TRIP TO GROUND ZERO

When Alice emerged from the subway station on Rector Street, her phone vibrated. It was a text from Nobu, apologizing for running late. He'd confused the date for their lunch. Should they cancel?

No, she texted back. *I'll wait for u.*

To kill time, she made a snap decision to walk a few blocks uptown to the 9/11 Memorial & Museum. The museum had been open for six years, but like most people she knew, she'd never gone. It was the fate of memorials that commemorate catastrophe to be visited mostly by schoolchildren and tourists. When she'd first moved to the city, she used to make a point of getting off at random subway stops to explore neighborhoods she'd never seen. (Something of the infinite is contained within the subway system.) The longer she lived here, the less she did this. Why? She was disappointed by how easily she'd slipped into the familiar grid of her routines.

She'd learned that, during the year of *Outdoor Piece*, the Artist often traveled by foot to this part of Lower Manhattan. From studying the maps he'd marked of his daily perambulations, Alice knew that he took a regular morning shit at an overgrown weed lot on the corner of Worth and Park, and sometimes on Peck Slip, a cobblestone street lined by old and dilapidated brick buildings where, two centuries earlier, trading boats used to dock.

It was also from these maps that she realized she'd mistaken the location of the waterfront piers that the Artist used to haunt. He wasn't uptown near the storied piers where Gordon Matta-Clark carved raw openings in an abandoned steel-trussed warehouse with a blowtorch. He was much farther south at the piers above what was now Battery Park City and a few blocks from where she stood.

The memorial plaza, an austere grid of white oak trees and low granite plinths, was emptied of people. Out of respect for the dead, the living had been zoned away. There were no blue and yellow Sabrett umbrellas with dirty dogs bobbing in their steaming vats; no caramelized scent wafting from the cart of an Argentinian peanut seller; no sandwich board hucksters handing out menus for nearby Chinese lunch buffets. Alice watched a handful of tourists pose with selfie sticks in front of the sunken pools set in the footprints of the fallen towers. The waterfalls roared.

To enter the museum she first had to pass through security—a room tricked out with metal detectors, X-ray machines, and body scanners. Once inside, all natural light seemed to vanish. As she made her way from floor to floor, she realized that it was possible to encounter different commemorations for the same victim many times over. You might see a digital transfer of a woman's missing persons poster projected on a wall; then see the woman again in another gallery in a touch-screen memorial of her life, the chapters of which you could advance with your finger. You could find her name stitched onto a sixty-foot quilt, and outside, etched in the bronze parapets around the memorial's reflecting pools. When Alice entered a dark video chamber, the same woman reappeared, this time in a montage of photographs, augmented by an audio narration by someone close to her. From this we learn she was a loving mother, a bowling enthusiast, and an executive secretary for a global provider of risk management services.

One day, decades from now, Alice thought, these digital tombstones might appear as distantly anachronistic as Civil War soldiers staring balefully from silver-tinted daguerreotypes. But for now, another audiovisual tribute is cued up, this time for a VP at one of the big financial firms that was headquartered in one of the towers. Alice viewed a slideshow of photographs of the man, slim, tall, with dark hair, while the voice of his sister flooded the dark room. The sister remembered her brother primarily as a person preoccupied with neatness. She described how meticulous he used to be about his grooming and appearance, and how, as a boy, he used a piece of tape to delineate his side of the bedroom. The VP probably never imagined he'd be summed up this way, deep in the bowels of a museum for all eternity. The memory of us will persist, if it does at all, in the fickle minds of others. Alice waited politely for his tribute to end before leaving the room to find the Survivors' Staircase.

Hundreds of people flooding out of the towers had taken the stairs that morning, which led them past the fire and wreckage on the elevated plaza of the World Trade Center to the relative safety of Vesey Street below. For years during the reconstruction process, the stairs remained at their original location, the only remnant of the WTC still aboveground. But developers eventually won the battle to have them removed and the entire granite slab was lowered by crane to its final underground resting place in the museum.

Alice found the Vesey Street stairs wedged between an escalator on one side and a flight of newly constructed stairs on the other. The top of the stairs was roped off with a sign that warned DO NOT TOUCH THE ARTIFACT. Museumgoers were encouraged to walk alongside the ruined stairs in a pantomime of the survivors' descent.

Later that afternoon over lunch, Alice told Nobu about the stairs. His eyes took on a distant look.

"It's too bad they didn't leave the stairs where they were," he said. "They would have made a very good Thomasson."

The two friends were in a booth on the second floor of Ho Yip, an old-school pay-by-the-pound Chinese steam table joint that probably hadn't changed its menu or decor in decades, having long ago achieved the exquisite balance between quality and quantity, grease and affordability. The restaurant was located in a charmless alley steps away from Zuccotti Park and a short walk from Nobu's art studio. Across from their booth, two postal workers sat together in companionable silence, bent over their buffet selections.

A Thomasson, Nobu explained, is a street artifact that has become useless and derelict because it no longer serves its original function. An outline of a window filled with concrete is a Thomasson. An amputated telephone pole is a Thomasson. A balcony connected to an entrance that's been bricked off. Stairs that lead to nowhere.

In the 1970s, the artist Genpei Akasegawa identified the phenomenon and named these hollow objects Thomassons after Gary Thomasson, an American ballplayer who spent the last two years of his career in Japan with the Yomiuri Giants, striking out so many times at the plate that the Japanese called him—not without affection—the "Electric Fan."

"Akasegawa thought Thomasson's record-making strikeouts were not a humiliation but actually quite marvelous," Nobu said. "Here was this guy who was paid a very good salary to do a job that he was never able to do." The *concept* of Thomasson as ballplayer was truer than his actual *performance* as a ballplayer. So it was with the phantom structures that bear his name, located somewhere between mind and metropolis, in the fault lines of a city's architecture.

Alice thought on this. "You could say the Artist's work is useless, too, at least in the traditional sense. But it isn't worthless."

She recalled that the Vesey Street stairs were not the only Thomasson stairs she'd encountered, if she understood the definition correctly. As a high school exchange student, she'd seen an installation of marble stairs inside a museum in Hiroshima. A sign explained that the stairs had once been attached to a bank in the city. Grafted onto the stairs was a murky, dark smudge left by—no—of a person who had been incinerated on the spot just after eight in the morning. Most likely the person had been waiting for the bank to open when Little Boy detonated.

On that same trip to Hiroshima, Alice had visited other atomic bomb memorial sites with a group of Japanese high school students. She remembered the group pausing frequently to pose for photographs—in front of the famous skeletal domed tower; by the river where people threw themselves to relieve their burns. The students beamed and held up their fingers, slinging their customary bunny ears while Alice, sunk by what she'd seen and too mortified to smile, tried pressing her lips together in a rictus of what she hoped was a look of dignified shame.

Nobu nodded. It made sense to him, he said, that a country like Japan that had been devastated by so many natural and man-made catastrophes—earthquakes, tsunamis, fire-bombings, nuclear attack—would be home to so many Thomassons. It made sense, too, that Japanese people would be partial to their peculiar, remnant charm, he mused. People who follow Shinto believe they are surrounded at all times by little gods that inhabit everything from the wind, the mountains, to the trees. Why not Thomassons?

"It's like the Thomassons can't forget their purpose . . . they can't let go of their original post," Nobu said. "Maybe there is an unused post out there in the world that can't forget its former life as a post!"

They laughed a little.

The doggedness of the Thomasson, Alice said, poking at a fatty piece of General Tso's chicken, reminded her of a story she'd read about the dancing bears of Bulgaria. The bears, trained by Gypsies to dance for money, had been freed so they could live out the rest of their lives in a wildlife preserve. Yet even now, years later, if a human being approaches them, they rise up automatically on their hind legs, ready to dance again.

That guy who suffered from *Truman Show* delusion never did make it to the Twin Towers.

Instead of heading downtown, he made his way north to the United Nations. Maybe part of him knew, in a pocket of his mind undisturbed by delusions, that the towers were gone. In any case, he switched tactics. He went to the U.N. to seek asylum from the show runners who had made a spectacle and lie of his life. Which was how he ended up as a patient in Bellevue and the subject of an article in a psychiatric journal.

At the museum, Alice allowed herself to be led by the building's architectural flow to the gift shop stationed by the exit.

When the gift shop first opened, she remembered how the critics had declaimed it, this exchange of money and goods in this sacred space. But wasn't shopping the American way of keeping calm and carrying on? People need their souvenirs. Alice scanned the shelves of stuffed toys and children's books devoted to the dog heroes of 9/11, the Survivor Tree tote bags, the Never Forget bracelets. She tried to picture the person who would buy the necktie designed with a pattern of the Twin Tower tridents, and what occasion he would have for wearing it. Then she pushed through the glass doors that opened out directly onto the street. The warmth of the afternoon sun touched her skin as she paused, taking in the honk and rumble of passing cars and the bright clang of the indeterminate present.

THE LONELINESS OF THE PROJECT

It was late spring; the days molted with gold. Alice had felt a sting of regret at having to leave New York in the precious weeks before the summer heat panted its wet tongue across the city. Once she landed in California, she found herself looking for evidence of the drought, now in its fifth or sixth year. Some people had let their lawns go brown; others had replaced their grass with rock gardens and desert plants. Amy said that she hadn't been taking her regular morning walks because the air quality was still bad from wildfires blowing in from the north—or was it the south?

At Solace Place, Alice signed in at the front desk, turned left past the complimentary coffee station, and down the corridor lined with paintings of sailboats and bouquets. It was Sunday morning and the facility was quiet and relatively empty; there were no patients roaming in the hallways with their walkers and no doctors and nurses making their rounds.

The Father had been moved to the facility's memory unit, which was separated from the rest of the building by an alarm-activated door. He hadn't made any meaningful improvement with therapy; Alice and Amy learned that finding a residential care home that would take him would be next to impossible. Once inside the memory unit, Alice smiled and nodded at the nurses and CNAs she recognized. She avoided the stone-faced woman in the wheelchair who haunted the corridor, always asking the same question—"What's the weather like out there?"—and who sucked her teeth in haughty disbelief no matter the answer you gave. The memory unit was a sad place, there was no getting around that, but it was also quiet and gentle, and Alice hoped it was a relief to the Father's brain, which had over time become even more easily aggravated by noise and movement.

When she saw he wasn't in bed, she stepped through the sliding glass door in his room that opened out to a narrow yard. The Father was slumped forward in his wheelchair and talking to himself. As she got closer to him, she realized what he was muttering was his own name over and over.

"He's been doing that a lot," Elias, the CNA on duty, told her. Elias was East African, Ethiopian, she guessed, based on his impossibly elegant features. His eyelashes were murderously long and made her shy to look at him.

Alice spent some time with the Father in the yard listening to the birds and the wind tossing the trees lightly before Elias wheeled the Father into his room and lifted him back in bed to check his briefs. Alice stepped out of the room while this happened. When she returned, Elias was rubbing down each of the Father's fingers with some kind of antibacterial wipe. She pulled up a chair. The Father continued talking about his wood shop, insisting that he had work to do.

"But you don't have to work anymore," she said, hoping to reassure him. "You're retired."

"But I have to work to make money," he shot back, full of heat. A worried look came over his face. "If I don't work, I won't know my name."

For years the Father had complained about his job and how he couldn't wait to retire. The people he worked with—the contractors, the architects, his coworkers in the shop—all drove him nuts. What he wanted, he said, was more time for his projects. He wanted to focus on his photography and his cooking. Above all, he groused, he didn't want to have to deal with people anymore. But, as it was with so many old men, when the Father finally did retire, his life emptied out.

"Liberty is frightening, and that is why the elderly man will sometimes refuse it," Simone de Beauvoir wrote in *The Coming of Age,* her sprawling five-hundred-plus-page book about growing old under capitalism—the stigma, the social isolation, the ragged safety nets. Our exploitation as workers—hidden from us for most of our lives by routine—is revealed in old age, she wrote, even as we are anguished to be excluded from it.

Beauvoir was in her sixties when she began writing the book. By then her partner Jean-Paul Sartre's health had begun its long downward spiral. He'd had a few worrisome falls; spots blocked his field of vision. His decline must have made Beauvoir, already finely attuned to her own age and appearance, even more anxious about losing her vitality. To measure the sharpness of her mental acuity, she devised little exercises and tests for herself, obstacle courses that she ran repeatedly in her own mind. As long as she was able to complete these mental tests, she could be assured that her faculties were intact.

One day—this was during the height of the sixties student protests—young people marched right under Sartre's apartment in the Left Bank. In an earlier time, Sartre and Beauvoir would have been on the front lines; now Sartre found he was only sought out by activists eager to wring his celebrity for media attention. No one asked for Beauvoir at all. That must have stung, but it didn't matter. They had their projects. In her case, the manuscript that would become *The Coming of Age;* for Sartre, a mammoth life study of Gustave Flaubert.

Reading Deidre Bair's biography of Beauvoir, Alice was moved to learn how Beauvoir hauled herself every morning to the Bibliothèque nationale de France, arriving early so she would be sure to secure a good seat at one of the library's long wooden tables, where she spent hours burrowed in her fortress of books and papers. Beauvoir was evangelical in her belief that irrelevance in old age and its attendant terrors could be spared by inhabiting projects. Having projects, she insisted, was even more important than having one's health!

Sartre, in the last decade of his life, would prove her point.

All his life Sartre had lived with complete disregard for his health. He smoked two packs of unfiltered cigarettes a day, punctuated by several pipes of tobacco, and consumed ferocious amounts of alcohol—wine, beer, vodka, whiskey. Alice never thought she would have cause to say this, but Sartre reminded her of her father. On top of that—and here is where Sartre outdid the Father—he popped amphetamines and barbiturates, which he washed down with endless cups of coffee. When he was diagnosed with diabetes, Sartre refused to let up on sweets and ice cream. His drug use, mescaline in particular, was likely the root of his persistent hallucinations. Specifically, he hallucinated crabs. The crabs, usually in a group of three or four, followed him wherever he went—in the street, the underground, the lecture hall. He began thinking of them as companions. In the morning, he'd ask the crabs how they slept. After delivering a stern warning that they behave themselves, he'd invite them to come to class.

Despite having reached this civil détente with his apparitions, Sartre remained fearful of suffering a nervous breakdown. He engaged the help of his young psychoanalyst friend Jacques Lacan. Lacan examined him and concluded that the crustaceans were a manifestation of his fear of being alone.

It fell on Beauvoir to make sure he never was alone. Projects are essential, but they are not enough. Most of us require companionship as fortification. In Sartre's final years Beauvoir orchestrated a daily routine for, and around, him. On weeknights she slept in the extra bedroom in his flat behind the Gare Montparnasse overlooking the cemetery; his adopted daughter, Arlette Elkaïm-Sartre, stayed over on the weekends.

Every morning Beauvoir made sure she got Sartre out of bed, shaved and dressed in time to have breakfast with his other female friends. She and Arlette took turns watering down his whiskey and emptying his ashtrays. Afterward she might read aloud to him. In the evenings, Maoist acolytes would be conscripted to take Sartre to lectures or political meetings. Along with Beauvoir, they kept him engaged in his projects, his research, his writing. In this way Sartre remained active—long past when his body had begun to give out. This should be the destiny of every old person, Beauvoir believed. If that were so, growing old would not be the cataclysm we all fear.

Could projects have saved the Father? Alice thought. Maybe. If his mind hadn't been so damaged by alcohol. Or maybe that was wishful thinking. Over the years Alice would ask the Father, "Do you ever think about making furniture again?"

The answer was always no. After a time, he must have known what she didn't yet realize: that his hands could no longer handle the tools even if he had wanted to.

While Beauvoir took care of Sartre, she was also keeping notes for a project that would become *Adieux: A Farewell to Sartre*, an unsparing account of the philosopher's last years. She wrote about his dental plate, his blindness and infirmities, the strokes that left his lips twisted, the drunken falls, the wet spots he left on chairs and the streaks that ran down his trousers, which he blamed, improbably, on pissing cats. After Sartre died, Beauvoir described her attempt to climb into his bed one last time to be with him. The hospital attendants interrupted her in the act and advised her to lie down on top of the sheets: his bedsores had turned to gangrene.

When *Adieux* was published, Beauvoir was decried for exposing Sartre at his most vulnerable. Deidre Bair joined the critics who faulted the memoir for being overly long and fatiguing. Unlike in her other scrupulously written books, Beauvoir had allowed "everything to spill out." And when that happens, Bair wrote, "the raw stuff of life with no refinement makes for bad art."

Arlette Elkaïm-Sartre was so outraged by the memoir that

she bought advertising space in the newspaper *Libération* so she could blast Beauvoir in an open letter: "You abuse your power brutally. You have gone too far."

But Beauvoir wasn't interested in refinement. She wanted all of it to spill out, the leaking, the stink, the bodily terrors, yet there were consequences to the code she and Sartre shared, to tell nothing slant. After he died, Beauvoir suffered a mental and physical collapse. Her cirrhosis worsened. She came down with pneumonia and fell into a depression fed by Valium and Johnny Walker Red.

Beauvoir, who had agonized over losing Sartre even when he was alive, was now alone. Well, not entirely alone. She had Sylvie le Bon, whom she'd met when Sylvie was a young graduate student, and adopted when Sylvie was thirty-nine. Sylvie was her insurance against her fear of falling under her sister's care, which would have led, she believed, to the inconceivable: leaving Paris. In Beauvoir's last years, Sylvie did the cooking and cleaning and the watering down of her liquor bottles, as Beauvoir had once done for Sartre.

It was only in her final years that Beauvoir finally let go of her looks and the fastidiousness with which she guarded her appearance. By then her skin and eyes had become yellow with jaundice; her abdomen was swollen from drinking. She could no longer be bothered to maintain. ("It can't be helped," Sartre would murmur after dribbling soup all over himself, which used to make Beauvoir so cross.) She rarely bothered to get dressed anymore, even to receive guests. Her daily uniform was house slippers and a frayed red robe. But her mind remained sharp. What would *Adieux: Farewell to Beauvoir* have looked like? Maybe she didn't see it coming, her own death. Alice remembered in the early days at Solace Place, after the Father had finished a good physical therapy session and she was wheeling him back to his room, how he'd become nearly giddy with the thought that he could, if he kept improving, get out his pots and pans and start making Chinese food again.

"Maybe," she said, letting the little balloon of his hope rise. How strong is the dream of the project.

KILLING TIME

In the memory unit at Solace Place there was, every day, a dead zone between breakfast and lunch when the residents, at least the ones well enough to get out of bed, were wheeled out to the hallway, where they faced each other as if in a receiving line. The first time Alice encountered this peculiar formation, she thought they were waiting for something. But they were just killing time.

Now the Father had become part of this routine, although, unlike most of the other residents, he was younger and had more energy. Restless, he dragged himself in circles in his wheelchair with the balls of his heels. Alice sat on a folding chair reading a book. Whenever he passed her, the Father grabbed saltines from the Tupperware container she held out with one hand.

Diversion came in the form of a tall, silver-haired man in a baseball cap who leaned over the counter of the nurses' station like a cowboy at a saloon. "There's Rob," the Father said, brightening, and wheeled himself over.

"Hey, Rob," the Father said.

The man looked down at him.

"Do I know you?" he said coolly. "You must have me confused with someone else."

Alice watched them, seeing the Father through this stranger's eyes. The Father's pajama pants were slightly open at the crotch, revealing the mound of his adult briefs. Across his shirt-front, a constellation of crumbs and stains.

The Father was confused by the man's reaction, then abashed by his blunder. He retreated without saying another word.

Later she spotted the silver-haired man in the activity room talking to his elderly mother. She overheard him explaining in a gentle but firm voice to her how she wouldn't be going home with him after all. She would be staying here.

Through the moves from city to city, hospitals to nursing homes, Alice and the Father sat together in rooms passing time. This wasn't terribly different from what they used to do when he still lived in Berkeley, smoking cigarettes and chewing the fat around his dining room table. Except of course now everything had changed, everything was diminished, and they were both sad but pretending for the other's sake not to be utterly miserable.

It was in the dead hours of these melancholy spaces that the Father would bring up his recurring idea of moving back to Alabama.

What if he got himself a small house with a front porch? He didn't need anything fancy. Housing was cheap there compared to California; he'd looked into it on the computer. He could live out the remainder of his days there.

"But who would take care of you?" she asked. The Father

didn't have an answer to this. Maybe he hoped his sister or brother would, both of whom still lived near their hometown. Or more likely he was envisioning an alternate reality where he didn't need to be cared for. Alice wondered sometimes—whenever some combination of her and her sister, the Father's Indian doctor, his Filipino caregivers, the nurses from Ethiopia, Bangladesh, the Ukraine, crowded around his bed—if he ever looked up at their faces and thought, Where am I, so far from home? But where was home? Home was so long ago. The idea of Alabama was a time machine.

THE OLD MAN

"The old man," Beauvoir wrote, "looks like a different species to others because unlike active members of the community he is not engaged in a project."

Once when Alice was visiting the Father at Solace Place, she stood to the side as two staff members lifted him out of bed and onto a wheelchair. They did this every day around noon so he could sit upright for lunch. Whenever this transfer went down, the Father would scream bloody murder. This time was no different.

"Sons of bitches!" the Father yelled through clamped teeth. After a few minutes when he was settled into the chair, he blinked and looked around him, wide-eyed.

"It's the old man," he said. "He's sorry."

Alice was astonished at this sleight-of-hand. The man who swore and shouted at people—surely he was someone else!

In many ways the Father had become someone else. There was a Before and After, and everyone who met him After didn't really know him at all. They would never know him, she thought. For a time, there was an In Between—Alice remembered an encounter from more than a year ago, a meeting she'd arranged between the Father and a local rep from a home care service. She and Amy had finally managed to convince him to allow a caregiver to come to the house a few times a week. The first step in this process was a meeting with a rep from the care service company who would do an initial assessment of the Father's needs.

The rep showed up at the Father's door dressed in a company-branded polo shirt and pressed khakis, his hair neatly combed. He was Asian and looked to be in his mid-twenties. Alice went over the care plan with him, mindful to include the Father so he had a voice in the matter. The Father seemed to follow along but was mostly quiet. Yes, they could have someone come twice a week, for starters. Yes, the caregiver could do some light cleaning and prepare a few meals. She could even follow recipes if we left the proper instructions. No, she wouldn't cut nails; that was against protocol.

The rep slung some marketing jargon with practiced aplomb and handed Alice a laminated folder of additional literature. He or one of his colleagues would be back in touch. As the rep was packing his briefcase to go, the Father peered closely at his business card, holding it right up to his eye. "Do," he said, reading the rep's last name out loud. "That's a Vietnamese name."

"Yes, that's right." The young man's eyes flashed. "Very few people know that."

He looked at the Father as though seeing him for the first time as someone other than a cranky old man who was falling apart in his house. The Father knew the things of this world. Alice felt a surge of pride.

After the rep left, the Father confessed that he wasn't comfortable with anyone else doing his laundry.

But why? she asked. To reach the laundry room, the Father had to negotiate a steep flight of stairs down the back of the house. The Father hung his head. It was because of his underwear. He didn't want anyone to see. He'd tried soaking them in the sink, but it didn't work.

She assured him professional caregivers were impervious to such things, that they'd probably seen everything under the sun and then some. She moderated her tone to sound casual. Inwardly she was gratified that he'd shared his sad secret. It meant his trust in her was bigger than his shame. Later, working on the Project, she would think about his dirty drawers and how ready she was to air them—for what, this dumb pun?

QUESTIONS

"What do you do?" the Father once asked Alice out of the blue, like small talk.

Alice was stumped. What *did* she do? She edited video. Sometimes she made projects. She failed at making projects.

"I take care of you," she said, a simple answer that didn't always feel true. This seemed to both puzzle and satisfy him.

Later she asked him, "Do you want me to scratch your back?" He used to love this, always.

"What day is it?"

"Thursday."

(A beat.)

"Then no."

"Is there anything you want?" she asked the Father before she left for the day. (She didn't add, *from the outside world.*)

A thoughtful look crossed his face. "Other than killing me in my head?" he replied.

EMOTIONAL LABILITY

At night, sleepless on the sofa bed in Amy's living room, she found herself reading up on frontotemporal dementia again, lit in the dark by the small glowing screen of her phone. Sometimes she scrolled through the same websites, reread the symptoms, the treatments, the causes, the seven stages of, the life expectancy, and so on and so forth, over and over again, as though to squeeze more insight from them. She read, with morbid fascination, a blog by a Chicago businessman who had been diagnosed with frontotemporal dementia. The first handful of entries swaggered with bravado. ("I'm not going down without a fight, damn it.") Then followed a spiraling eddy of setbacks. He fumed at his employer. He yearned for more sympathy from his daughters and ex-wife. And then a catalogue of frustrations and regrets before the blog posts stopped abruptly. The last entry was written three years ago.

One dementia website described a classification of symptoms known as *emotional lability*.

Labile, as in unstable, as in readily or continually undergoing chemical, physical, or biological change or breakdown.

Only Alice kept misreading *lability* as *liability*—as in a person or thing whose presence or behavior is likely to cause embarrassment or put one at a disadvantage.

The more removed the Father became from the outside world, the less liable he was for his outbursts. He lived in a sick place surrounded by people familiar with his sickness. He could shout, "Shut up, you moron!" which he did many times a day, and no one would blink.

The first few times he shouted this at her, Alice's impulse was to laugh with admiration at the candor of his feelings. Also, she supposed, because she preferred dealing with this ornery side of him than the one that cried.

THE MUSTACHE

Alice had come to say goodbye to the Father and drop off a jar of Vaseline and baby oil before her flight later that night. When she entered the Father's room, he was propped up in his bed. There was a strange blankness to his features that took her a few seconds to register. His mustache was missing. All her life she'd never known him not to have a mustache.

"Hey, you shaved your mustache," she said.

"I did?"

"It looks good." Although she didn't think so. She wanted the mustache back.

Someone in charge of the Father's hygiene and grooming must have shaved it off. His face had turned into a hotel room, furnished with only the most basic items to facilitate cleaning and maintenance. Did he feel it, this erasure of his personal vanity? The effect was that he looked less like himself and more like his father.

———

Around this time the news was saturated with stories about football players and the epidemic of traumatic brain injuries they had sustained on the field crashing into each other with brute force. The *Times* ran a big feature on a study of more than a hundred autopsied brains of former NFL players. All but one brain had signs of chronic traumatic encephalopathy, a neurological disease. The symptoms—problems with impulse control, depression, declining executive functions, unsteady gait, tremors—made Alice think of her father.

It was the Father's outsized aggression that worried her and Amy the most. They worried he would be kicked out of Solace Place for bad behavior, and that they would have to keep searching and searching for other facilities willing to take him and he would end up somewhere that was more like nowhere, some remote town in the Central Valley that would take hours for them to drive to and where he'd be an exile twice over. This possibility loomed larger and terrified them more than his death.

Various medications were attempted, including one whose name sounded like a tree, and another, which sounded like a monster from Greek mythology. It was hard to tell if these drugs were designed to ground him in reality or spare him the horror of it. It was also hard to tell if any of the drugs helped in the end. Alice didn't know and she would never know. She only knew that they seemed to make him calmer. Or was that just her?

KNOWLEDGE

On her last visit the Father had said while she was sitting by his side, "I don't want my little girl to see me because I'm a big fat idiot."

Later that same day he said, "I'm tired of being a fat boy"— even though by then his skin was hanging from his bones.

She wondered if he was traveling back in time to his boyhood. Had he been teased as a kid for being overweight? He'd never mentioned it before, and now she couldn't ask and expect an answer. Everything she knew about her father was what she already knew.

HO YIP

Even after all these years in New York, Alice's intolerance of the summer humidity had never abated. The Californian in her was suffocated by it; her skin broke out in protesting rashes. She was relieved to see that the forecast was only in the low eighties on the day she had arranged to meet Nobu for one last lunch at Ho Yip. His residency was ending in a matter of days. She climbed the stairs out of the subway station at Rector Street, navigating her way through a clutch of German tourists who had gathered around the stone retaining wall that wrapped around the Trinity Church cemetery. When she turned into the alley, she saw that Nobu was already there and that the rolling steel doors to the restaurant were pulled down.

The last time she'd been to Ho Yip, there had been a "C" rating taped to the window. At the time, she'd shrugged it off. She had a theory about this—that you were more likely to make allowances for a certain threshold of questionable hygiene if the establishment served food from your own people. But that had been months ago. Had health inspectors shut it down?

Nobu nodded toward the shuttered door. On his way over

he'd run into Wojciech from the residency, who told him Ho Yip had lost their lease—the building was being sold. "I figured to meet you here and then decide where to go." They agreed to cross the street to investigate the food trucks that rimmed Zuccotti Park.

The midday heat bore down on the lunchtime crowd that had gathered at the park, people in shirtsleeves and open-toed shoes bent over their Styrofoam containers. A whiff of cannabis cloyed the air.

They found a spot on a low slab bench. Nobu had good news to share: Someone had bought one of his found grocery list portraits after a few of them were exhibited at a group show in a Lower East Side gallery. They clinked their soda cans. Nobu picked at his pad see ew. Despite the good news of the sale, Alice could tell he was in a funk. When she pressed him, he said that his visa was set to expire soon. This wasn't a surprise; he'd already begun the tedious process of accumulating all the paperwork and letters of validation he'd need to renew it. But he'd spoken recently with his lawyer, who warned him that, under the current administration, all visas were being scrutinized, and he shouldn't take anything for granted.

"I wish there were something I could do," she said.

Nobu shook his head. "It's okay." Then he smiled, probably to make her feel better, Alice thought. "It is very hard to keep proving my extraordinary ability."

Alice, meanwhile, was doing nothing extraordinary. The Project had begun to feel, like so many of her previous projects, mucked. Spinning its wheels, lightless at the end of the tunnel—such clichés seemed apropos. She was swimming in material—text, images, video, interviews, notes, so many notes—but the form of the thing, how the project would come together, how it would take, eluded her. At one point she considered throwing everything against the wall, or rather, into some kind of mixed media installation. But who would give her the space to stage it? She'd read that the Artist had been trying for years to interest a museum in mounting a retrospective of his life's work. He'd never been entirely satisfied with the representation of time in the shows where his work had been exhibited. His concept was to translate the passage of time—including his final per-formance, which involved thirteen years of making art without showing any of it—as gallery space. So far no one had taken him on up it.

She missed James. It had been months since they'd spoken. His responses to her emails and texts were curt and then some-times he didn't respond at all. He had said he had a lot going on, but what was going on? Was he even in New York anymore? She got the message and backed off, gave him his space.

A month or so ago she thought she spotted him in the street. It was a miserable afternoon; rain was driving hard into the pavement. She had a meeting in Midtown with a new client and had been making her way to the H-Mart in Koreatown when she spotted what she thought was a familiar figure—James with the hood of his jacket pulled forward. She couldn't see his face; it was the way he moved that caught her eye, like James, pitched slightly forward as though weighed down by an immense backpack.

She quickened her pace to catch up with the hooded man

before he rounded the corner. She could have sworn the man recognized her from the corner of his eye before turning away. A big man in a heavy leather jacket shouting into his phone blocked her path; by the time she maneuvered around him and the rampart of garbage bags at the curb, James or Not-James had vanished. From a few streets away came the Doppler cry of an ambulance. Her hands were cold; the wind shuddered along the spine of her umbrella, threatening to turn it inside out.

THE ENIGMA OF A BACKGROUND

In the exhibition catalogue of *Outdoor Piece* is a photograph of the Artist gazing out from what looks like a lifeguard chair. Nothing else is in the frame except the Twin Towers looming in the distance behind him.

Only later would she figure out that the chair was not a chair but a wooden staircase, and that the staircase was not only a staircase but a sculpture created by the artist Donald Lipski.

The sculpture was installed on a stretch of Lower Manhattan now known as Battery Park City, a neighborhood of blocky glass buildings overlooking an aggressively serene riverfront. Back when the photograph was taken, the area was a landfill bank created when mounds of soil and rock were unearthed to build the World Trade Center and a massive water tunnel.

In the late seventies and early eighties when the economy was shit and development projects in the city were at a standstill, artists took over these urban sandy dunes along the Hudson. They staged music and dance performances and built sculptures from old refrigerators, busted TVs, and driftwood. None of it was meant to last, including the beach.

Lipski's original concept was to string ropes attached with colorful flags from the top of his stair sculpture to the roof of the World Trade Center. He'd even consulted an engineer for structural advice and purchased two half-mile lengths of rope. The city wouldn't go for it.

Through the optical illusion of forced perspective, when you climbed the twenty or so steps of Lipski's sculpture to the standing platform, you looked to be at the very top corner of the North Tower. It would have made for an excellent selfie. If the sculpture were still there today, you'd climb to the top of the stairs and reach a spot of empty sky. The staircase or the sky is the Thomasson.

THE FUTURE OF THE FATHER

In August the Father's doctor informed Alice and Amy that it was possible the Father had a year to six months to live. Arranging for hospice, she said, was something they ought to consider.

Alice had always imagined that, if a doctor were to make such a prognosis, her tone would be serious, hushed, and that she would deliver it in a sitting room designed specifically for the conveyance of such portentous information. Instead, the doctor spoke briskly and matter-of-factly in the corridor of the memory unit as CNAs and patients milled around them. Well, actually Alice wasn't even there; she had joined the conversation by speakerphone from Brooklyn.

Her disembodiment from the conversation made the news even harder to believe. Also confusing was the absence of any malfunctioning major organs or other vital signs that would have indicated the Father's dire state. Was it death itself that couldn't be comprehended? (Beauvoir: "My mother had always been there, and I had never seriously thought that some day, that soon I should see her go. Her death, like her birth, had its place in some legendary time.")

When she hung up, Alice recalled all the other times in the past few years when professionals they'd consulted—about housing, health insurance, caregiving—tried to foretell their father's future and when his life would end.

In the beginning it was even harder to know who, or what, to believe. It seemed so long ago now, but back when the Father was still recuperating at the skilled nursing facility in Oakland, Alice and Amy had toured an assisted living facility that stood out in her memory for its size and relative grandeur.

At the facility, they were greeted by the general manager, who walked them through the various common rooms and the grounds of a pleasantly shaded outdoor garden with planter boxes filled with flowers. The general manager looked to be in his late forties, trim and toned like a runner, with a sharp patrician nose. Alice wondered why he looked so familiar, before realizing she'd seen him in a promotional photo on the facility's website, dancing with one of the residents.

The available room was on the second floor, a sharp left off the elevator and across from the in-house barbershop and beauty salon. She tried to imagine the Father there in that spare white room alone in front of his TV or sitting down for a meal in the dining hall downstairs, where yellow cloth napkins had been folded at each setting in the shape of swans. Amy raised her eyebrow. She was skeptical that the Father could navigate by himself to the common areas on the first floor. And how would he know when it was time to eat?

"We come upstairs and knock on all the doors," the general manager assured them.

After the tour, the general manager led them to his office for the hard sell. He explained that there was a base fee for room and board, and on top of that there was a point system for additional services the Father might need, with associated costs. They included:

Assist with dressing	15 points
Food cutting at meals	18 points
Reminders to toilet	4 points
Oral medications	36 points
Delusions	1 point
Time/place orientation	6 points

The numbers were making them uneasy, he could see that. He'd been here many times before with other family members.

"If I may be frank," the general manager said.

He explained that someone in the Father's condition was looking at a life expectancy of five, maybe seven years, max. He whipped out a sheet of paper and drew a chart with a jagged line.

"In his later years," he said, "your father may move to our memory unit, which means he'll be able to share a room. This would be a cost savings to you, and, by that stage, privacy really won't be an issue."

Alice thanked him. She told him he had given them "much food for thought." She shook his hand, thanked him again for the tour. Amy pressed the packet of information to her chest and they left. Alice hadn't been offended by his prognosis, just incredulous. Hadn't the Father proven himself impervious to death? Despite his drinking, his two-pack-a-day habit, his standard meals of Fritos and pork rinds confettied with peanuts, his lungs had remained pink and his blood pressure and cholesterol levels normal. Just like they were now.

Six months! How could anyone possibly turn into a dead person in so short a time?

PROJECT FOR A TRIP TO VENICE

The ride on the Alilaguna from the airport to the island was draped in fog. Alice peered through the window of the ferry, blinking hard as though to clear the mist away.

For months she'd sat on the knowledge that the Artist had been selected to represent Taiwan at the Venice Biennale. For months she'd been unsure if she should spend the money to go. If she didn't go to Venice, would she be missing essential plot points for the purposes of the Project? And yet the cost of Venice, the tourist hell trap of Venice. What if something happened to the Father while she was away in Venice? Maybe she didn't need to go at all. Kafka, after all, wrote an entire novel set in Amerika without ever having set foot here.

Then the thought of not going to Venice started to feel more and more like a future problem. The Project had gone fetid; it needed fresh air, to arrive somewhere. Maybe Venice could be that destination. The Artist was scheduled to give a closing talk there in November as part of his exhibition. Flights, it turned out, were extraordinarily cheap around that time because late fall was the peak season for acqua alta, the time of year when heavy rains typically flood the city. Factoring in costs for a place to stay, the whole trip would weigh heavily on her credit card debt. But this was the research budget for the Project, she decided, which relieved her from having to think of the trip as a vacation, a true squandering of money. She booked a single round-trip ticket.

From her seat on the ferry, Alice could see snatches of her surroundings through the fog—the edge of a landmass, the top of a tree. Everything looked otherworldly. Later, after she'd spent a full day in Venice, it occurred to her that the island was not otherworldly so much as other-timely. Out on a walk, she'd see a child chasing a pigeon down the stairs of a footbridge and her mind would flutter across the thousands of years and the thousands of children who must have chased a thousand pigeons across this very slab of flagstone.

She'd read in a guidebook that Venice had been built entirely on water using wooden columns and platforms cut from trees harvested and somehow transported from forests in Croatia. This was marvelous and nearly unfathomable. So was the silence of Venice, which wasn't really the absence of noise so much as the absence of the clamor of cities—the roar of cars, the bleating of horns and sirens, the hammering and buzz of construction, pop music thumping from open-air cafés. Without that din, Alice was astonished to hear water trickling from the spout of a public fountain. When she turned another corner, she could hear the wind tangling with a plastic shopping bag that hung from the doorknob of a flat.

In the evening as the crowds dissipated, Bangladeshi buskers took over the campos, selling cheap propeller toys, the airborne version of fidget spinners, which they set off high into the night sky to the delight of the children below. It was so quiet you could hear the whoosh of the toys in flight. The quiet was ancient. The quiet amplified ordinary life into plot: at night Alice's footfall on the narrow stone paths clattered like film noir.

The novelist Masahiko Shimada, who returns to Venice every few years or so from Japan, wrote that Venice seems not to change, which is how he knows it is he who is aging. The first time Shimada visited the city, he was twenty-eight. Now he was in his fifties. And yet, "the fact that I am able to get older is proof that I am still young," Shimada wrote, "unlike Venice, which no longer ages and is already well on its way to becoming a fossil."

One way Venice was changing was the thirty million tourists who descended on the island every year, even as the number of Venetians continued to dwindle. In recent years Venetians had deplored this imbalance with street protests. "Ocio ae gambe che go el careo!"—"Watch your feet, I've got my grocery cart with me!" they shouted in the dialect of their city, hoisting shopping trolleys and strollers above their heads—too heavy and clunky for carry-on or check-in—that marked them as locals. Some Venetians had even tried blocking cruise ships with a battalion of small boats.

But this late in the season, Alice saw no outward signs of protest apart from a handful of posters in the windows of apartment buildings of an ocean liner with a red bar slashed across it.

A pharmacy near the foot of the Rialto Bridge flashed an electronic sign that counted down the city's shrinking population: fifty-five thousand.

The dominion of shops that serviced tourists triggered in Alice a peculiar sub-genre of sightseeing: the search for businesses whose primary customers were Venetians. Strolling past innumerable storefronts hawking Murano glass and masquerade masks, she'd gawk with amazement at the sight of an ordinary hardware store in a side alley, a defiant barrel-chested carpet-cleaning machine planted in its window; or a butcher; a Laundromat; a gondola repair shop.

By the time Goethe visited, indeed by the time Thomas Mann checked into the Grand Hotel des Bains on the Lido, Venice was already a tourist trap. Venice was over then and continues to be over—over and over. Over as in, the Hotel des Bains was being converted to luxury condominiums over. Over as in, the Chinese were arriving in droves, even in the lowest of low season over. Chinese people, in fact, were nearly the only tourists Alice saw, floating in gondola convoys on the Grand Canal; clustered at the vaporetto landings; snapping selfies in front of the Bridge of Sighs. Most of them seemed to be from her parents' generation, the women with short sensible haircuts and the men in puffy coats and newsboy caps. It pleased Alice to think of elderly Chinese people enjoying their holiday or retirement, even as she fretted that they were stiffing the gondoliers with bad tips because they were—like her—shit people.

Shit people! A few years ago, the chef-owner of a celebrated Brooklyn restaurant, the type of establishment with a fixed menu at a fixed price and limited seating and impossible-to-get reservations, made headlines when his employees filed a lawsuit accusing him of stiffing them on overtime and tips. The complaint also claimed—and here's where things got spicy— that the chef discriminated against certain customers—namely, Asians—whom he allegedly referred to as "shit people."

Shit people! Alice hadn't realized how much this catch-phrase had been missing from her life. Shit people who dress head-to-toe in the latest designer labels yet possess no personal style of their own; foodie shit people with undeveloped palates who bucket-list Michelin-starred restaurants and take photographs of their plates; shit Olympic figure skaters whose routines demonstrate impressive technical proficiency and shit classical musicians trained to execute the most difficult, virtuosic passages—artless, soulless trophy chasers, all; shit people with multiple degrees from top-flight schools who will never be capable of true ingenuity; shit people at the water park wedged together within an inch of their lives in goofy flotation devices waiting for the artificial wave machine to carry them aloft. Like the nouveau riche tourists from America in the nineteenth century before them, today's Chinese tourists, flush with first-generation capital, were the new vulgarians.

At this moment in time, Alice found herself in a peculiar position as a citizen of a nation whose empire appeared to be crumbling (the current President, far from being the cause of this decline, was merely its symptom), even as her Chinese-ness allowed for loose affiliation with the empire that was rising. Or so she thought, as she got lost, tracing and retracing her steps from one alleyway to the next in a city that had been a global power seven centuries ago.

The Artist's afternoon talk was at the Fondazione Querini Stampalia, not far from Alice's rented room in a pensione above a costume store. As she crossed a small square, Alice was charmed to see children bouncing a rubber ball against the wall of a Baroque parish church, their laughter bouncing off the stone facades that enclosed the campo. At the Fondazione, Alice entered the event space, a softly lit room with theater seating, and joined about twenty other people in the audience.

On an elevated stage at one end of a long table sat the Artist, along with three other panelists and the moderator. The Artist was dressed in a pressed shirt that he wore buttoned at the wrists. He looked at ease. A young female translator sat at attention by his side with her hands in her lap.

The Artist was the first to speak. He explained his philosophy and approach to his work. (*Life is a life sentence. Life is passing time. Life is free thinking.*) To illustrate this point, he projected, across the enormous screen behind him, a Snoopy cartoon. Over a series of panels, Snoopy lies on top of his doghouse without incident or words. In the last panel, Snoopy, still atop the doghouse but with his head pointed in the opposite direction, reflects in a thought bubble: *Life has changed.* The audience chuckled.

Next to speak was a stern-faced philosopher from Frankfurt.

It's impossible, she said, to reflect on radical and emancipatory art, without raising the issue of labor—not to mention the subjectivities of time and place in which we live.

She described the Artist's performance works as propelled into a distant future, as though conceived *then* for an audience *now;* predictive of certain conditions that have consumed contemporary life—the 24/7 work cycle and our lives, regulated and accelerated by capitalism, under constant surveillance. The robots, the cloud, the data—we're living, she continued, in the age of the Fourth Industrial Revolution. Soon there won't be enough work for many people, and then what? These were the truths the Artist exposed by rendering life into the theatrical. Was it Rancière who said it is the artist who turns the ordinary into the extraordinary? Because in the Artist's work, the line between art and life has completely eroded: to live is to perform; to perform is to live. What does it mean, then, in our post-factual moment, to keep a promise to oneself and others about a Life Practice, to perform an act of faith that seems so alien at a time when deceit and disappointment have become the forces that govern the laws of life?

When the philosopher finished, the audience clapped, which she did not appear to acknowledge in any way, just as she had kept her eyes focused on her notes throughout her talk, as though to separate herself from the vulgar yet necessary display of public performance. There was a respectful pause and some shuffling of papers. An art theorist from Taiwan, a man who looked to be in his thirties, with a thick sweep of black hair and wire-framed glasses, spoke next.

He began with a reflection on the subject of deserted islands. After the Communist takeover of China, Taiwan became a deserted island of a kind, expelled by the United Nations. Soon after, Japan cut off diplomatic relations, followed by the United States and others. One could argue, he said, that Taiwan's history of being deserted stretches back to the late 1800s in the First Sino-Japanese War when the Qing Dynasty ceded the island to Japan.

He paused. What can we learn from this recurrence of desertions?

This history, the theorist argued, seeded in the Taiwanese people skepticism toward the very notion of modern nations. The Artist's work, he argued, is implicitly connected with this era when Taiwan became an orphan within the global community. The performance pieces that thrust him apart from the rest of society—being locked in a cage, constrained by a ferociously unyielding time clock, exiled from the art world and the community he had made for himself—were manifestations of this abandonment.

In Deleuze's concept of deserted islands, the island is constituted not by geography but by the imaginary, he said, just as in the Artist's work—and here he made reference to the Artist's method of devising mental maps to delineate the spaces of domestic living, both in the confines of his cage and in the streets of Lower Manhattan. Just as Robinson Crusoe painstakingly re-created the trappings of bourgeois life from scavenging and cultivating his deserted island, the artist, too, must re-create everything based on the reserves of capitalism. He has to re-begin . . .

The last panelist was a British social anthropologist with the tweedy, disheveled aspect of a professional thinker. Peering over his reading glasses, he began by announcing that he had only met the Artist just a few hours earlier, and, in preparation for this talk, he had read some background materials about the Artist's work, and just that morning had gone to see his exhibit at the Taiwanese Pavilion.

After this crash course, the anthropologist said the question that had surfaced top of mind for him was this: Has this man got a sense of humor? Because what he saw at the exhibit was a man who looked tired and miserable and sleepy. A man in a cage, his head buried in his hands. A man tied to another artist and looking rather fed up with his colleague. Is there humor? the anthropologist wondered. Is there release? Is there a freedom of the spirit in this work?

So imagine how pleased he was when he finally did meet the Artist, who greeted him with a radiant smile. That smile gave ballast to his conviction that the Artist's work does, in fact, raise, rather than repress, the human spirit. How can this be so, when his performances impose on themselves a repressive regime? That is the central question embodied in his work.

And here the anthropologist made a meta-gesture toward the activity of the panel at hand.

When confronted with work like this, particularly if the artist is not inclined to do much interpretation himself, legions of academics and critics tend to descend on it like a murder of crows, each eager to offer an interpretation—whether it's to claim the work as a critique of capitalism or neoliberalism, military oppression, and so forth—that spins on the idea that the artist is most certainly making a point.

No doubt, he said, underlying the work is a great unhappiness with how the world works. But to marry it to a singular interpretation turns the art into a mere instrumental force. And yet the only way to change the world in the long term is to do work that *is what it is*—not work that stands for something else. The work must reach beyond the instrumental and become exemplary.

The anthropologist paused. I want to describe a concept of waste, he said, by way of anecdote.

One day at the university where he teaches, he and his colleagues arrived to discover that all the waste bins had been removed with no notice. Everyone was told they'd have to make "alternative arrangements" for their garbage. The reasoning for the abrupt banishing of bins was that waste was seen as a sign of inefficiency. Ideally, all inputs should be turned into outputs, data and knowledge into published work, all without a shred of waste!

What the bean counters hadn't understood, the anthropologist went on, is how inefficiency is the very essence of creative practice. Whether one is a blacksmith or a poet, one is bound to produce enormous quantities of waste to make a thing. Wasting time only has a negative connotation when we accept the narrow idea that time is money: wasted time is wasted money and therefore must be inefficient.

But what if we were to adopt a different understanding of production and time? What if wasting time were not negative at all, but the very essence of what it means to be creative and live a life? The production of such a life would have nothing to do with commodity.

Turning his head slightly to face the Artist, the anthropologist said he understood the Artist's maxim—that he worked hard to waste time—to mean that he was working hard to live, and that the living of life had to come first. He, too, cited Deleuze, specifically his thinking on immanence. The anthropologist recounted a passage from Dickens that Deleuze himself used to define this concept:

In the Dickens story, a man nearly drowns in a boating accident before he is saved by strangers. The man, we learn, is an unsavory, disreputable character, yet his saviors, who know nothing of this, gather with hushed reverence over his sickbed as the reprobate hovers feverishly between life and death. When the man awakens and reveals himself to be the nasty person that he is, the spell is broken; the reverence he commanded hours earlier vanishes.

In that man's early, liminal state can be found a pure immanence that does not emanate *in* something or *to* something, but is absolute, and nothing else. Deleuze called this a complete power, a complete bliss. Life goes from A to B to C—that's one way of seeing it, the anthropologist said, his voice rising slightly as his argument crested. But there is another life, a more essentialist life that runs between these points, like a river that flows between two banks. Deleuze describes this quality of life, its immanence, as very fragile. It is the life we feel on the borderline of death—it is life playing with death—hanging by the slightest thread. That kind of living is like walking on cobwebs. Your work, the anthropologist said, turning again to make eye contact with the Artist at the end of the long table, is this river . . .

The audience applauded and rustled in their seats. A brief intermission was announced, and people began spilling out into the foyer, where a small reception had been arranged with sweets and coffee. As Alice constructed a ziggurat of cookies on a tiny white dish, she watched, from the corner of her eye, the Artist posing for photographs with other Chinese people. She stood alone with her tottering snack and tiny cup of espresso for what felt like an eternity before everyone was called back into the theater for the Q&A.

The first person to raise her hand was a middle-aged woman with a French accent a few rows behind Alice. The bangles on her wrists clinked as she gesticulated.

It is really shocking, the woman said, her tone wounded, indignant, that the Artist's work would be considered art.

She compared the Artist's performances to the spectacle entertainments of gladiators in the Roman Empire. She demanded to know the Artist's immigration status: Were you a refugee or an illegal immigrant? Why didn't you try to get another job? Did you try to get help from the government? Surely your art was a political gesture and not an artistic one. It is insane what you do.

Necks twisted in the room. The air crackled. Alice gripped her pen suspended above her notebook.

The Artist attempted an answer in the dialectic mode: *When I say one thing, you have to think in the opposite direction to get the whole thing. When I'm talking about wasting time, when I answer you one way, you have to think of it the opposite way. I only can say one thing.*

Then from one of the first few rows an Asian woman spoke up. Alice saw mostly the back of her head, a smart bob balanced on a slender, elegant neck. The woman explained that she was a native of Taiwan and lived in Brussels now. She told the Artist that she had first heard about his exploits as a girl. She remembered reading the headlines when he was arrested in New York during the making of *Outdoor Piece*. She mused that it had taken forty years for his work to achieve the recognition that he now enjoyed, and it had taken her thirty years to understand it. So now, she said with a smile, we are equal.

From the seat next to her, an older man, his silver hair buzzed close to his skull, cleared his throat to speak. By way of prefacing his comments, he explained that he was not an artist himself, nor did he make it a habit to follow all the goings-on in the art world. In fact, he has a Ph.D. in chemistry. He was here this afternoon because of his daughter.

I think you have done something very good, he addressed the Artist approvingly, in that manner of old men assured that their opinion will be taken for wisdom.

You have created emotion, the man continued. The work touched me and touched other people, and it is good. The human being is the master of the earth, he said. Yet we are becoming the slaves of time. In the past, ninety percent of our time was spent planting and creating food. Now we've gone way beyond that, and yet we imagine ourselves to be extremely busy!

A voice called out. It was the same unhappy woman in the back.

Are we all aware of an incident that occurred at the start of the Biennale? the woman demanded. A group of young Belgians—naked and perhaps drunk—had leapt into the canal. The mayor of Venice responded with fury, rightly so, by slamming the young people with fines.

The woman then addressed the Artist directly. Art like yours—if it can even be considered art—is just the sort of act that would inspire such rash, self-harming behavior in others. This risk of contagion must be stopped. The Belgians were not artists, just young and drunk; this made them highly suggestible and susceptible to self-destructive behaviors, she said, her voice warming up to her own outrage. Allowing an artist to damage himself is dangerous!

At that moment the panel moderator, a rakish, bearded British art critic with a leonine head of hair, descended swiftly like a schoolyard monitor and began steering the conversation to more neutral territory.

The highest function of art, he reminded everyone in a calm but authoritative voice, is to question what art fundamentally is. As the tension in the room dissipated like a fart, the moderator hurriedly thanked the panelists and audience for the richness and quality of the talk and drew the event to a close.

Now it was late in the afternoon. Alice took a short vaporetto ride to the Giardini, where most of the Biennale pavilions were housed. It was the last day of the festival: the art world crowd had long ago come and gone, and there seemed to be relatively few people there except for groups of Italian schoolchildren and straggling tourists like her. The ground was damp with dirt and fallen leaves; the mood, vespertine. Even the Doberman pinschers at the German Pavilion, one of the year's most buzzed-about exhibits, were padding about in their metal cage like common housepets instead of oppressing people with their loud barking as everyone hoped they would.

Alice made the rounds, snapping a few photographs here and there, and then took leave of the area to see the Artist's exhibit at the Taiwanese Pavilion, which was housed at the Palazzo delle Prigioni, a stolid white limestone building on the promenade at a considerable remove from the Giardini.

Alice climbed two flights of stone stairs to the gallery space of the Palazzo. One wall of the largest of the rooms was covered entirely by the time cards the Artist had punched every hour for the duration of *Time Clock Piece* more than three decades ago. Projected against a bare wall was the six-minute film he'd made of the piece, playing on an endless loop. Alice waited for the film to start from the beginning so she could record with her phone the film the Artist had made from his photographs—for what purpose she didn't yet know, except that it felt essential to the Project.

But of greatest interest to Alice was a glass vitrine that contained nearly everything the Artist carried on his person during the year of *Outdoor Piece*. Among the collection: a transistor radio; Swiss Army knife; spoon; pair of small scissors; toothbrush; plastic soap container; three pens (black, green, red); knit cap; pair of woolen gloves; tan-colored canvas coat; winter coat with a fur-lined hood; pair of jeans; two pairs of socks; winter boots; black Converse sneakers; fisherman's sweater; rubber handball; and a knapsack with a weather thermometer dangling from it. The clothing appeared shiny and hardened with dirt; black streaks ran along the collars and shirtsleeves. All the objects gave off the air of having been exhumed.

The last room in the show led her back to the front of the gallery, where she nearly did a double-take: the Artist himself was seated there on a folding chair. He sat with an ankle propped against his knee forming a rhombus with the air of a man surveying the street from his front porch. For a second Alice half thought he was part of the installation, that visitors were meant to travel through the rooms of the gallery and their archives of the past to be confronted, at the end, with the real-life incarnation of the Artist in the present.

Alice and the Artist looked at each other; in that narrow space, it was impossible not to. Did he recognize her? Surely he had no reason to remember their chance encounter at his restaurant. If James were here with her, she thought, he'd be jabbing the small of her back and hissing, *Now's your chance. Tell him you've come all this way and you're working on a project about him, for god's sake!*

But James wasn't here. Alice turned to face the Artist. She murmured, "Thank you," in a low voice, and bowed slightly. He dipped his head in acknowledgment. What she wanted to say was too big for saying. The two words she'd managed to get out were its context.

Alice read in a news article saying that the Artist had initially thought to turn down the invitation to represent Taiwan in the Biennale. Then he changed his mind. He said he realized that if he didn't say yes to Venice, he might never see Venice in his lifetime. Alice had thought the same thing about her own trip to Venice. Once she found herself in Venice, she became preoccupied with the idea that she'd probably never return to Venice, given how little she traveled and how many other places there were in the world where she'd never been and probably ought to go instead of revisiting places like Venice. Such were the thoughts of a person who was, by actuarial tables, most likely halfway dead.

The Artist, interviewed about his time in Venice, said that, during the day, he performed the activities required of him, greeting people, responding to questions. But in the evening when his obligations were finished, he ate dinner alone and returned to his hotel room alone. Every night in Venice he ate the same thing: spaghetti alle vongole. It wasn't that he didn't manage to enjoy himself. *Probably that's my life*, he mused. *My real life existence is that way.*

The Palazzo delle Prigioni was completed in the 1600s to relieve overcrowding at the prisons in the Doge's Palace. On the tour she took of the palace, Alice paused on the covered bridge that connected the two prisons across a narrow canal and peered through the thick bars at the sun's reflection flashing on the waters of the lagoon. Marco Polo, she'd read somewhere, might not have written *The Travels of Marco Polo* if it hadn't been for prison overcrowding. Three years after Marco Polo returned from the Far East, Venice and Genoa were at war and Marco Polo was captured in a battle at sea and thrown into a dungeon. While imprisoned, he told his life story to his cellmate, a native of Pisa who became his ghostwriter.

Viktor Shklovsky, the literary theorist, critic, and writer, has imagined Marco Polo in his twilight years, strolling along the algae-streaked canals with the aimlessness of a man whose greatest adventures and achievements are behind him. On his deathbed, a priest urges the old merchant to repent for the fabrications he's told and for daring to suggest that the foreign lands of the East were grander and more sophisticated than those of Europe. Marco Polo—whose nickname among the locals is Marco Millione, for the countless tall tales he's spun—refuses. "I moved backward not only in space, but also in time," he says in Shklovsky's account. "All that we see here is already history for China."

Shklovsky, who'd survived the Bolsheviks, Stalinism, revolution, multiple wars, and multiple periods of political exile and outlived most of his family and friends, no doubt felt immensely for Marco Polo the old man. Shklovsky ends his second-to-last book, *Bowstring: On the Dissimilarity of the Similar*—another one of his indefatigable montages of memoir, literary criticism, history, and biography—on a wistful note. He has a wish: that the manuscript taking shape under his pen be set and bound by the venerable publishing house Aldine Press, once the most powerful and celebrated printing house in Venice, its signature colophon a dolphin curled around an anchor. Shklovsky used to own a few Aldine books, all gone now. There's a slight complication to his wish, he concedes, which is that the press hasn't been in business for over five hundred years.

Some critics have come down on *Bowstring* for being yet another vessel for Shklovsky to rehash his pet theories and ideas, among them, ostranenie, or to "make strange." This was the term Shklovsky coined to describe the formal decisions an artist makes to shake people from the stupor of received meaning so that they might emerge trembling and radiant from the encounter, and find themselves capable of insurrection. This was the transfiguring purpose of art. It's true Shklovsky makes his point about ostranenie over and over again across multiple books. What of it? Most people are probably only capable of one or two big ideas in their lifetimes. Alice, for one, was starting to think that her only subject was time, and however she might construct provocations around this subject, her only real idea about time was that it passes and that this is sad.

SUICIDE

After her trip to Venice and while going over her notes and graphic files for the Project, Alice got it in her head that she should read Deleuze. But, as always happened when she attempted to read philosophy, comprehension eluded her. She quickly devolved to consulting secondary sources, which included listening to a reductive podcast of bantering philosophy bros that made her feel even more regretful about the limits of her intellect.

Here's what she learned: Not long after publishing his essays on immanence, Deleuze killed himself by jumping from the window of his fourth-story apartment in Paris. His health problems—including a weak heart and a chronic breathing problem that made talking and writing difficult—were widely believed to have played a role in his decision to take his own life. This decision seemed to sync with his conviction that life was worth living so long as one possessed the will to will, to use one's power to the limit. It wasn't worth being alive, according to Deleuze, if one was no longer capable of acting and *becoming worthy of what happens*.

"There is but one truly serious philosophical problem," Camus wrote in *The Myth of Sisyphus*, "and that is suicide."

Suicide is the subject and title of the book Édouard Levé is best known for. Levé previewed the concept for the book years earlier in *Oeuvres*. It's Number 527:

"A book describes the life of its author in the present tense. It is factual recollection up until the moment of writing, then fiction up until the author's death. Both of the book's parts, separated as they are by the weeks of its writing, have the cold style of an official statement. Later, the author can decide to live what he had foretold."

Ten days after mailing the manuscript of *Suicide* to his publisher, Levé killed himself.

To know this chain of events and to read *Suicide* is to feel illicit somehow—as though Levé premeditated your complicity in a crime. But what is the crime?

Sontag wrote in her journal that she didn't want her life to be reduced to her work. But nor did she want her work to be reduced to her life.

"My work is too austere," she wrote. "My life is a brutal anecdote."

Before he left Taiwan for New York, the Artist painted a portrait of his father as the old man lay on his deathbed.

Alice was afraid that if she didn't put the Father inside a project, he would disappear from all time.

The Father lacked the nerve to kill himself. But maybe, very slowly, he had been doing so all along.

The Artist said: *It doesn't really matter how I spent time: time is still passing. Wasting time is my basic attitude to life; it is a gesture of dealing with the absurdity between life and time.*

Levé was once asked in an interview, "How does art serve you?"

"It lets me love life while preparing to die," he replied.

ASYLUM

It was around this time Alice's next-door neighbor sent her an email.

The email said her cat had entered his home several times that week through a cat door. Her cat had sprayed his closet, clothes, shoes, rugs, and furniture. He'd also sprayed the back door, his patio area, plants, etc. He'd been spraying the backyard, in fact, for some time. But now it's getting out of control, the neighbor wrote.

She took the cat to the vet. The cat, it should be said, must not have had cancer all those months ago or he'd be dead by now. Most likely he had irritable bowel syndrome, which Alice kept in check with medications and a special protein diet of canned duck or rabbit, the cost of which made her feel ludicrous. The trip to the vet this time was to determine whether a testicle had failed to descend when he was first neutered, which might explain the spraying. The vet quickly disavowed that theory. A certain number of cats that are fixed continue to spray, the vet explained, and her cat was, regrettably, a member of this minority faction. Alice suspected the spraying was the reason the cat had come to be abandoned by his original owners in the first place.

Why the cat was spraying now was a mystery. Maybe it was simply that he'd discovered that the neighbor's cat door was a portal to a new territory, one rich with reserves of unrestricted kibble. His spraying was a manifestation of his imperialist tendencies.

But now this unfortunate marking behavior had doomed him to a life indoors. That the cat did not know he had condemned himself saddened her. For the remainder of his days, he'd never be able to roam freely outside. The whole situation made Alice think of the Father, silly and distasteful as it was to do so. The Father, too, was living a life of confinement. Instead of spraying, the father drank too much. Spraying and drinking resulted in the same fate for cat and man: the loss of their freedom.

The sociologist Erving Goffman characterizes the asylum as a *total institution*—a place where individuals, cut off from society for an appreciable period of time, together lead an enclosed, formally administered round of life.

Once, the Father asked Alice in a shy, wistful voice whether it would be possible for him to move away from the facility and live somewhere else. Alice had held her breath, afraid he would say he wanted to move in with her or Amy. It turned out what he had in mind was the type of place where he remembered his aunt Bonnie had lived out her last years.

"You know," he said, "what people used to refer to as an old folks' home."

"But you're in one right now," she said with brittle brightness.

This was true and not true. Early on, before the Father's dementia got much worse, Alice had also had a similar vision of a peaceful place where old people chatted over meals, sunned themselves in gardens with blankets across their laps, played checkers and canasta. But since then, she'd toured the inside of many nursing homes and had yet to witness a single game of canasta.

If the cat had to live the rest of his life confined, she reasoned, at least he was getting on in years and his future wouldn't be long. In fact, the cat was fourteen years old—eighty by human years, according to the internet. The Father was old, too. Although in his case it was not his age that was the problem but that the frontal lobes of his brain were eroding like time-lapse footage of melting ice caps.

The problem with asylums: One can't control how the other residents behave. The Father did not want to be surrounded by sad people acting strangely. Alice remembered at the nursing facility in Oakland how he'd tried at first to chat with other patients. But each time he realized the person was not all right in the head in some way, he would draw back without another word and limit his interaction to a polite nod if he passed them in the hallway. Now he'd become a sad person who acted strangely.

Goffman wrote an entire a book on the subject of total institutions, drawing partly on his experiences as a young man working at a mental ward in Washington, D.C. In *Asylums: Essays on the Social Situation of Mental Patients and Other Inmates*, he argues that all spaces of confinement—think nursing homes, orphanages, convents, internment camps, homeless shelters, prisons, ICE detention centers, refugee camps, rehab centers, Foxconn, Guantánamo, all share a set of common characteristics:

1. Each phase of the member's daily activity is carried on in the immediate company of a large batch of others, all of whom are treated alike and required to do the same thing together.

In the beginning of his time at the asylum on Solace Place, the Father was wheeled at least once a day to a common room where there was a piano, a TV, and a large fish tank. Fixed to the wall were activity boards—faucets, doorknobs, and light switches—for residents to practice with so they wouldn't lose their familiarity and facility with instruments they no longer had any use for. Reflexively, when she thought no one was looking, Alice took a quick snapshot of the boards with her phone for the purposes of the Project, not that anyone cared.

All the residents in the asylum gathered in the room around lunchtime. Most were wheeled in; a few could walk, but not many. They waited around a number of round tables, sometimes for forty-five minutes, for their meals to arrive. The waiting, too, was considered a form of activity.

2. All phases of the day's activities are tightly scheduled, with one activity leading at a prearranged time into the next, the whole sequence of activities being imposed from above by a system of explicit formal rulings and a body of officials.

The first time Alice saw the Father in the common room surrounded by a large batch of others, she was stunned. He had always insisted he wanted to be by himself, to watch TV alone, eat his meals alone. He hated the noise of other people, which set his brain on edge and made him irritable. But there he was, stationed at a round table, lifting a fork to his mouth. She watched him through a glass pane for several minutes with a mixture of dread and pride like a parent observing her child adjusting to his first day of school.

On the mounted TV played an old-fashioned variety show featuring country music performers. At least that's who she assumed they were, based on the hairstyles and lapels and the long gowns on the women.

She flashed back to a time in another common space in a different asylum—the SNF in Oakland. That asylum was older and poorer. But it did have Netflix.

She remembered sitting with the Father in an activity room one afternoon in front of a big-screen TV with two other men. The lights were off and they were watching a remarkably violent film. Every other scene seemed to feature bone-crunching fistfights and AK-47 carnage. At the time, she was both shocked and amused that a film like this would be playing at a supposed sanctuary of healing and recuperation. The men seemed to enjoy it.

In the memory unit at Solace Place, however, the TV aired nothing except anodyne variety shows, which made her appreciate the freedom the residents at the Oakland asylum were afforded. They could at least choose their own dumb movies. The absenting of violent entertainment struck her as a loss of manhood.

3. The various enforced activities are brought together into a single rational plan purportedly designed to fulfill the official aims of the institution.

Three times a day, covered meals were rolled into the memory care unit on multi-tiered carts. Diapers were checked every two hours. There were set schedules for bathing, nail clipping, shaving. A bedside button could be pressed to express a need or request, but most people in the unit, like the Father, could no longer comprehend its purpose and shouted or cried instead.

In another era the Father might have ended up at Agnes Developmental Center a few miles away, a sprawling Mediterranean Revival–style compound of stucco and tile that dated back to the late 1800s when it first opened as an asylum for the "chronic insane." As with other mental asylums of the period, people were committed there for any number of alleged deviant and disturbed behaviors, according to hospital records, from epilepsy to vagrancy and masturbation. It was home to *imbeciles, dotards, idiots, drunkards, simpletons, fools*—a place where *burdens to families* could be sloughed off.

Alice had some history with Agnes. As a high school student, she used to volunteer there on occasion, hoping to demonstrate to institutions of higher learning that she was thoughtful and kindhearted.

The volunteering sessions typically lasted an hour and involved handing out seasonally themed cookies in the shape of pumpkins or Christmas trees. The experience was nothing like she thought it would be, no one seemed remotely brightened by the whole glum affair. Most of the residents looked down at their feet, stared vacantly in the distance, or worked their jaws in silence. They didn't look as though they dressed themselves. Otherwise, she didn't remember much about the place except a little girl who was born, the volunteers were told, without a mouth. The girl no longer lived at home, if she ever did. The Father no longer lived at home. He lived in a home.

One distinction between living at home and living in a home is the ability to escape from large batches of others. The Father had long ago stopped being shy or embarrassed about having his briefs changed or being seen naked in the bath. This didn't mean he'd lost perspective on the difference between private and public: he no longer called Alice by their family's name for her—Mei—as he had their whole lives together.

Some years ago, Agnes shut down, part of a national trend of mental institutions closing, replaced by smaller care facilities that blended more easily into the community. The last time Alice checked, the Agnes compound had been turned into a tech company's corporate headquarters. She'd more or less forgotten about it, although all these years later she still occasionally found herself thinking about the little girl with no mouth and wondering what was in the center of her head in place of a mouth. Was the space packed solid with matter, like a pot filled with dirt?

4. In our society, [asylums] are the forcing houses for changing persons; each is a natural experiment on what can be done to the self.

The above being one of Goffman's all-time weirdest sentences.

The Father was a *changing person*, no question. The *changing* compels the *forcing*, which can, in turn, force other kinds of changing, bad changes that make things worse. This describes the essential conundrum of the asylum.

In a moment of lucidity, the Father once turned to Alice, who was visiting again from across the country, and asked, "I'm never getting out of here, am I?"

She looked right into his eyes. She would give him the truth, not the false cheer she knew he hated, and said, "No, I don't think you are. You're too sick."

What can be done to the self—embedded in the syntax is the inherent derangement of the asylum. The more things are done to the self, the more one loses what Goffman called the *personal economy of action.*

Which, in the Father's case, was to watch his favorite shows on Netflix, chain-smoke, and drink Jim Beam.

What the cat wanted to do was to kill small creatures, defend and test the boundaries of his territory.

Yet how easily one adjusts when there is a recession in one's personal economy of action. The cat did not cry all day to be let out as Alice feared he would. Mostly he seemed preoccupied with marshaling his next meal. Sometimes Alice would open a window for the cat, leaving the screen shut. The cat's entire being would thrust forward—eyes, whiskers, ears, nostrils—every nerve ending thrilling at the phenomena of the world. But more and more the cat spent a great deal of time sleeping, like the Father.

TRACE EVIDENCE

Here she should mention that, for months now, she'd been accumulating surveillance reports on the Father.

10:27   *Clocked in > Received patient awake and talking*
         about his little girl > Folded his sheets and pulled
         his clothes in place
10:40   *Encourage him to drink water from time to time*
10:50   *Brushed his teeth and gave him a shave > Wiped*
         his face with a warm cloth > Wiped his hands with
         antibacterial hand wipes > Cleaned his ears

The reports became a thing after the Father did something bad, or rather, a series of bad things: he'd raised his arm and threatened to strike a nurse; he tried to bite someone's finger; he got out of bed on his own and fell to the floor. The staff at Solace Place strongly suggested that Amy and Alice retain an additional caregiver and were given the number of a private service to call.

Was this an ultimatum? By then the sisters had read up on the law: a nursing home can't easily remove a resident against their wishes. But there was no point in making enemies. This was what the Father's house money was for: caregiving and safekeeping. Carekeeping? The caregiver service, they learned, required their employees to send daily reports of the Father's ~~progress~~ behaviors. These reports, sent via text, described the Father's activities of daily living, from his bathing schedule to what, and how much, he ate at every meal. The reports doubled as evidence of their labor.

11:18   *I gave him some peanut butter crackers for snack >*
         Encourage him to drink water
11:36   *Patient went back to sleep*
12:30   *Lunch is served with corned beef, rice, veggies and*
         fruits. Patient ate 100% of his meal including
         fluids. Encourage him to drink lots of water.
2:00   *I took my break and came back at 2:15*

After a few weeks of different caregivers coming through, the sisters settled on Elpidio as the caregiver who would come most often. They liked that he sometimes included details in his reports like the topics that the Father talked about. They learned from chatting with Elpidio that he commuted every morning by UberPool from Fremont, and that he and his wife had both been nurses in the Philippines. Their daughters were grown, one in Singapore and the other in Toronto. But the Father remained the center of conversation between Elpidio and the sisters. He was the reason their lives had crossed.

3:15 *Patient woke up*
   > Encourage him to drink water and he is talking
   about the army

5:30 *Dinner is served with bread, pasta, veggies and*
   fruits. Patient finished 100% of his meal including
   fluids. Encourage him to drink water

Alice used to half dread the ping of her phone that signaled the arrival of a new report. Her MO was to scan the entire report hurriedly to make sure nothing terrible had happened. Then she would read the contents more slowly, savoring the details. Not that the details revealed much. Like the Artist's punch cards, cassette tapes, and maps, the reports authenticated events in time but were otherwise frustratingly opaque, delivering none of the information she actually wanted: What was the Father thinking? Was he ever happy? What did he live for, or was he beyond such thoughts?

Over time, receiving and reading the reports became part of her daily routine. She'd catch herself reviewing them like a researcher in lab, taking mental notes and making adjustments as needed based on the data. (*Order more petroleum jelly. Remind nurses he doesn't like protein shakes.*) Sometimes, after reading the recap, she'd compared notes with Amy as they tuned in to the show of his life.

6:27 *Patient is asleep*
   > Clocked out

THE OLDEST LIVING POLAR BEAR
IN AMERICA

The Father was sleeping when Alice arrived that morning at Solace Place. Someone had drawn the blue curtains across the sliding doors in his room and the early November sun shone through them, casting a stippled pattern across his bed. On the tack board next to the Father's head was a collage made from magazine cutouts of vegetables and a chef bent over a frying pan—probably the work of the memory unit's activity director, who must have figured out from talking with the Father that he once enjoyed cooking.

Alice settled into a chair and scrolled the news on her phone, pausing on a story about a polar bear who had just turned thirty-seven, which made her the oldest living polar bear in America. The bear's name was Coldilocks and she lived in the Philadelphia Zoo.

When the Father opened his eyes, Alice drew the curtain back to coax his interest in the world outside. He wasn't having it. Instead, they sat companionably together watching TV. On-screen, a reality show involving two men setting out somewhere with rifles, to hunt most likely. Something about the show stirred the Father's imagination. He gestured at Alice to lean in close.

The Father could no longer speak in complete sentences but it was possible to piece together his meaning like a mosaic from tiles of loose nouns and verbs. With considerable energy, he described his plan to survive some kind of apocalypse or hostile invasion. The plan involved making sure there was plenty of water—that was critical. He muttered something about peanut butter and roller skates and gestured repeatedly at the space under his bed: that was where he kept his rifle. He and Alice working as a team would need to round up the others, including his brother in Alabama.

"Oh, okay," Alice said, nodding. "Got it."

In the wild, polar bears can live to be twenty-three. Klondike, who had been Coldilock's companion at the zoo for three decades, died at age thirty-four. As a special birthday treat, Coldilocks received a cake made of peanut butter, honey, raisins, and fish. Was the Father only alive because he lived in captivity?

FACE TIME

For days Alice barely left her apartment, emerging only for liters of Diet Coke and plastic tubs of pre-made Asian noodles from the corner grocery. Since returning from California, she'd been on deadline, tightening up the latest installment for *Bring On the Feels*. The episode was a story about an organ donation. The donor was an ex-Marine who'd died in a car crash. The recipient was a chubby kid, nineteen or twenty years old, with a goofy grin and an advanced case of Type 2 diabetes. The donated organ was a kidney.

The organ recipient was responsible for much of the footage Alice was editing, which he shot with his smartphone. He recorded himself reflecting on his diabetes; his love for his hard-working parents who had sacrificed so much for him; his methods for staying positive when he was down; the joy he felt the day he learned that a kidney had come through. He and his family had prayed and prayed, and now the dream was real!

The money shot in the segment was the first-ever face-to-face encounter between the organ recipient and the organ donor's widow. Even though Alice had seen the scene more than a dozen times, her eyes watered every time despite herself. The kid towers over the widow, who is thin and papery. Grief has aged her. After a heartfelt embrace, they stand apart, facing each other. The widow has her palms pressed against the kid's love handles, gently, as one might touch a pregnant woman's belly or a large vase. Under different circumstances, her gesture would have come across as overly intimate. But her husband's kidney was pumping inside another man's body: this gave her rights. You could see the kid sensed this, too. He let himself be the breathing, beating vessel of this strange reunion.

Alice finished the edit, changed out of her sweatpants into a pair of black jeans, and dabbed furiously at the cat hair on her legs with a strip of Scotch tape. Her plan was to drop in on her client contact so they could go over the edits on the segment together. Alice was being handled now by Mona, a mid-level account director whose job it was to attend project management meetings so her bosses didn't have to. For the past few months, Mona's emails had become more sporadic and with none of the friendly exclamation points that marked their earlier correspondences. Alice figured she could use the face time.

When she arrived at the marketing firm's office, she was kept waiting in the front lobby. Alice always felt sorry for the young woman—it was always a woman—whose job it was to sit alone in casual business attire at the reception desk, a small island isolated from the mainland of her coworkers, sometimes with a houseplant or a jar of candy for company. Maybe the receptionist preferred it that way, using the isolation to her advantage to work secretly on her own projects. The receptionist at this office, who Alice guessed was only a few years out of college, stared at the screen in front of her and tapped urgently on her keyboard. Alice gazed at the Blue Note album covers decorating the wall until Mona strode into the room. She was a strikingly tall woman of impeccable proportions, which she offset with a pair of clunky glasses that nevertheless reinforced the indestructibility of her good looks.

Mona explained that an emergency situation with another client had come up, and she wouldn't have time to meet after all. The shape of her eyebrows conveyed warmth and regret. She said she appreciated the fact that Alice dropped by, and they absolutely should get together for coffee soon.

Alice smiled. Of course. No worries. But she was kind of worried. Her mind flickered on the box of nondenominational holiday cards in her desk drawer at home that she'd bought with the intention of cultivating greater professional intimacy with the people who paid her. *Are we drifting apart?* she wanted to half joke but didn't.

It was lunchtime. The elevator was crowded with office workers in a dizzying array of designer sneakers. The combination of their youth and the proximity to food made the air inside the cabin vibrate with the giddiness of recess. Alice stood with her back pressed against the back of the elevator. When she stepped out and felt the sun on her face, she was seized, despite the cold, by the sudden desire to have the sandwich she'd packed outdoors overlooking the water, and not in a café hunched over a laptop and iced coffee as she'd originally planned. She veered right, to the street that would take her to the edge of the East River.

She wasn't entirely sure, but she believed this street was a location shot from *Film*, one of Buster Keaton's last movies.

Samuel Beckett wrote the screenplay, his only one, inspired by a dictum by the Irish philosopher Bishop Berkeley: "esse est percipi"—to be is to be perceived. There are two leads in the film: Keaton plays O, the perceived, and the camera itself plays E, the perceiver. Keaton hadn't been anyone's first choice for the role. After several other actors took a pass, Beckett suggested casting him, as he'd once pushed for Keaton to be cast in *Waiting for Godot*. (To that offer, Keaton had said thanks, but no thanks.) Beckett intuited, as had James Agee, that Buster's *thing*, unique among the silent comedians, was his refusal to allow sentimentality to gum up his work. "Thrumming under the grandeur and foolishness of his comedy was a freezing whisper not of pathos but of melancholia," Agee wrote.

By the time he signed on to *Film*, Keaton was in his seventies and an incorrigible alcoholic. He'd read Beckett's six-page script and didn't think much of it. He couldn't imagine the movie lasting longer than four minutes, tops. Before production began, Beckett arranged to meet Keaton in person in a Manhattan hotel room. It was a hot July day in 1964. The meeting was awkward. Little of importance was exchanged and Keaton spent the whole time drinking beer and watching a baseball game on TV. He was a fiend for television: it was his habit to watch eight or nine hours a day while chain-smoking and dealing himself hands of solitaire.

The filming of the opening outdoor scenes along the waterfront in Brooklyn was plagued by the sopping summer heat and production problems. Keaton's character has an unpleasant run-in with strangers in the street and flees, only to be cornered by an angry neighbor in the vestibule of his building. Everyone recoils from O, and he from them. Once inside his shabby room, he banishes a Chihuahua and a cat, throws a cloth over the bird-cage, and covers the mirror with a drape.

He then turns his attention to a sheaf of photographs: they are of himself and people he knows. These he rips to pieces. Relieved to be alone at last, he collapses in a chair, only to encounter a phantasm—his double—observing him impassively as his own mouth gapes open with horror. The film ends as it begins, with a close-up of Keaton's eye. The camera zooms in so tightly that the flesh of the eyelid is revealed as a series of tiny folds, shiny as turned meat.

By all accounts, Keaton was exemplary on set. He hit his marks and did as many retakes as requested without objection. It's possible Keaton did the film because he needed the pay-check: decent money for a three-week shoot. All his life he'd never been good with money. He spent extravagantly when he had it and just as much when he didn't. Or maybe it wasn't about the money at all but because acting gigs at his age were hard to come by and he didn't know what else to do with him-self if he wasn't working on projects. He'd worked since he was a child, the youngest member of a rough-and-tumble vaudeville family; when he was three years old, as part of a bit, his father used to grab him by the seat of his pants and toss him into the orchestra pit for laughs.

When *Film* screened at the Venice Film Festival, Keaton received a raucous standing ovation that lasted for ten minutes. How the old man must have relished the waves of applause that washed over him! Afterward Keaton gave an exultant interview. His friends from the silent era lived in the past, Keaton lamented to the reporter. They hadn't kept up with the times. They'd never even listened to a Beatles record! No wonder four of them were dead within a year. "They simply had nothing to do, nothing to occupy their minds. I have so many projects coming up I don't have time to think about kicking the bucket."

Five months later Buster would be dead from lung cancer. No one realized how sick he'd been during the making of the film.

Deleuze considered *Film* the greatest of all Irish films.

Beckett proclaimed it an "interesting failure."

Pressed by a reporter, Keaton summed up *Film* this way: "A man may keep away from everybody but he can't get away from himself."

When the eyelid shuts, so does the movie.

2018–

The work is the death mask of its conception.

—WALTER BENJAMIN

How hard it is to sleep
in the middle of life.

—AUDRE LORDE

TEHCHING HSIEH 1986-1999

December 31, 1986

STATEMENT

I, Tehching Hsieh have a 13 years' plan.

I will make **ART** during this time.

I will not show it **PUBLICLY**.

This plan will begin on my 36th birthday December 31, 1986 continue until my 49th birthday December 31, 1999.

Tehching Hsieh

PROJECT FOR A JOURNEY TO FAT CITY

New York City empties out over the holidays. The streets and subways are less crowded, the restaurants and cafés buzz at a lower register. Those who stay behind remark on the change, how much easier and more pleasant it is to go about one's business and how they wish it was quiet like this all year-round. Alice's video work had crawled to a halt as it usually did that time of year and she'd spent most of the month alone in her apartment, tinkering with the Project, watching movies, and curled up with a memoir written by an American expat who'd lived in China before the Japanese invasion. Her family was not big on Christmas and she had no plans to return to the Bay Area until early spring of next year.

When she, Amy, and their mother did a three-way call, Amy reported that she and Ezra had both come down with the flu over the holidays. She'd heard from Solace Place that the flu had spread among the facility's residents, too, possibly transmitted from an influx of visiting relatives. The Father had suffered a slight fever, but he seemed to have bounced back: his appetite had returned and he was back to eating well—and yelling. He was sleeping more, too, but that was to be expected given his recent illness. The Father would be fine, their mother assured them. "You don't need to rush to visit. Make sure you're totally healthy first." Then she and Amy talked about whale-watching and whether that was something Ezra, who was prone to motion sickness, could enjoy. Alice wondered how the Father's experience of time now affected his measure of it; did he have a sense of how long it had been since someone had last visited him, or had time become endless and without measure?

On the first Saturday of January, Amy felt clear enough from the effects of the flu to drop in at Solace Place. She was still at the nursing home when she called Alice. Her voice sounded uncertain, worried. There was some fluid in their father's lungs, Amy said, she could hear him gurgling as he breathed. The nurse said she'd had to give him his meds through a syringe earlier that morning because he was having some trouble swallowing. No one at Solace Place seemed to be raising alarms about it. But the sisters felt a current pass through them—something had shifted.

Alice told her she'd look into flights and they hung up. Days earlier an unusually brutal winter storm—a bomb cyclone, the headlines blasted—had walloped the Eastern Seaboard with frigid wind gusts, snow, and ice. New York was still digging out from under it. Sub-zero temperatures had frozen equipment at the local airports, creating a snarl of canceled and backlogged flights. Alice had seen reports of planes colliding on a runway at JFK. The earliest flight was days out. Alice bookmarked a few and clamped her laptop shut.

Her thoughts went fatherward. It was the Father who had led her to the memoir she was reading. The memoir's author,

George Norbert Kates, had written another book, *Chinese Household Furniture*, a copy of which the Father owned and Alice had kept, the Dover paperback edition with its pale yellow cover. There were only a handful of English-language books devoted to the subject of traditional Chinese furniture, and that was one of them.

The Father was in his twenties, newly discharged from Vietnam, when he first fell hard for Chinese furniture. An American friend he met in Taiwan who was studying art history at the time turned him on to it. The Father's love for Chinese furniture was the kind of love that could not be satisfied by admiring the craft from a distance: he had to work it with his hands, the way a person might be moved to learn piano after hearing "Ruby, My Dear" or "Clair de Lune." When he returned to the United States, he apprenticed for a while with a craftsman based in Napa who specialized in eighteenth century Chippendale furniture. He took what he could use from that man and taught himself the rest. He did the woodwork by hand, using the type of interlocking joinery techniques and waisted corner leg construction that typified the classic Chinese style.

Kates's *Chinese Household Furniture* describes over a hundred tables, chairs, desks, stools, and chests—simple utilitarian pieces that furnished ordinary Chinese homes in the 1930s. Each piece is represented with a black-and-white photo and a short write-up—a little historical background, a description of the design principles at work, and the materials used. Alice was thrilled to find a version of the first piece of furniture her father ever made (Plate 38), the narrow rosewood table, two feet and seven inches tall. Kates describes the table as standing on "horse-hoof" legs, "relieved from absolute rectangularity only by the remarkable delicacy of its proportioning."

Who was George Norbert Kates and how had he become an expert in Chinese furniture? Alice turned up just two photographs of him on the internet: an effete-looking man with a receding hairline, round glasses, and a full mouth. He could have passed easily for a banker, an accountant, or a professor, but he was none of those things. The son of a Polish-Jewish industrialist father and German mother, Kates was educated at the most elite universities and worked for many years as a consultant in Hollywood, advising American filmmakers on the correct décor and aristocratic manners for French and British period films and helping European stars like Maurice Chevalier cross over. This consulting work proved lucrative and unsatisfying; eventually Kates quit the industry and withdrew to Rhode Island with his savings and his large collection of books.

It was during this time that he fell under the spell of Tang Dynasty poetry. The spell was so strong that he made the decision to move to China, determined to improve his Mandarin. By then it was 1933: money, too, had become a factor. The stock market crash had plundered his savings and a move to China would allow him to extend his life of leisure.

Kates was one of only a handful of Jewish students at Harvard in the 1920s, and probably gay. Alice imagined he was accustomed to singularity, and that this might have made moving to China—a place he'd never been to and where he knew no one—less daunting and possibly even more freeing than it might have been to others. Once in Beijing, Kates eschewed the urban cloister where all the other foreigners lived in favor of a neighborhood north of the Forbidden City. He rented a dwelling that was once a storehouse for the palace candles from a eunuch who had once served the Empress Dowager Cixi. For the next seven years, Kates would live happily in China attended by two servants, until the Japanese invasion forced his retreat back to America.

All of this is recounted in his memoir, *The Years That Were Fat*, one of the few personal accounts of pre-revolutionary Beijing written in English. The title referred to his years of tranquility, abundance, and good fortune. (The Father use to say, "Fat city!" and clap and rub his hands together whenever there was a grand plan that had earned his full endorsement.) In his memoir Kates offers learned accounts of the Forbidden City, the imperial lakes, Confucianism, the Chinese systems of names and of keeping time. But the book truly crackles to life when he describes the quotidian goings-on just outside his courtyard walls—the cacophonic orchestra of street merchants, each calling out their wares (Kindling! Silk! Fresh persimmons!); the routine procession that passed through his gates—the water carrier; the barber with his ear-picks; the foot messengers who doubled as human telephones, bearing "chits" between households and unloading neighborhood gossip along the way.

One morning Kates awoke to find that the lane outside his front gate was blocked by a line of camels laden with coal from the outer provinces. He would stay in China long enough to note how, in spring, the camels' coats peeled and grew mangy like scorched leather, and how by autumn, their hair would grow lustrous in preparation for the cold season ahead.

He was keen on many things Chinese, but he especially loved Chinese furniture. Not the fussy curios made for imperial chambers but the workhorse variety found in ordinary people's homes. These pieces were open in design and elegant in their functionality—tables, chests, and chairs of hardwood so dense that it was said to sink in water, beautiful in grain and surface like the backs of old violins.

From the Father Alice had learned a handful of things about how traditional Chinese hardwood furniture was made. For example, the joinery of a traditional table was so expertly constructed as to make nails superfluous. The legs of one popular style of low table were built so they could be easily collapsed: the originating purpose was so one's servants could carry it through narrow mountain passes in pursuit of the perfect overlook to enjoy tea and conversation. In museums she'd seen ancient scroll paintings of just this scene, two tiny robed figures at their cups in the mountains, dwarfed by the vast reclusiveness of the landscape.

Kates loved Chinese furniture so much that, when he left China, he arranged to have thirty-five pieces, many from his Beijing home, shipped back to the States. A selection of his hardwood chairs, tables, and armoires became the centerpiece of a show he curated at the Brooklyn Museum after the war, the first time such furniture had ever been exhibited in this fashion.

In the ensuing decades Kates had become mostly a forgotten figure, except that, every few years or so, someone seemed to rediscover him. Alice found a recent biography of him, written and self-published by a Dallas finance lawyer and Sinophile. A decade earlier, the journalist and historian Fergus Bordewich— disillusioned by the drab, modern-day incarnation of China he encountered while working for a Beijing news agency—read *The Years That Were Fat* in a swoon and was so taken by Kates that he set out to learn more about him. Much to his surprise, Kates was still alive; his search led him to a nursing home in Connecticut where Kates lived. There, Bordewich found a very old man, exceedingly polite, tucked in a wheelchair and dressed in khakis and a blue tie patterned with tiny carrots. All his precious Chinese furniture had long ago been sold off or donated. At the request of his guest, Kates extracted from a cabinet in his room what remained of his treasures from China: a few ivory and lacquer boxes; an ivory needle case; and a ring he'd bought from a pawnshop at the Great Wall.

What had happened to Kates between the museum show and the nursing home? For many years he continued to live modestly off dwindling stocks and bonds. He stayed in cheap hotels and rented rooms and published articles here and there about Chinese history. At some point, he moved abroad again, this time to Innsbruck, Austria, where he spent years researching the life of an obscure fifteenth century archduchess. The manuscript never found a publisher, or perhaps was never finished.

Then, in the early eighties, his life took a bad turn: while on a trip to Scotland, he fell down a flight of stairs and broke several bones. This marked the end of his independence and the beginning of his confinement in an institution.

The Father's journey was different from Kates's, yet their fates had been similar. The Father entered Solace Place able to stand and shuffle forward on two feet, albeit slowly and leaning heavily on a walker. He could still bring a fork to his mouth. None of that was true now. Alice remembered crying in a stairwell on the phone with a rep from his insurance company who told her that their appeals hadn't been successful: the Father had officially plateaued, according to his therapists. By then Alice was under no illusion that he would improve; she simply hoped that ongoing therapy would help him retain, for a bit longer, what muscle memory he still had. The rep, who had a musical Indian accent, was not unkind, and somehow the quiet sympathy she extended made Alice feel worse.

Was that what life amounted to, a series of plateaus? A year ago, when Alice was turning the Father's house upside down searching for the combination to his gun safe, she came across a small lacquer box in a dresser drawer, the kind of box where one stores Indian Head pennies, stones from sentimental walks, and keys to long-forgotten doors. She thought she'd struck gold. In the box was a folded piece of paper with the Father's handwriting. Only it wasn't the combination to the safe but a draft for an advertisement:

CHINESE FURNITURE

Reproductions of Traditional Chinese Furniture

using traditional hand joinery

Chinoiserie custom furniture in the Chinese style

PALACE REPRODUCTIONS

Folded in the slip of paper was the yellowed clipping from the newspaper where the ad eventually ran. Alice didn't know how long the Father kept at furniture making before he realized no one wanted what he had to offer.

When she'd first read about Kates's research into the archduchess, it saddened her to think his scholarship never saw the light of day. Instead, all his years of research existed in print solely as a coda in Bordewich's book. But lately she'd come to revise this view. Kates, surrounded by his books, his archives, and his notes about the archduchess, must have felt that the intrigue and magnitude of her life and times enlarged his—especially as his own circumstances began to narrow. Alice liked to imagine him quickened by the feeling of burrowing into a project, returning to it day after day, grooming it, feeding it, worrying and bleeding it, as he slipped into that fugue state when it's just you and the project, a project that no one is waiting for or cares about other than you.

Alice began mentally packing for her trip to California, which coat she ought to bring, how many rotations of underwear and socks. She thought that she might bring *The Years That Were Fat* and read it aloud to the Father. She knew that very sick people who might not appear outwardly responsive could often still hear, still comprehend. She could at least make sure he heard the sound of her voice. The book would give her words to say.

She imagined that, by the time she got there, the padded mats on the floor by his bed would have been removed; he likely lacked the strength to propel himself out of bed anymore. She would turn the chair to face the sliding glass doors so she could look out onto the yard and the line of trees and benches where no one ever sat. She wondered, as she always did each time she returned after an absence of months, whether he would recognize her.

That night she could feel the cold press against the windows of her apartment. She heated up leftover lentil soup and toasted an English muffin for dinner. She gave the cat his daily steroid folded into a Pill Pocket for his inflamed bowels. She read, watched a little TV. Then, around one-thirty in the morning after she'd fallen asleep, Amy called in tears to tell her their father had died.

What happened? He'd had trouble breathing; fluid must have been building up in his lungs. When did it happen? Who was there? Alice's mind kept catching on these questions, her thoughts racing in circles, wild, flapping, refusing the terminal destination, as though the telling of how he died, the details of it, what time it was (was it Saturday his time, Sunday hers?), could make his dying more real. What she didn't ask was what his last words were. Most last words don't realize they're the last. A person might say, *I'm thirsty*, and die. Alice only knew the last words she heard the Father say. This was in November as she was leaving Solace Place for her flight back to Brooklyn. She leaned over the bed to kiss him goodbye on the cheek. His skin was soft, freshly shaved, and nearly translucent for lack of sun. She made her way past the foot of his bed. By then he was no longer capable of smiling or laughing. His affect was as thin and unchanging as the line of his mouth. But his eyes followed her.

"I think she loves me again," he said as she reached the door.

THE NEW MILLENNIUM

On January 1, 2000, the Artist emerged from his thirteen-year silence. On the day he'd turned thirty-six, he launched what would be his last performance work. More than twenty years had passed since he first announced himself to the New York art world by locking himself in a cage. In the intervening years he had carved out a singular if modest reputation as a boundary-pushing artist. His next move was to diminish whatever currency he had by taking himself out of circulation.

Now it was the new millennium. He'd just turned forty-nine. To mark the end of his thirteen-year project, the Artist organized a press conference at Judson Church, a progressive ministry in Greenwich Village with a history of hosting art, dance, and theater events. It was chilly and overcast that morning. The city was quiet. Yet a sizable crowd had turned out at the church to see what the Artist had to say.

Onstage was Martha Wilson, an artist and the director of Franklin Furnace, the downtown avant-garde arts space that had exhibited the Artist as part of a group show years ago. From a large black dossier, Wilson withdrew a slip of paper. It was the

Artist's official statement. The audience hushed and focused their attention. Wilson read a single sentence out loud in a clear voice, letting each word carry its own weight: "I kept myself alive."

The statement hung in the air. Then a confused murmuring swept through the crowd like a wind dragging across the surface of a lake.

"Was that it?" someone said, indignant.

"Haven't we *all* kept ourselves alive?" another grumbled.

Alice tried to imagine who was present in the crowd that day and their state of mind. Most were probably friends or colleagues. There must also have been people who had never met or seen the Artist's work firsthand but knew of his legend. Surely many of them had taken part in bacchanals the night before, and before that, endured an entire year's worth of anxiety and hype over the Y2K changeover. Historians and futurists had pontificated over it; engineers and programmers had been tasked with making sure servers did not melt down. In the end, nuclear missiles were not accidentally triggered; traffic lights didn't jam and cause head-on collisions; planes and elevators didn't plunge people to their deaths. The countdown began, the second hand advanced, the 1999 parties were just okay, and here they all were, the same people, the same friends, the same jobs, the same neuroses and afflictions. Only time had changed, and they had yet to feel it.

The Artist stepped forward. He explained that he wouldn't be sharing any of the art he'd made in the thirteen years he'd been away. Whatever had happened to him, whatever he did in those years—that was personal. The crowd rumbled some more.

Was this a midlife crisis?

If it was so personal, why even invite people to this event?

What was his definition of *art*, exactly?

That's when the Artist dropped the real bombshell: From this moment forward, he said, he would no longer make art.

Alice wondered what she would have thought if she'd been in the audience that day. She would have wanted more without knowing what that more was. She would have wanted at least some flicker of light to illuminate the hole he'd slipped through for more than a decade. It wasn't hard to understand why some people might have thrown up their hands when he announced he'd no longer make art. The whole thing was like being slapped in the face before getting doused with a bucket of cold water.

Later, much later, the Artist would explain that he didn't have a choice in the matter. From the beginning, all his performance pieces had followed an inevitable progression. Once the pieces were set in motion, there was no possibility of turning back. In his first four works—starting with locking himself in a cage and ending with the year he tied himself to Linda Montano—he'd worked hard to waste time and showed himself doing so. Yet he considered these works mere footnotes to the two pieces that followed. With *No Art Piece* he jammed up the means of production entirely by making nothing and having nothing to show for it. He shifted the focus away from how he passed the time toward the passing of time itself. That was the project.

But maybe it was too perverse and painful, even for him, to not be making projects at all. Yet he couldn't return to the kinds of performances he'd done in the past. To reach the next level, he'd have to keep carving into his raw material: time. So that's what he did. He kept carving and carving until what fell away was his audience.

No audience meant no more performing. No trace evidence. No before and no after. Just time, emerging.

Dear Tehching: What is it about you that makes people want to write you letters? I think part of it must have to do with the enigma of your refusal, your self-described "missing adaptor." In the monograph of your life's work, there in the very back pages, are a series of letters written to you by art critics and other artists. None of them really knew you, just as I don't know you, and just as you didn't know all those strangers you wrote to all those years ago to inform them of your intention to seal yourself in a cage for a year.

So I'll do the same, write you a letter. I'll write a letter that tries to fill in what isn't known about the thirteen years you disappeared—a letter of speculation. We don't have to start from zero. We know a little about what transpired during the *Thirteen Year Plan* from what you've shared in more recent interviews. We know, for example, that your original plan was to head to Alaska.

By going to Alaska, you had in mind a "double exile": the terms of the performance piece effectively exiled you from the art world; leaving New York would deliver you further into an exile from everyone and everything you knew. Your plan was to pick up itinerant work along the way—carpentry, dishwashing, sweeping floors—the kind of low-wage jobs you used to do when you first immigrated to New York. This is all we know of how you passed the time. The rest will have to be fabricated; the Project is a fiction, after all. According to Tolstoy, there are only two possible stories: a man goes on a journey or a stranger comes to town. So start with your journey. The most direct route you could have taken from New York City to Alaska would have been Interstate 80 to Chicago, followed by Interstate 90 to the Pacific Northwest. Since the journey was part of your project, it's possible you didn't take the most efficient route. Whichever route you took, once you left New York City, the country that had been your home for over a decade must have revealed itself to be vaster than you could have ever imagined. You'd seen photographs, movies, TV shows, maps, of course, but nothing quite prepared you for the sheer size of this country. The road, the sky, the land—miles and miles of flat plains stubbled with needlegrass and sagebrush, long stretches with no buildings or people in sight—all of it producing an exhilarating emptiness you could feel in your stomach. And the clouds! Fattened and pinned to the sky, they reminded you of old comic books about Sun Wukong, the Monkey King, and how he flew through the air by balancing on clouds as though riding a cumulus hoverboard. You stayed in motels, sometimes weekly-rate efficiencies with a small kitchenette where you could boil water for Sanka or tea. To save money, you sometimes slept in your car in the parking lots of churches. You missed white rice. You missed gai lan, and spaghetti with clams from your favorite Italian restaurant in the Village. You avoided bars despite the loneliness that sometimes clung to you like a stink when night fell. On the interstate two boys leaned out the window of a Buick station wagon and made Chinky eyes at you as they sped by. Outside a sandwich shop, a pretty stranger with cat-like green eyes smiled at you—rare blossoming thing—but it turned out she was just trying to get you to join her church. One night after a long day of driving, you bought a large can of beer from the only open gas station in town and settled into your motel room, drinking and watching TV until there was nothing on but televangelists and infomercials for sex talk hotlines. (*Get personal right away . . . you never know where it might lead.*) The next morning you walked from the parking lot to the diner next door, sat down at the counter, and watched the U.S.-led aerial bombardment in Kuwait on a mounted TV. Volcanic flames and black smoke belched from torched oil wells—a *Screw you, too*, from Iraqi forces in retreat—the images on-screen hellish and mesmerizing. Another cheap room with gray pillowcases and stained carpets. A rainstorm so violent one of your windshield wipers sheared right off. Jobs laying roof shingles, breaking walls and installing Sheetrock, working in the backs of restaurants with people with felony records and migrants without papers. Being on your feet all day made your ankles ache (they'd never fully recovered from that two-story jump you made decades ago in Taiwan, an early foray in performance art); the analgesic cream you applied at night made your eyes water. When you felt things starting to get too familiar, you moved on.

As night fell on a heavy day of driving, the sky opened up like a fountain and you pulled into a small town at the Washington and Idaho border, nearly missed the glowing chop suey typeface of a Chinese restaurant through the rain battering your windshield. The restaurant was modest, its interior outdated but clean, and the family that ran it, kind. As you chatted, the wife waved the gweilo menu aside and insisted on cooking you the good stuff (a long-held fantasy, I admit, of my own). While you waited for your meal, you watched a pair of silver angelfish coasting back and forth in the aquarium by the restaurant's entrance. You read the faded specials written on paper plates taped to the walls. Our children, they won't learn Chinese, the parents complained, but with barely suppressed pride at their girls' Americanness, gesturing toward the two black-haired heads bent over their schoolwork at the oilcloth-covered table closest to the kitchen. What brought you here? Work, you said. Orange slices and beer while the father smoked low-tar Salems. They tried to send you off with more food, which you begged off, smiling and waving your hands in protest. Mostly people left you alone. *Disappearance Piece*: you could feel yourself vanishing further and further into a place where no one knew you or thought of you other than as a back and a pair of hands.

You kept at it for six months, making it as far as Seattle. Then you abandoned the project-inside-the-project. You were willing to disappear from the floating world of the art scene. But to disappear from your own life—that was too great a sacrifice. The project was, you said, *against myself.* So you came back to New York. By then it was 1991, which left another eight years before the end of your project. What happened then? I won't speculate any further except to ask: With each day, each month, each year, did you start to feel that you were no longer within the project? If so, did you feel sorrow or relief, or had you entered into a different zone entirely? A year was one thing. Thirteen years was something else altogether. It was impossible to go back; you could only move forward.

The last time I saw you was in October, the month before my last visit with my father. I'd been out drinking with friends at a bar off Fulton Street, a celebration for Julia's layoff from the school where she worked. She'd been meaning to quit; the administrators were borderline abusive, but she loved the kids, and then there was the health insurance, the best she'd ever had. Even dental! But the team meetings were escalating in frequency and aggravation, the doodles she drew in these meetings more and more Satanic. She'd even started smoking again, and her fingers stank all the time, and so it was just as well that she was let go.

What will you do now? we all asked her.

"I'm not sure. But I think I'm done teaching for a while. Maybe it's time to learn instead. I want to be selfish with my brain."

Around nine, our group split up, with one contingent headed to the nearby McDonald's, inebriation having triggered a craving for the Breakfast All Day menu. I begged off. I couldn't bear the thought of being under bright lights. I needed to walk.

Without thinking, I found myself taking a circuitous route home, a route I must have known would take me to you.

I want you to know that I hadn't been doing any kind of active surveillance on you. I told myself that, for the purposes of the Project, a certain distance was necessary, and that keeping this distance was something I was convinced you preferred as well. But I did remain curious about your life.

When I turned the corner and your building came within sight, I saw that the restaurant had closed for the night but the lights were still on. Through the storefront window I could see that you were alone. You were running a mop across the floor with a vigorous, practiced stroke, a bucket on casters at your feet. As I stood there watching you through the glass door, you looked up suddenly, as though you sensed that you were being observed. I froze, I might have even held my breath. Your eyes looked out. The glare from the glass must have reflected your own image back at you, leaving me unseen.

I'll leave you here, which makes this a goodbye letter.

For some time now I've wondered where this Project was going. I don't know, but I keep taking notes:

—From a fortune cookie at a Sichuan restaurant in Chinatown: *If one only knew the value of a day.*

— In the subway station, a poster of an elderly Japanese man in a fishing vest: he has dementia and has been missing for two weeks.

—A letter from a man who's spent the past seven years in solitary and wants westerns, romance, suspense, and a pen pal.

—The TV shows I've watched, a sitcom about a band of misfits navigating the afterlife; a rebellion by artificial intelligence robots; a treatment center for military veterans that begets forgetting.

—An email from Amy: *Ezra wants to see bears, so Yellowstone, but I'm thinking we should go to Glacier instead before it disappears?*

—The prompts I receive on my father's birthday and on the anniversary of his death from the online company that hosts his digital memorial: *Leave a new tribute, add a new photo, or share a recently remembered story.*

—A news brief about a polar bear, starving and caked with mud, who strayed hundreds of miles from the tundra into Norilsk, a city of nickel smelting plants in northern Siberia where most people die by age sixty.

In the first few months after my father died, I surprised myself by how much I missed the reports from his caregivers. It used to be there was a delay of a day between when the reports were filed and when my sister and I received them. But when I read them, the events they described made my father feel close; his life had shrunk but still he imprinted himself on the present.

When the reports stopped, I was struck by the immense absence of my father's effect on the world; there would be no more new utterances or thoughts, only memories of what he'd said and done. It was as though Munin continued to return, but not Hugin.

I felt—bereft. Yes, that is a good word.

My father would have said of the Project: *Take your time.*

But a project must have a beginning and it must have an end.

I thought I could go on like this indefinitely, assembling and rearranging the current of my days for the purposes of the Project—for the purposes of keeping my father near. The Project had given all that was happening in his life—my life—a shape, a form. But life already has a form: death supplies it.

I asked Nobu: If a project falls in the forest and no one hears it, does it still exist?

Nobu thought on this. Not every project needs to be known by the world. It can be private and still worth doing.

I said: Every time I think I've finished the Project it changes shape. I'm not even sure it's ever going to end.

Nobu said: Maybe there is a project that is like the monster star of all projects, the one that makes all the others possible?

I said: What if the project is the forest?

Dear Tehching, you said you haven't finished your art but you won't be making art anymore, and you haven't for more than two decades now. *The only thing I'm sure about is that I'm still in the process of passing time, as I always am,* you said. *Life becomes open and uncertain again.*

MYRTLE AVENUE

The winter cold clung on for months before the trees began releasing their blooms. The sky was sheathed in its crispest cerulean; people liberated from the weight of their winter coats walked freely in the street. Unseen in the trees, newborn birds shrieked with the shock of their own hunger. Every spring a few unlucky hatchlings fell to their deaths onto the pavement, their skulls tiny and translucent as grapes.

There were days when Alice could expect to talk to no one. She could do her work, take the subway, do her laundry, shop for food—all without having to say a word. The hours took on a meditative quality; her mind drifted like the octopus she'd seen in a nature documentary gliding along the ocean floor.

Today was one of those days. She turned the corner onto Myrtle Avenue. Her first task was to deposit a *Bring On the Feels* paycheck, the last such check she'd receive, at least for a while. The media company was rethinking its strategy. Not enough click-throughs. *Could mean more animal friends vids, could mean something else*, Mona's email said. *In any case, TBD. Thanks for all your hard work and we'll be in touch. Best.* Alice passed by what was once her dry cleaner's, a storefront that had been vacant for over six months now. She used to nod hello to the owner through the big glass window, an older Chinese woman who was often bent over her sewing machine. Once Alice brought a torn shirt to repair and the owner waved her away. "Can't fix! Buy new shirt!"

"Are you going to relocate somewhere else?" Alice had asked her when she first spotted the FOR LEASE sign in the window.

The woman laughed as though she'd been told a good joke, her silver fillings flashing. She shook her head. "Going back to China!"

Alice walked through the sliding glass doors of Walgreens. The seasonal aisle had been restocked since her last visit with flip-flops, tanning lotion, and mosquito repellent. As she stood in line, a mother in front of her snatched a chocolate bar out of her child's hand. "How many times do I have to tell you, I said *no.*" The girl stuck out her lower lip, thwarted but not repentant. Back on the street waiting for the light to change, Alice heard in the distance the rolling jingle from a Mister Softee ice-cream truck—*Dada dada da da-di-dum dada dada di-dum-dum.* A few years ago she read the obituary for the man who wrote the Mister Softee jingle. Before he became an adman for the *creamiest, dreamiest soft ice cream*, he worked in sheet metal and flew planes in World War II. Did the jingle man know he was writing the anthem for summer? Down Myrtle Avenue past the bulletproof Chinese that wasn't technically bulletproof anymore, and the discount furniture store where a canned recording issued from a tinny speaker in Spanish and English about deals on the installment plan. She reached the edge of the park, where the smoothness of the sidewalk gave way to older Belgian block paving that reminded her of crooked teeth. Ahead of her, sometime in the future, she'll see James. They'll agree to meet there along the row of benches that flank the edge of the park. Seeing him after so long a time, even at such a distance, will make her flush: her first instinct will be to look away. But James will have seen her, too—he'll stand up from the bench in the shade of the ash tree and rest his headphones on his shoulders. His face will be too far away to read. They'll have made no plans beyond meeting face-to-face. Some things can only be felt out in person. They'll walk a slow loop around the park, climb the stairs to the foot of the monument to Revolutionary soldiers, a Doric column planted on top of a crypt. They might head west, make their way back down to the footpath, and pause to admire the blazing gold of the forsythia bush before descending to the street below, past the cheap pizza joint and Tex-Mex Chinese takeout where, on her countless walks to and from the subway station, Alice often passed workers in scrubs grabbing a bite between shifts before heading back to the teaching hospital across the street. On the corner of Flatbush, they'll admire the cheesecake displays in the window of Junior's and slip into one of the orange booths in the back. They'll talk about James's father, who's moved in with James's sister on Long Island: he's set up in what used to be the bedroom of his college-age grandson, the old man replacing the child. Alice will tell James that Ezra is now into robots, and James will turn to Alice and say, Before I disappeared, I meant to tell you a story. It's an old Zen fable about a swordsman and a cat that I first heard about in high school. I'd seen Bruce Lee and

Kareem Abdul-Jabbar in *Enter the Dragon* and was wild for kung fu. Nah, I didn't take lessons—there was actually very little to zero martial arts training involved. You could say I became a disciple of Golden Harvest movies on late-night TV. I also started tuning in to the old kung fu heads in the neighborhood, most of them vets like your dad. One of them turned me on to Richard Wright's haiku. Did you know in the last year of his life Wright wrote more than four thousand haiku? Anyway, this same dude also told me the story I'm about to tell you. It was a long time ago, so don't quote me, but it went something like this: A swordsman is terrorized by a rat in his home. The swordsman has a cat who knows he's no match for the rat, so he enlists a band of local cats to handle the job. Yeah, you got it—like *Seven Samurai, The Magnificent Kittens*. Anyway, each cat is like its own Marvel franchise: one can leap seven feet straight up into the air; another one can squeeze through quarter-sized holes. But every single one is brought down by the General Woundwort of rats. Mass humiliation. The swordsman brings in one last fighter, a real small cat, not much to look at, but she's a legend. This old cat strides into the house, and then—blam!—she nabs the rat by the neck in a lightning move. O shit is right. The other cats all crowd around, they all want in on her secret. First, they try to impress her with their own slaying techniques, but the old she-cat yawns, unimpressed by all this meow-meow contrivance, and lays down the truth: they got their ass handed to them because none of them had figured out how to let go of the self, the ego. That's the real foe, not the rat. What you've got to do, the old cat said, is to surrender to the flow, the Way, whatever you want to call it, Drunken Master.

Alice will nod. She thinks she gets it and will tell James as much. The truth is she's never been very good in the moment, the now, at least not yet—always there is too much of it—that's why she's making all this up, having James tell this story wreathed in the words she thinks he might use, because it wasn't James who disappeared on Alice, but Alice who disappeared on James, Alice and her faithlessness. They aren't right with each other and Alice isn't sure when they will be, but for now, this is what she can do—she can place them in that booth in the diner in this memory of the future. She can describe the waitress clearing their plates and setting the bill facedown on the table with a nod—*Whenever you're ready*—she can pan to the picture window, where twilight, that fugitive duration between daylight and darkness, is descending, and rest on their half-empty coffee cups growing cold on the table; she can show how the booths one by one are emptying out around them, two city dwellers together on a leisurely Sunday as they wander through the arcades and moraines of their minds, losing all sense of time.

Will there be another project?

ACKNOWLEDGMENTS

Thank you:

Tehching Hsieh, for your life's work.

Brian Leahy for introducing me to Hsieh's abandoned "torch piece" and Boris Groys for "The Loneliness of the Project," which helped shape this work. Adrian Heathfield, Andrew Rebatta, Sesshu Foster, Steven Boone, Peter von Zeigesar, NYC Books Through Bars for sources, signposts, and stories.

At Norton, Drew Weitman, Ingsu Liu, Dave Cole. Jill Bialosky: few writers get an editor who's also a poet, novelist, and essayist—I am lucky. To Molly Atlas for her expert timing.

Anelise Chen and Eugene Lim for talking it through and reading earlier versions. Thank you: Wah-ming Chang, Markus Hoffman, Madhu Kaza, and Alejandro Varela. Sunyoung Lee for the Thomassons. Nobutaka Aozaki for agreeing to his fictional avatar and for his art, which is real. My Center for Fiction crew— T'ai Freedom Ford, Anu Jindal, Melissa Rivero, Samantha Storey, Ruchika Tomar, and Nicola DeRobertis-Theye for her generous spirit.

For space and support—Beach 64 Retreat, the Blue Mountain Center, the Lower Manhattan Cultural Council, the Rona Jaffe Foundation, the Center for Fiction, and the Saltonstall Foundation for the Arts. To the editors of these journals where parts of the novel appeared in different forms: *Brick, The Common, Guernica, Ninth Letter Online, StoryQuarterly, Seneca Review, Sonora Review,* and *The Threepenny Review.* Lyn Hejinian, for permission to reprint an excerpt from *The Fatalist.*

My family, to which much is owed. To Andy Hsiao: I love life through you. (André Gorz).

WORKS CITED

Many sources were consulted in making this book. Special thanks to these invaluable works:

Akasegawa, Genpei, *Hyperart: Thomasson*, trans. Matt Fargo (Kaya Press, 2009).

Carr, Cynthia, *On Edge: Performance at the End of the Twentieth Century*, rev. ed. (Wesleyan University Press, 2008).

Goffman, Erving, *Asylums: Essays on the Social Situation of Mental Patients* (Doubleday, 1961).

Heathfield, Adrian, and Tehching Hsieh, *Out of Now: The Lifeworks of Tehching Hsieh* (MIT Press, 2009).

JOMO, "Caring on Stolen Time: A Nursing Home Diary," *Dissent* (Winter 2013), https://www.dissentmagazine.org/article/caring-on-stolen-time-a-nursing-home-diary.

Kates, George N., *Chinese Household Furniture* (Dover Publications, 1962).

———, *The Years That Were Fat* (MIT Press, 1967).

Leahy, Brian T., "Art Without Work: Tehching Hsieh's No Art Piece and the Ethics of Laziness" (master's thesis, School of the Art Institute of Chicago, 2015).

Shklovsky, Viktor, *Bowstring: On the Dissimilarity of the Similar* (Dalkey Archive Press, 2011).